Anise

Other books by Maren Henry

Fiction

Dead Juliets

Anise

Maren Henry

WILDSIDE PRESS
Doylestown, Pennsylvania

Anise
A publication of
Wildside Press
P.O. Box 301
Holicong, PA 18928-0301

www.wildsidepress.com

FIRST EDITION

To John and Kay.

Chapter One

Laurice used to say that my love was like a thunderstorm, falling on everyone equally in a roar and a flash, and that Daddy's love was a deep, still lake that no one ever saw. Daddy's love was dammed, she'd say, and for years I thought she meant damned. She would have laughed at that. She had such a love for words.

I begged Daddy to use one of her poems for her headstone, but he insisted on Beloved Daughter, and to this day that's what it says above the grave that keeps her from me: Beloved Daughter, not sister, not poet, just daughter. Daddy tends to see things from his perspective only.

Did he love us both then, back when I was twelve and Laurice had not yet degenerated? I try to remember, but all I can see is his face at the gravesite. He cried for her. He never cried for my mother, or for me.

At the breakfast table, on my seventeenth birthday, my plate of steaming waffles sat alone. Marce had covered them with apple frosting, and stuck a candle in the top, but I couldn't rally a smile, not even for her. She looked from me to the meal, and smiled for both of us.

"Seems I only blinked and you grew up when my eyes were closed," she said. "You're beautiful, Anise, and you have the heart of a lady."

"There's no place setting for Daddy," I said, and Marce knew to smooth back my hair, smoothing, soothing.

"He gets off at noon today, early, just for you."

I wanted to believe her, but I didn't.

Daddy came home at a quarter after two with an armful of helium balloons and a sly smile that detracted some from his handsome, tanned features. Daddy was an administrator, the head administrator at the Tampa Degeneration Institute, so of course his work was very important, but so was I.

"I thought we were going to the art museum today," I said.

He made a sweeping gesture to brush away my concerns – and it worked, it worked, because his smile was in full force now. He concentrated on me as if I were the only human alive on the planet. He should've been ridiculous, like a clown with those oversized bright blue balloons, but he looked like the President of the United States, so serious, so handsome.

"A great thing has been decided," he said. "Let's find somewhere private, shall we?"

He gave the balloons to Marce, seized my hand, and led me through our grand home. I hated the cold marble floor beneath my feet. If I dared, I would tear off the silk wallpaper, and the velvet that lined the staircase. To him, our home was a symbol of his success. To me, it only showed how he prioritized work over everything, including me.

His private office, the one Laurice and I were never allowed into as children, was in the west wing. Laurice's portrait dominated the room. She had in death gained access to Daddy's office, the one I still rarely entered. Laurice's presence was only fitting. If not for her, there wouldn't be a Tampa Degeneration Institute.

Daddy settled into his high backed leather chair behind his broad, empty desk. He rarely brought work home – he'd rather stay late and finish it – so this office was more for his private thinking than anything else. I sank into the visitor's chair, the one that took an inch or two off the relative height of any claimant to Daddy's attention. I curled my legs up beneath me and managed to even our heights. Daddy still had that mischievous look.

"You should know better than to think I'd work on your seventeenth birthday."

He'd worked on my sixteenth, was that so different? I thought this, and maybe my lips pursed, but I held the thought in. The path to Daddy's love did not lie in mouthing off.

"What were you doing?" I asked.

"I was at the notary public. Jonathon Denvers was with me. Such a terrible cough, he has. I almost called the whole deal off, even though I know it's something he's done to himself with the cigarettes. The cigarettes, not the genes."

"What are you talking about?" When he mentioned genes, I had a sinking feeling that he might mean a promise contract, but no, surely it was too soon for that. I had only turned seventeen today. I'd never even kissed a boy.

"Marriage." He clasped his hands before him on the desk, leaned towards me. "Orson Denvers, Jonathon's only son. Scored ninety-nine point eight five on the degen measure. It doesn't get better than that," he said, his voice wistful, his gaze not on me but on Laurice.

"When?" I asked.

"Don't you want to know what he's like?"

"I want to know when," I said, my voice small even to my ears.

"Not until you're eighteen, I insisted on that in the contract. He's good-looking, Anise, even I can see that. Twenty-one years old, attends Harvard, really quite a find. Ninety-nine point eight five on the degen measure."

He beamed at me expectantly. I was supposed to say, "Thank you," and say it with feeling, and not reveal through tremble or tears how I really felt.

"Thank you, Daddy," I said, but my voice choked.

"Ninety-nine point eight five," Daddy repeated, and he dug out his wallet. From the wallet came a picture that he slid across the desk to me. My fingers trembled just to touch it, and so I knew I daren't risk looking at him, this Orson, this fiancé.

"May I be excused?"

I hadn't pleased Daddy, that was clear, but he held up and said, "Of course, Anise. We can do the art museum tomorrow."

The art museum was closed Fridays.

"Thank you, Daddy," I said, and slipped out of the room.

I found Marce at the grand staircase. She had tied a blue

balloon to every post and still had five in her hands. She held them out to me, and I threw myself into her arms.

"Daddy's marrying me off," I cried, and even as I said it I felt Marce stiffen.

"Whoever to, child?"

I gave her Orson's picture. She peered close at it – her eyes weren't what they used to be – then gave it back to me without a word. I sat down on the grand staircase, feeling so very less than grand myself, and I looked for the first time at this man who would be my husband.

His hair was not just blond but almost white, like the frost I'd seen just once on a childhood trip to Vancouver. It was a vibrant color, but it also made him look older, and twenty-one looked so old to begin with. He held himself proudly, perhaps arrogantly. It was a posed photograph. He wore a Harvard sweater over a stark white buttoned-down shirt. The only thing whiter than his hair was that shirt and the cornrow of gleaming straight teeth revealed in his posed smile. The posedness of it bothered me; if I could get a candid shot, or better yet, a videotape, I could get some sense of who this Orson was, but the photo told me nothing.

Marce wanted to talk, but I escaped to my room, and I spent the rest of my birthday curled up on my bed, reading of other places, other problems than my own. Daddy never even knocked.

At breakfast the next day – banana pancakes with Marce's apple syrup, and it tasted much better than it smelled – Marce made a point of bringing out a pitcher of water or a new cloth napkin every few minutes. On her first trip, when she delivered the pancakes, she said, "Used to be that women married for love, and some didn't even marry at all, but times are different now, you know that."

On her second trip, she said, "It seems like you're too young, that was my first thought, but you grew up the day Laurice died, didn't you? One more year might make all the difference between a child and a woman."

On her third trip, when she refilled my nearly full water glass, she said, "There's worse-looking chaps, that's for certain," and I said, "Please stay."

She joined me at the table. A bit of flour sprinkled from

her hands onto the satin tablecloth, and before she could brush it away, I drew a heart.

"Daddy married for love," I said.

Marce didn't answer, didn't have to answer. We both knew what had happened to Laurice's mother, same as it happened to Laurice. They'd shared the same genes.

"He loved my mother too," I said. The ice clinked in Marce's pitcher. I took a bite of pancake to collect my thoughts.

"Or perhaps he grew to love her," Marce said.

Would I grow to love Orson? What kind of name was Orson, anyway? He sounded like someone out of the nineteenth century, not the middle of the twenty-first.

"Your daddy informed me that there will be an engagement party next Saturday. Not much notice, but I can pull it off." She seemed to want a response from me, but I couldn't imagine what. My bite of pancake had turned to dust in my mouth. Orson would surely come to his own engagement party. "I can pull it off," Marce repeated. "Can you?"

I took a sip of water, but my hands shook, and I spilled water down the front of my shirt. Clumsy, embarrassing. I was sure to do the same – or worse – at this party, this important party, only a week away. If Orson liked me, I'd be unhappy; I wasn't ready for a husband. But if he didn't like me, then I'd have failed Daddy and I'd be just as unhappy. There was no way to win. Even Marce had joined Daddy's side.

"You were on my side yesterday," I said.

"I still am. Oh, child, it's just that I've had time to speak with your Daddy. He can't bear the thought of another child lost. Not his granddaughter or grandson. Ninety-nine point nine, he kept saying, ninety-nine point nine on that soul-breaking degen measure."

"Ninety-nine point eight five," I said.

"He was in a hurry to get to work, but he took the time to tell me about all the thought he'd given this. He's sure he did the right thing."

Of course he was sure. Everyone had to see things from Daddy's perspective, and Daddy didn't have to see it from anyone else's. I laid my napkin on the table. If only I could walk away from this engagement as easily I could from my banana pancakes.

Belatedly, I realized what Marce had said about Daddy hurrying in to work. So it didn't matter that the art museum was closed today. Daddy had forgotten me.

Chapter Two

The following week, I took my tutoring from eight a.m. to noon, an hour earlier than my norm, so that I was free to plan for the party in the afternoon. Marce took care of the dining arrangements while I took care of the extra touches: a bride-and-groom ice sculpture, dishes of rose petals to set all over the house, even a calligraphy rendering of "Double-Blinded Love," Laurice's heartfelt poem about scientists in love.

By Wednesday, all that was left to arrange was myself. My hair, long and dark, shone when it was down, but perhaps it would look more grown-up in a French Twist. And what about my dress? I considered something casual, but Daddy would prefer a more sophisticated look, like my working-woman's blazer-dress – unless Orson would prefer something slightly daring, such as my off-shoulder red silk sheath? Or would he prefer something conservative? I didn't know Orson, and I didn't know what he'd like.

I left my room in shambles, dresses strewn all over my bed. At Bannings I found a dress I liked, a simple floral sheath that had this season's uneven hemline. I charged the dress on Daddy's gold card, along with a pile of cosmetics and five extra pairs of silk nylons, in case of runs.

That was Wednesday. Thursday went slowly, Friday slower yet. The night before the party, I couldn't sleep, I just kept thinking things like: he's a college man, surely he'll want me to go to college – for I had decided long ago that I would get a degree in Spanish. Laurice would've gotten an English degree, and I'd have translated her poems and novels so all the world could read them.

He'd want me to go to college. Would he want children right away? Perhaps that had been worked into the promise contract. Perhaps I was to be a brood mare.

My worries wove their way into my dreams, so it hardly mattered if I slept or not; I woke unrested. But I wanted to speak with Daddy about my fears, and wearing my robe and slippers I hurried down to his office.

I knocked and waited, feeling for all the world like a child of eight not trusted to enter the magic portal, the gate to the adult business world. My feet twisted, a familiar twisting, a sign of my self-consciousness. It was all right to be self-conscious, but it was not all right to show it.

"Come in," came Daddy's voice. He sounded funny, stifled, and when I opened the door I saw why. Tears streamed down his face. He sat in his chair, staring up at Laurice's portrait. They streamed, those tears, like a river, like a waterfall.

I didn't know what to do, so I did nothing, just stood in the doorway with my father crying before me. Only once before had he cried in my presence. Only at Laurice's grave, on a long-ago Saturday.

"She was so good," he said, "but her genes were bad."

"She was good," I agreed.

He looked at me, blinking as if he didn't recognize me. "Did you need something?"

"No," I said, and I left him alone with his grief, alone with his Beloved Daughter.

My nylons did not run when I pulled them on. The dress fit a little looser than it had in the store – I hadn't been eating well this week – but it still looked nice. I carefully applied foundation, using a wet cotton ball to make it go on lightly. Even so, I felt a bit clownish when all was done – the rosy cheeks, the brown eyeliner – but I tried to convince myself that only I would see the tall, nervous girl in the mirror as clownish.

With Daddy away six days out of seven, Marce and I normally had the house all to ourselves. Not today. A cavalcade of servants had arrived, hired from some temporary service to facilitate the party. To make room for the guests, half our furniture was relocated to the off-limits west wing. I thought of Daddy still in his office, maybe still crying, and made sure the servants left a clear path to his office door. Marce bustled in and out of the kitchen, too busy for more than a quick, "You look beautiful, child."

A tent was pitched in our back yard with its view of the bay. The bride-and-groom ice sculpture was mistakenly unloaded in the hot morning sun. The sunshine fell particularly hard on the ice bride's face, so that her features smeared together, her nose receding, her eyes blanking over. I had the ice sculpture moved to the shade of a palm tree, but her face was still lost, and I found myself strangely affected by that.

Or perhaps it was Daddy's tears that had made me feel this way. I wanted to run tripping up the stairs, into my room, into the world of Dickens' London, a confusing place, yes, but not so confusing as this one.

I couldn't run, not from my own party. I greeted Mr. and Mrs. Anderburth, the first guests to arrive, and I melted like the ice sculpture under Mrs. Anderburth's hot, curious glances. Oh, there was one good reason not to run and hide. I had seen only a photograph of Orson, and here I would see him, hear him, know him, and then I would know what my life with him would be like. If he were attentive, if he were kind, if he looked into my eyes and saw me, then all my fears would blow away.

The Anderburths were early, as were the Quinns. The band arrived next – I hadn't even known there was to be a band – and they played their soft jazz in the far corner of our property, down near the bay. They were only a few yards away from our family graveyard. Laurice was buried there. I imagined her to be enjoying the music. Jazz had always been her favorite.

Daddy emerged at last from the west wing, his eyes clear and joyful. So joyful, in fact, that it seemed to me I must have imagined his crying, except that his tears struck me far deeper than any imagining, any fiction, ever could. This was no mere storybook hero, this was my Daddy. He held my hand tightly as we waited for the Denvers to arrive. He'd done his best to do well by me, and he was a skilled administrator, so he must've made a good choice. How I hoped he'd made a good choice.

He squeezed my hand. We moved to the shade of the overhanging eaves in front of the house, where we could easily greet our guests. Daddy wanted me there, and so did I. When the Denvers' black limo finally pulled up on our red cobblestone drive, I couldn't breathe. There had to be more to Orson than the number ninety-nine point eight five. He was a person, not a number, but would he be a person I could love?

The limo driver emerged, a Hispanic teenager with an ominous green-tinged splotch stretching from his left eye to his chin. He opened the back door on the side facing away from us. I craned to see over the limo. A woman emerged, soft blond hair coiled high. A man next, older than Daddy and not nearly so handsome. He raised a handkerchief to his mouth, and coughed vehemently. Cigarettes, Daddy had said. Mr. Denvers was a smoker, and it showed in the pursed wrinkles around his lips and eyes. He had been handsome once, I thought. His coughs died off, and he eyed me appreciatively.

I became aware that I'd childishly risen to my tiptoes. I stayed on my tiptoes – they'd never know from the other side of the limo and Orson was the only one left to emerge. It seemed he'd never come out. I felt like an Academy Award nominee on the dazzle night. *And the winner is. . .*

The shiny black door nearest me swung open. I fell at once back to my soles. Orson stepped out into the sunshine. Blond hair. An arrogant twist to his lips. All my trouble over finding a perfect dress, perfect shoes, and he wore that wrinkled shirt, those ugly brown trousers? It only took one look. I did not like him. I turned away with some vague thought of retreating back into the house, but Daddy's hand clenched shut, Daddy kept me here.

"A pleasure to meet you, Anise." Orson's voice was like a lawyer's, smooth and emotionless. I flushed hot with embarrassment. He took me in, his eyes scanning down my face, my chest, the glimpse of nyloned leg, all without any feeling revealed in his face. I felt like a fax being scanned, a cut of meat being weighed. Perhaps Daddy felt it too, for his grip loosened. He gestured for them to enter our house.

"Welcome," Daddy said.

I murmured an assent, too soft for words. Words would've given away my dismay. As soon as they were inside, safely out of hearing, I told Daddy, "I don't like him."

He was silent for a long moment, and in that silence I formed the words in my mind that I wanted him to speak: we'll call it off then, honey, because I'd never make you marry someone you don't like, you're all I have left, I'll keep you home with me forever before doing that.

Instead he said, "Did you see their driver?"

"He was a degenerative," I obediently answered, but my heart rebelled. I didn't need a speech on degens, I needed understanding.

"You saw his face? He'll be lucky if he lives out the year. Anise, listen to me. I loved my first wife, and I loved the daughter she gave me. I lost them both. Laurice scored sixty-five point two and she didn't even make it to your age."

"I lost her too," I said.

"There's not many young men out there with scores in the upper nineties and the proper social background. I'm not saying this engagement has to work out, but you need to give it a chance. Can you do that for me?"

"I don't know," I said.

"I know you'll do the right thing," Daddy said, and I saw the glint of a tear on his lower right eyelid. He wiped it away as quickly as he could. Another limo had pulled up. The Easterling clan stepped out and instantly overwhelmed us.

Daddy squeezed my arm. "Anise, it's your party, you must want to go mingle."

"Oh, yes, absolutely she must," agreed old Mrs. Easterling. She was at least seventy, from a time before the degen virus swept like wildfire around the world. She had been a widow for five years, but still dressed in black. Now that was the sort of love I wanted. Did I have any chance of finding it with Orson?

"Go on," Daddy urged.

Mrs. Easterling's sons, grown men in business suits, trailed behind us. The grandniece, a five year old in a pinkly polka-dotted dress, skipped ahead of us.

Emptied of most its furniture, now filling up with Daddy's elegant business associates and friends of the family like the

Easterlings, our house was barely recognizable. Daddy hadn't had more than twenty people over at once since Laurice's funeral. In fact, that was the last time I'd seen many of them, including the Easterlings, the Sandts, the Westons. From the dining room Mr. Weston studied me, his face unreadable. Perhaps he was thinking how beautiful Laurice had been, like a movie star, and that I fell so short in comparison. She had been petite, and I was lanky. She had been joyful, worry-free. Oh, I was forever the supporting actress to Laurice's starring role, but I didn't mind. She had been special.

"You must be so happy," Mrs. Weston gushed.

"Of course she is, the dear," said Mrs. Easterling, and she swept me onward. Onward, out of control, adrift on a treacherous sea of smiles. We went through the great room with its marble floor, into the bar, and on into the back parlor. Everyone we passed cast glances at me, some less kind than others.

"My son-in-law scored only eighty-one." Daddy's secretary, Rebecca, spoke to the gentleman beside her, but she kept her dark eyes fixed on me. What had Daddy done, gone trumpeting through the hospital hallways that his future son-in-law had perfect genes? Rebecca ran her hand appreciatively along our kidskin couch. She was probably jealous of that, too. She didn't understand that not all the money in the world could bring back a Beloved Sister, or make the guy with the perfect genes into the perfect guy.

We went out onto the patio and I was able to breathe easier. I settled Mrs. Easterling into the best chaise. She had perked up when she heard the jazz music and now had a soft smile on her face, as if she were remembering good memories of old. I thought I'd keep her company, but old Mrs. Easterling insisted I go enjoy myself.

What enjoyment? I moved from group to group; they all acted the same and asked the same questions. Where would the happy couple reside? How had we met – or worse, from those who knew how we met, how had Daddy found such a find? "So that's why he's worked at the Degen Institute all these years," said one fat old man, his eyebrows raised lecherously. "He's had access to everyone's measures. I guess my scores weren't good enough for you."

"He works there because of Laurice," I blurted out. A sophisticated black lady in the group choked on her champagne, then looked away in embarrassment, but whether for me or her, I didn't know. I didn't even know her name, I didn't know the fat man's name, and I didn't want to talk to any of them.

I fled back into the house, but Daddy intercepted me just before the staircase. He talked loudly of the cake and the cutting. People, dressed laughing perfumed people, followed us into the dining room. Too many people. I felt pressed against on all sides. Orson lounged indolently at the dining room table, seated in Daddy's seat.

With an air of deliberate boredom, Orson rose and joined me before the cake. It was three tiers high and entirely covered with frosting flowers in every color, yellow, red, violet, like a field of wildflowers. Marce had made it. Orson showed no interest. He did not appreciate the artistry before him. I wanted a fiancé who would gasp in delight, as I would have had I not been crowded, nervous, miserable.

"How happy you must be." Only I heard him mock everyone's favorite phrase. Only I felt how cold his hand was on mine as we slid the knife through the cake; only I knew how utterly disinterested in me he was. He bowed, making a show of it to those clapping around us, but his eyes were as cool as his hands, as cool as his heart. I couldn't breathe. Daddy steered me toward Orson's parents, but Mrs. Denvers wore a look of pity. How unhappy you must be, that's what her puckered face said. She stretched out her arms to embrace me. I felt a sob rising in my chest. I couldn't maintain my mask, and I couldn't humiliate Daddy by breaking down here, now. I had to get away. I brushed past Orson, and escaped into the hall. I wanted to go up the staircase to the safety of my room, but Daddy would find me there, drag me back down. Not safe. I hurried instead into the west wing, to the very door of Daddy's office. There I slid to the ground and clasped my arms around myself; I shook, but I did not cry, had to keep my face pretty, had to be braced because at any moment Daddy might come for me, Daddy who'd want me to understand my embarrassing departure from his point of view.

I couldn't turn to Daddy with this. No matter what I said, no matter how I explained the indifference I saw in Orson, Daddy would hear only one thing, ninety-nine point eight five, and all he'd say, no matter what words he used, was ninety-nine point eight five – oh, and Laurice, he'd say ninety-nine point eight five and he'd say Laurice, Laurice degenerated, Laurice.

I clutched the carpet with my fists. I couldn't turn to Daddy, but I had to turn to someone, I had to share this pain and ask for guidance. Not Daddy. My mother had been religious, my mother whom Daddy had loved less than Laurice's mother, my mother who'd swum out too far one sunny June day when I was five. She had worn a cross around her neck always, even when she swam. If she were here and I had turned to her, she would have counseled me to pray.

"God," I said out loud. "Help me, God, please help me. I don't like him."

"Well, at least she's honest," came a whisper. I startled back against Daddy's door, knocking it open, but I caught myself before I fell any further.

Orson stood before me.

Chapter Three

"You followed me," I said, half accusation, half gratitude.

"It was the right thing to do." He held out his cold hands to pull me to my feet. I hid in my lap instead. He had done me a kindness, and I had done him a wrong.

"Did it hurt you?" I asked.

"You running away? Why would it?"

"No, what I said. About not liking you. It's not even true."

"Of course it's true," he said. "If we're going to have any sort of relationship, you need to tell me the truth."

I felt like I was being lectured. "Please don't treat me like a child."

"You are a child." He brushed past me into Daddy's office. I was too stung to stop him. Had he really just called me a child?

"There's such a thing as social niceties," I said with as much venom as I could muster.

He only laughed. I peeked into Daddy's office. Orson had sat on Daddy's desk, and was tossing Daddy's glass duck paperweight, the one Laurice had given him, from hand to hand.

"Who's that?" He pointed at the portrait of Laurice, and the paperweight tumbled into his lap. I retrieved it at once. The touch of my hand against his ugly brown trousers did not excite me, nor him as far as I could tell. He wasn't even looking at me, but at Laurice's portrait.

"That's Laurice," I said.

"She's beautiful."

"She was a poet."

"Recite me something."

"She was a poet. She's dead now."

"I caught the 'was,'" he said.

I wanted to slap him. Anyone, anyone at all, upon being told I'd lost my sister, would've said what a shame it was, how sorry they were to hear that, or that old stand-by, at least she's in heaven now.

"Who do you think you are?"

"Don't you know any of her poems?"

"I lost my sister. It hurts me every moment of every day. My Daddy works seventy hours a week and he thinks that if he finds a cure, then it's as if he cured her, but he's wrong. She's gone forever. She was like the sun and now she's set."

"Terrible analogy. The sun rises again every day." He pursed his lips, deep in thought. "Better to say she was like a supernova and now she's exploded."

"That's horrible," I said. I clutched the glass duck all the tighter. I wanted to throw it at him. If it weren't from Laurice, I would have done it.

"You don't want to marry me," he said. He kept his eyes on Laurice's picture, just as Daddy always did. "I don't want to marry you either. But there's money involved. If I don't marry you, I don't get my inheritance. I don't get my senior year at Harvard and I don't go to graduate school. I get a job, that's what I get, a back-breaking job like every other joe in the world."

"Is that so bad?"

"It would be as if I had the world and lost it."

I was stunned. That was just how I felt about Laurice. I was about to say something, tell him again about Laurice in a way that would make him listen, when the glass duck slipped from my hand. It fell for miles, for two stopped heartbeats, before it landed on the thick plush carpet. It didn't break.

He laughed. I was mortified. I had taken it away from him, and then dropped it myself. "You should be more careful with that," he said.

"Get out of my Daddy's office," I said.

"This engagement is just a matter of being a good Catholic. You've got to put procreation ahead of selfish concerns."

"I'm Lutheran," I said, and because he wasn't leaving, I

marched to the door. In my last glimpse of him, he was bent over, picking Laurice's glass duck up off the carpet.

I made it to my room intact, threw myself onto my bed, then got up at once. I did have someone left whom I could turn to. In the top drawer of my dresser was an old leather-bound diary. When Laurice had known that she hadn't much time left, she had come to me with it. She wanted me to know her, not as an older sister but as an equal, and she pressed her diary into my hands. She had asked me not to read it until the day I turned seventeen. Then I'd be old enough to understand what she'd done.

I read it the day after she died. I was twelve, I knew it was wrong, but I missed her so desperately and here was a part of her. I read it from cover to cover and then, ashamed of what I'd done, I hid it away. I hadn't opened it since, although I held it from time to time and thought of my dear sister, the real Laurice, not the fantasy Daddy had built up in his mind.

Of all people, Laurice would have understood what I was going through. I opened the diary to the last two entries, the ones I remembered so well from my first reading.

> Saturday, March 22, 2046
>
> Daddy doesn't know this, but Jimmy and I made love last night.
>
> Daddy doesn't want to admit that my degeneration has begun. The doctors, the ones he's made me visit twice weekly so long as I can remember, they tell him so and he says, "Make it stop," with such a convincing air that really, it seems as if the doctors must make it stop and give me a future. Little Anise will have a future, a blessed wonderful future, and I hope she goes to college and marries and has children and all the things that I'm going to miss out on. I want to be up in heaven and look down and see her smiling, see Daddy cradling a grandchild on his knee, and know that everyone's happy. I have been blessed these past sixteen years, I have lived every moment God gave me, and I've even been so

fortunate as to fall in love and have the man I love, love me back. His name is Jimmy. We met on the beach four months ago. He has the bluest eyes, the most giving heart. He says he wants to marry me, but I tell him he can't, for he's going to live a long, happy life, long after I'm gone.

We went to the beach last night, the very strip where I first looked up and saw him looking down at me. I told him how weak I've felt lately, and he held me close. The stars twinkled above us, and the waves were crashing, crashing, and I felt a tear slip down my cheek as I told him that I didn't want to die without ever knowing love. He kissed me then, first on the lips, then on the tears spilling down my cheeks. He'd never had a girlfriend before me, but he knew just what to do, how to touch me so that my gasps rose above the sound of the waves crashing, and all the time it was Jimmy's face I was looking into, his blue, blue eyes, and it felt as if I'd live forever so long as I had him.

I turned the page, my heart heavy with what was to come. My problems were nothing, compared to what Laurice had faced – and yet, she had tasted love, and so my joys were nothing, compared to what Laurice had known.

Sunday, March 23, 2046

Jimmy was supposed to be waiting last night, waiting at our usual place at the end of the drive. I was going to read him my poem, oh, but I can't bear to think of that now. He wasn't there. I called his house this morning and his mother answered. It took her an eternity until she was able to get the words out, but I knew from the moment I heard her voice. Jimmy was gone. He'd been at a florist, picking up roses, oh, roses for me, and a degenerative man came in with a gun. There was a young couple with a baby in the store, and the man pointed the gun at them. Oh, Jimmy, I know you had to save them, I know it was the right thing to do. You tackled him. Somehow that man looked into your blue, blue eyes, from a distance no greater than what was between us last night, and he pulled the trigger. I can't believe he did that. I can't believe you're gone.

Your mother wanted me to know that your last words were of me. "Tell Laurice I love her. Tell her, tell her I'll be waiting for her."

You'll be waiting for me, Jimmy? It's not how it was supposed to be – you were supposed to go to college and find someone to marry and live forever, Jimmy, forever. Oh Jimmy! But I'm not afraid to die now. I've lived and I've loved. I have you waiting for me on the other side. I love you, Jimmy. I love you forever. I wouldn't be this sad if I hadn't known true happiness with you, so I'm going to be grateful, Jimmy, grateful for what we had together. Oh, Jimmy. It wasn't supposed to be this way.

Oh, Laurice. The rest of the diary was empty. She had died on April 15, three weeks after penning her last entry. Neither Daddy nor I had known that there had even been a boy named Jimmy, but after I had read Laurice's diary, I looked up the newspaper record of his death. He had been extraordinarily handsome, and honorable-looking besides. He had looked like a man worthy of my sister.

The sounds of jazz floated in the open window. The party was still going on. Daddy might be expecting me to compose myself and return.

I found a pen on my desk. Not a disposable pen, but my Kennington uniball. It had the most beautiful dark flowing ink. It was a good enough pen to use in Laurice's diary. I turned past Laurice's last entry to the first blank page, and I wrote the date at the top just as she had:

May 10, 2050

Daddy wants me to marry Orson for his genes. Orson wants to marry me for money – not even my money but his own. I want to marry for love, the sort of love you had, Laurice. If I marry Orson, I'll never have that, never. Such a cruel word: never. I'll never see you again. Isn't that enough never for one girl to bear?

There was a knock at the door. Daddy. I tucked Laurice's diary into my pillowcase even as the door opened. The pen was still in my hand.

"Anise, you've got to come back down. People are asking about you. It doesn't look right."

"I talked to Orson," I said. "He's marrying me for money."

"Well, we've got plenty of that," he joked. He *joked.* He wasn't even listening to me. I threw myself flat on the bed, let the pen roll from my hand and clatter to the floor. How could I trust Daddy to make choices for me when he didn't even listen?

"Anise, honey," he was saying. "When you ran away from the cake-cutting, Orson ran right after you. That says so much about his character. He'll make you a great husband, I'm sure of it."

Daddy was always so sure of his opinions.

"Now come back down to the party. Honestly, you can't run away every time you're unsure about something."

Run away. I looked out the window, at the jazz band and the blue bay beyond. The eyes of Laurice's love had been that blue. Run away, Daddy had said. A whole world lay outside that window, just waiting for me. If I married Orson, I would never taste what might be out there.

I got off the bed, composed my face, straightened my dress. Daddy smiled. He thought I was giving in, and that just confirmed his belief that he was right. He'd never change. He crooked his arm out for me and I took it, but behind me the jazz music still whispered through the open window.

Run away, I thought, and I tightened my grip on Daddy's arm.

From that moment on, I pretended to love my prison. The day after the party, Daddy presented me with a two-carat solitaire diamond. The Denvers had dropped it off with him at the hospital. It fit loosely on my finger, so that it swung around to the inside and cut into my palm if I clenched my fist – and, oh, how often I clenched them as Daddy went on and on about it being a woman's duty to repopulate the world with healthy babies. The degen virus had been eliminated years ago, but it had left behind damaged genes in its wake, and as Daddy emphasized over and over, as if I were hard of hearing or perhaps not as intelligent as Laurice had been, he didn't know if there'd ever be a cure.

I let Daddy talk, for I couldn't change him. I couldn't make him love me. All I could do was watch out for myself.

Marce caught me smuggling dried fruit and rolls out of the kitchen, but she only sighed and offered to make me something less rich than the veal we'd had for dinner. Daddy noticed immediately that the framed picture of Laurice and him was missing from the mantle, and I had to put it back and satisfy myself with a picture just of him. I packed Laurice's diary, of course, and a few days worth of clothes. I had three hundred dollars hidden away inside my favorite book, *Pride and Prejudice*, by Jane Austen. I had to take my extra shorts out to fit the book in.

Even with my bag all packed, I hesitated, and I didn't go on Thursday, nor on Friday, nor Saturday or Sunday. I thought I might just tell Daddy that I meant to run away, and that might be enough to shake this Orson madness from him.

Monday night, Daddy was supposed to take me to Diablos, the new restaurant on Tamiami and Sugar Palm. I waited cross-legged on the front porch for him to come home from work. I had it all figured out. Once he knew I was serious about not marrying Orson, so serious that I would plot my runaway, and had marked out the bus route to the heart of the degen ghetto, then he would hold me tight, and tear up that promise contract. With the sound of that tearing, in mind, I waited eagerly, impatient, twisting my ring back and forth on my left hand. I would be rid of it soon.

The katybirds took up trilling from opposite sides of the driveway. They alternated politely, back and forth, and I joined in with my best katybird call. I sat there for an hour as the sun sank from the sky, and the night grew cool, and the crickets replaced the katybirds. I sat alone in the dark for another two hours. At last I hobbled in, ankles sore, hands trembling. Daddy had forgotten me.

I took my time packing my things. The pack's strap cut

into my shoulder and pulled my dress out of line. When I returned to the front porch, Daddy still hadn't come. A stray katybird trilled suddenly. I tried to trill back, but my voice was too heavy, and I made an awkward sound, like a crow's caw, like a door's slam.

How could Daddy have forgotten me? If I ran away, would he even notice that I was gone? Years ago Laurice had waited for her Jimmy at the end of the drive. I walked in her footsteps, slowly, slowly. The willow trees made a proud line between our home and Bayshore Boulevard. In their shade they must've kissed, Laurice and her true love.

Orson was not my true love. I picked up my pace.

Something rustled from amongst the willows. A ghost? No, surely it was a rabbit, a squirrel, not Jimmy's ghost waiting, waiting all these years. I squinted, but our drive lights were too far back, and the boulevard lights too far ahead.

The rustling came again, and then a katybird trilled loudly, sweetly, not two feet from me. As if it had been waiting to guide me this far, and now that its job was done it had more pressing katybird tasks to attend to, the bird took off, up above the tree line, away. Away.

The boulevard stretched empty in both directions. Daddy would come from the north. Daddy would come with an apology, or the claim that our date was for Tuesday, not Monday, or he'd come with nothing, nothing at all, and unless I reminded him that we'd had a dinner planned, he'd never even know. Daddy would look at me and think of Laurice, of Orson, of perfect-gened grandchildren, but he'd never look at me and think of me. Just me, imperfect emotional me! Oh, Daddy, I'm just me, and maybe that's not enough for you.

The bus stop was four blocks to the south, on 210th Street, a street lined not with mansions but elegant Old Florida two-stories. No one from our neighborhood took the bus, no, we had our limos, our Honda Deluxes. The bus was to bring our servants to us, and to take them away again. Marce was unusual in that she lived onsite, but then again, Marce was unusual for being a lifer, not a degen.

I found the bus bench and it was cold, and I was cold inside. But that was good. After awhile, I found that I could just be cold, feel the cold, and not have to think. Whenever a thought tried to form, I forced it away and thought cold.

When at last a fully formed thought made it past my defenses, it was a doozy: the bus should have come by now. Following on the heels of that thoughts, as if to be sure to sneak through while the door was open, was the awareness that the man across the street was staring at me. He had been staring for quite some time.

He was at least thirty, with shaggy blond hair, no shirt and faded black jean shorts of unequal lengths. When he saw me stare back at him, he jerked his hand out of his jeans pocket. I had no idea what time it was, except that it suddenly felt very late, and the street very empty, and myself very alone.

The man shuffled a step away, but then he too seemed to realize how empty the street was. He peered exaggeratedly up the street, down the street, and then began to cross. His eyes remained on me the entire time, not on my face but on my chest. He was staring at my chest and crossing the street toward me and I had to get out of here.

I jumped to my feet. No doubt my chest bounced prettily, for his eyes widened. "Don't follow me," I said, and I ran. Half a block later, when I glanced behind me, he still stood in the middle of the road, as if with me gone he'd lost all sense of locomotion and would stand there until a car struck him down.

I couldn't help him, but as I jogged out of the residential area and onto Tamiami Trail, replete with banks and businesses, I wondered about that man, how he'd ended up on the streets. Did he have any place to go? Would I end up like that?

I reached another bus bench on the corner of Tamiami and 14th. Next to it, secured to a post and protected by a layer of grimy glass, was the bus schedule. I saw the problem at once. All buses ceased to run after nine p.m.

Oh, how poorly planned this had turned out to be! I couldn't even turn back, for that scary man would still be back on 210th Street, still frozen, still wondering where I'd gone. Not that it mattered, because I wasn't going to turn back.

After what felt like a mile, my feet grew sore. After two

miles, I developed a limping gait. After four miles, I could go no further. I hadn't reached the degen ghetto, but I found a small baseball park, and I curled up on the sand beneath the bleachers, and somehow I slept.

I was not alone when I woke.

Chapter Four

I came fully awake and scrambled out from beneath the bleachers before I realized that the boy standing atop the bleachers was just that, a boy, nine years old at the most. When I stood up, me on the ground and him on the bleachers, we seemed of equal height. He looked like a young Huck Finn: wild dark hair, brown eyes, full grin.

"You don't look like a bum," he said.

Give me a few more days of this, I thought. Out loud, I said, "I'm Anise Hunt."

"Jake Cowboy," he said, and swung an invisible lasso. "Caught you!"

I pretended to twist within the lasso. He loved it. His friendly face, his easy movements, all put me at my ease.

"Are your parents nearby?" I asked.

"I haven't got parents," he said. "Want to play baseball?"

We were in a baseball park, after all. I'd made it just within the city limits of Tampa, a fair distance from our Bayshore community. The park stretched green and treed around the small dusty baseball diamond. A few morning joggers ran among the trees, but other than that it was fairly empty, and safe-feeling. This was still a good part of town.

"I used to hit a mean home run," I told the boy. It was true. Laurice and I had often played in our back yard, and I always knocked them into the bay. *Giving the fish concussions,* Laurice would say. I hadn't even known what a concussion was until I looked it up after her death.

"You okay?" asked the boy.

"I'm fine. A little stiff from too much walking yesterday,

but lapping the bases should take care of that."

"You looked real sad, for a moment there," he said. He handed me a tree branch. Oh, it had been stripped of its leaves, and sanded smooth, but it was distinctly a tree branch.

His ball looked as if it had been fished out of a swamp, and perhaps it had been; it was water-stained, ripped, pungent. I was afraid it would fall apart the first time I hit it.

"Let's play," I said.

My blue cotton dinner dress was hardly appropriate for a ball game, and my navy flats wouldn't do at all. I slipped them off at the edge of the bleachers – bare feet would serve me better – and then I twisted off Orson's ring and let it fall into the shoe's heel. If I had slid it down into the toe, it would be better hidden, less likely to be stolen by one of the morning joggers. I left it visible.

Jake and I didn't specify any rules for our two-man baseball game. I swung and missed until I got the hang of the branch-bat, and when I at last hit the ball and made it to second base, I was declared the pitcher, Jake's turn to hit. The sun heated my scalp and the back of my neck, both covered in my thick brown hair. At last I insisted on a shaded break.

"Seventh inning stretch," Jake declared, and he pulled a sandwich out of a faded green backpack. "Want half?"

It was peanut butter and jelly, and Jake told me proudly that he'd made it himself. I had guessed as much, because it was a child's dream: overfull, gloppy, delicious. My hands were a purple and tan mess when I finished.

Jake wanted to get back to the game, but the break had gotten me thinking again, about my own circumstances – Daddy probably hadn't noticed my absence yet – and about Jake's circumstances too.

"Do you live near here?" I asked.

He tossed the ball from hand to hand with a boyish grace. "Depends on what you mean by near," he said coyly.

Parsing words. Laurice would've loved it. "Near like those houses over there." Two subdivisions, all tiled roofs and spacious yards, bordered the park on the east and south sides. "Or perhaps the houses on the other side of the road?"

"Nope," he said. "Where do you live?"

"I don't live anywhere," I said. The admission brought

more sadness than I wanted to deal with, and I tried to push it away. Who was I to care if Daddy didn't love me as much as Laurice? This boy had no parents at all to love him.

"I'll tell you a secret," Jake said. He looked down at the ball being tossed from hand to hand, an endless circle, like the sun setting and rising eternal. "If you got something to do, it keeps you from being sad. Like playing ball. You did pretty good for a girl."

"You did pretty good for a boy," I said, but my heart wasn't in the teasing. He was a perceptive boy, he knew just when I was sad. How much sadness had he known, that he could identify it so readily in others?

Unexpectedly he tossed me the ball, and I kept the circle going, and it was a good distraction. But the time came when I had to be on my way. The sun was nearing noon.

"Do you know where a bus station is?"

Jake's freckles danced on his cheeks. "Course I do! I only ride it an hour every morning, and an hour back again at night. It's this way!"

I did not follow him, I was too horrified. "Shouldn't you be in school?" It didn't feel like a Tuesday, it felt like Run Away Day One, but it was Tuesday, Tuesday noon, all good boys and girls in the schoolroom.

"Don't like school. But I like you. Let's play ball again, please?"

"Only if you answer my questions." *Are you a degen,* that was what I wanted to ask, but I couldn't bring myself to find out. He was such a winsome boy, smart and social, and so excited about attention. He was just a boy, out here all alone. "You said your parents have passed away. Doesn't anyone take care of you?"

"My brother Tom does. I'm not really supposed to tell people about it." He sat cross-legged on the grass, grinning up at me until I joined him. "But you're not a stranger, you're Anise, and you hit a mean home run."

Leave it to him to remember the one good hit I'd had, and not the dozens of misses and grounders. "Where's your brother now?"

"Right now, he's probably on lunch break, enjoying the sandwich I made him. I make lunches real good, you know."

"Yes, you do, real well," I said.

"Tom works at a factory. He makes furniture, real fancy stuff that rich folks buy."

I cringed at the wistfulness in his voice, the soft jealousy of the rich folks who could have fancy furniture and real baseball bats and whatever else they wanted.

"Want to meet him? We catch the four o'clock bus together. Sometimes the four-thirty if I talk him into a ball game."

I did want to talk to this Tom, I discovered. Maybe it was my own neglect at Daddy's hands, but I couldn't stand the idea of this boy squandering day after day in this park when he should be in school.

"I'll wait around to meet him, if you'll let me play baseball some more," I said.

Jake was happy to oblige.

When Tom rounded the bleachers, we both lay sprawled on the bleachers, I reading my Jane Austen novel, Jake reading a Bible, of all things. Jake sprang up into a hug, which Tom energetically returned, but the whole time he kept his eyes open, watching me, suspicious. I lay down my book, not needing a bookmark when I'd read it so many times before.

"Who're you?" Tom said. He looked like a grown-up Jake, a full-sized Huck Finn. He had to be about eighteen, with a rabbit's nest of curly black hair and a sprinkling of freckles, just like Jake. His eyes were large, dark, and at the moment, squinted against me.

"This is Anise," Jake said excitedly. If only some of his excitement would pass over to Tom, but it didn't. Tom warily nodded to me, then gathered Jake's things into his backpack.

"We played ball, and I showed her how to whistle."

While Jake whistled to demonstrate, Tom said to me, "Very kind of you to look after him."

"We had fun," I said. I had planned to lecture him on child neglect, but he didn't seem to need it. Jake swung back and forth on Tom's arm, whistling happily. If Tom could put up with that, then he surely loved him, and I'd waited the whole day for nothing.

Unless he was just being nice because I was here to see it, and Jake would get punished later, punished for telling a stranger that he was alone. "If I may ask –"

"No, you may not," Tom said, suddenly cool.

"Now I can take you to the bus station, Anise," said little Jake. He smiled at me, a child's full grin, and I found myself asking anyway, despite Tom's disapproval.

"Why isn't he in school? Don't you know what could happen to a child alone?"

"Jake, get your shoes on," he said, ignoring me and my impertinent questions. Who was I to ask – and yet, for Jake's sake, I had to ask.

"Isn't there anyone who could take care of him?"

"Tom takes care of me," Jake said, glancing from his brother to me, aware of our conflict. He was trying to be peacemaker, taking my hand and Tom's hand and squeezing them both. Such a sensitive boy.

Even Tom softened. "Bus station's this way," he said.

I hurried to pull on my own shoes, when I saw that the diamond ring was missing and cried out in surprise. Tom was at my side in seconds, pulling the ring out of the toe of my shoe. Apparently he'd seen the ring and couldn't help but slide it down, hide it out of sight, even before he'd rounded the bleachers and seen me with Jake.

"Thank you," I said. I slid it on my finger. I didn't like the ring, but I appreciated how considerate Tom had been.

Tom flushed a light red as he said, "Whoever gave you that spent a fortune. You should be more careful."

Jake walked between us, holding both our hands, as we made our way to the bus stop. They had missed the four o'clock bus, and would have to wait for the four-thirty. I checked the bus schedule; Jake and Tom's bus was exactly the one I wanted, to take me to the heart of the degen ghetto. By now Marce had to have noticed that I was gone, and she'd have informed Daddy. He might be calling his friends in the police department right now.

The bus couldn't come fast enough. Tom might not like me, but he still insisted that Jake and I take the two-person waiting bench. He stood behind. His hands drummed the bench close to my back.

"Want to come see my pet rat?" Jake asked.

Tom spoke before I could answer. "Girls don't like rats."

"Or baseball either?" I asked. I hated it when people assumed girls wouldn't like something just because they're girls.

"Anise likes baseball," Jake squealed.

"But I bet Anise doesn't like rats, does she?" Tom said softly.

"No," I admitted. He obviously didn't want me anywhere near his place, wherever it was that he and Jake and the rat lived. And that wasn't a problem. I didn't need his help. I didn't need anyone's.

The bus pulled up, a silver steaming monster with "Tampa Pride" printed in purple letters along its side. Tom marched Jake right up the stairs, swiped a plastic card twice through a slot. They were admitted.

"How much?" I asked the bus driver.

He spoke around the cigarette in his mouth. "Dollar eighty, like it always is. Ain't you ridden the bus before?"

"No, I haven't," I said, and I dug a twenty out of my backpack.

He gaped at the bill, his cigarette hanging loosely from his lower lip. "You gotta be kidding. Exact change, missy, or get off this bus. You don't want to go where it's headed anyway."

"Can't you make change?"

"Of course he can't," said Tom roughly. He had returned to swipe his card through the slot one more time, for me. I followed him to where Jake sat, certain that the whole bus was looking at me, laughing at me. But when I looked up, the handful of tired-looking folks seemed immersed in their own business, or in the passing scenery.

I tried to give the twenty to Tom, but he refused. So proud, when one look at his faded work shirt and stained trousers, and Jake's ripped jean shorts, and you just knew they needed the money. I gave the twenty to Jake when I thought Tom wasn't looking, but he intercepted it and gave it back.

"We don't need a rich girl's pity," he said.

"It's repayment, not pity," I said, and then, "What makes you think I'm rich?"

"Of course you're rich. You left your ring lying about like it's nothing. It could feed my family for a year. You never rode a bus before, you got a fancy dress and fancy shoes and you think a boy like Jake should be cooped up in some school when he would rather be enjoying what life he has."

"I don't like school," Jake said softly.

An old man sitting in front of us turned sideways to hear more. I didn't know what to say. Tom wouldn't meet my eyes, and Jake was staring wide-eyed at me. I smoothed down Jake's hair, not that those curls stayed put between one smooth and the next. "I loved school," I said. I meant my tutoring, but they didn't need to hear details that would just convince them further that I was a rich girl. "Learning makes us human. Can your rat learn?"

"He sure can," Jake said. "He knows I'm going to feed him when I tap the glass."

"That's pretty impressive, for a rat. But your rat can't learn your name, or the president's name, or what a democracy is. That's reserved for humans, and that's why school is important."

"She's right," said the old guy in front of us. At Tom's glare, he faced forward again.

"We're degens," Tom said softly. "What do we care who the president is? He doesn't care about us. You take a look at Jake's school when we drive past it. You'll know it's a school because of the bars on the windows, but other than that it looks like any one of the abandoned buildings in the dungeon."

"The dungeon?"

"Degen dungeon. That's what I call everything from Washburn to Koontz on the other side. If I were you, I'd ride right on through to Koontz. You'll stand out in the dungeon. A rich-looking, lofty-talking girl like you, they'll think you're carrying hundreds, and they'll see how pretty you are under all that hair. It's not safe for you. Go through to Koontz," he said, and he slumped down in his seat. Two thoughts crossed my mind: first, that I was indeed carrying hundreds, and next, that he sure had a gruff way of complimenting me.

"I didn't mean to come on so strong about the schooling," I said. I tucked the twenty back into my backpack, so he'd know I wasn't going to force that issue. And I ran a hand over my hair, smoothing it down.

Jake visibly relaxed. Tom took to staring out at the passing scenery, Jake to tossing his ball from hand to hand. I followed Tom's lead and watched as the streets passed, each one with more and more deteriorated buildings, more people on the street – not going anywhere, just lounging about, alone or in small groups. I saw an old gas station with every window shattered and lime green graffiti over its door. *Degens Be Gone*, it said, with a skull and crossbones painted underneath for good measure. I saw one young boy, no older than Jake, push a black boy into the street, and our bus veered around into the oncoming traffic lane to miss him. I saw a prostitute, all teased hair and sky-high red heels, prancing the streets at this bright hour. My shock must've shown on my face, because Tom leaned over and said, "Not what you expected, is it?"

"Not at all," I admitted.

He pointed out Jake's school, a rundown one-level building with a fenced-in, grassless yard and a gaunt blue sign that read, "We do not tolerate drug users in this school." It was an elementary school. I would never leave a child of mine in such a hopeless place.

"In another half hour, you'll reach Koontz Street and the eastern suburbs." Tom reached up and pulled a dirty cord that ran the length of the bus. The brakes squealed out their agony. Tom ushered Jake up, into the aisle. This was their stop, this hideous uncared-for stretch of town. No one should have to live here, but it was their stop. I steeled myself, and despite the churning in my stomach, I followed Tom and Jake down the aisle.

This was my stop too.

Chapter Five

My heart sank as I stepped off the bus onto the littered sidewalk. Even Laurice would've been hard-pressed to find pretty words to describe this ugly, ugly place. The air smelled of decay, and the buildings looked as if they might tumble down in the next strong breeze.

"Walk like you know where you're going," came Tom's stern advice. The bus pulled away to reveal three guys idly watching us from across the street. One smiled wide, too wide, when he caught my glance.

"Aw, Christ," Tom said. "I knew you'd stand out. Follow us."

He walked quickly down the street, Jake's small hand in his, me a step behind. We turned down an alley where what looked like a kitten sat gnawing at a black garbage bag. But it wasn't a kitten, not with those beady eyes and cordlike tail.

"My Mr. Rat is much cuter than him," Jake said as we passed the rat, the disease-ridden creature that could, if it chose, jump right on me. I shuddered, and Tom saw.

"The bus runs until nine o'clock," Tom said. "Anywhere you go is better than here."

"I can't go back," I said.

Out the other side of the alley, across a one-lane street, rose a tall rundown apartment building. The front door had a lock, but was propped open with an overflowing garbage can. Tom moved it away so that the door closed after us. We took the metal stairs. They bounced beneath us, and it scared me to see Jake run up them two at a time. When we emerged on the third floor, Jake already waited impatiently before the first apartment door on the left.

Tom, however, went to the right, and knocked on apartment 305. When the door opened, two small children bounded out. Tom reached inside and brought out a third child, a yawning pink-cheeked infant girl. The other two children, a boy and a girl, both identical in height, saw me and hid behind Tom's legs.

"Don't be shy, this is Anise," said Jake.

"That's not a name," said the little boy.

"Of course it is," said Tom. "Don't mind Kenny, he's our little thinker. You'll have to prove anything you say to him, starting with your name. On the other hand, Kelly here will believe anything."

"Will not," piped Kelly.

"Will too," said Kenny.

"You take care of them all?" I asked Tom.

"They're family," he said. He handed me the baby girl while he fished out his keys. "That's our little Honey, or Hannah if you want her given name."

Honey settled into my arms as if she belonged there. The other children all had dark hair, but she had soft wispy blond curls that framed her heart-shaped face. She smelled faintly of baby powder, and her rose petal skin was soft against my arm. It hurt to think she was a degen, this brand-new, perfect child. She wouldn't live but a fraction of the years she deserved. Someday she'd bloom and then wither, like the roses she resembled. I was glad when Tom took her back, glad not to have that soft dear weight against my chest.

Their apartment was starkly, dreadfully small. The crayon drawings that hung everywhere did little to soften the near physical blow of the gray walls, gray kitchen, gray carpet. An inlet no bigger than my closet served as their living room. I thought of our living room back home, and I wanted to cut it off of our home and paste it onto theirs.

As soon as everyone was settled in, Honey in her crib and Jake, Kenny, and Kelly playing in the living room, Tom took me aside. "You really haven't got anywhere to go?" he asked.

I assured him I didn't.

"And you're not a criminal? You didn't steal that pretty ring?"

"Of course not," I said, indignant. I hesitated, but his stern glance demanded honesty, and the whole story flowed out of me. I told him about Orson, and that I didn't care how other women chose their husbands, I didn't want to marry anyone I didn't love. "You only live once. That's something Laurice taught me," I said.

"Laurice knew what she was talking about," Tom said. "Degens don't live long, but we make up for it by living fully." He glanced back at the children in the living room. Even in his casual glance, his love for them shone through.

"I could use a place to stay." It took all my bravery to admit that, and he only looked at me, impassive, as distant as Daddy always was. I stumbled on. "I don't mean as a freeloader. I could keep the place nice, not that it isn't nice already – oh, I could take care of the children!"

"My own little rent-a-wife?"

I didn't like how he'd said that. It was insulting, like something Orson would say, and Tom seemed so different than Orson. Unless he thought I was offering myself physically! "I'd sleep on the sofa, of course. And –"

"Don't get too carried away. I pay Ms. Tilton across the hall forty dollars a week to watch Kenny, Kelly, and Honey."

"I'd watch them for free," I said, but it was obvious he didn't want me here. The shame of having begged him to take me in was overwhelming. I couldn't meet his eyes, and I fumbled past him toward the door.

He caught my arm. "Don't go. You saw how those men looked at you. I'd feel responsible if something happened to you out there."

"I'll be fine," I said, but he slid past me to block the door with his own body. Jake left Kenny and Kelly to watch us, a worried look on his face. Nine-year-olds shouldn't have worries.

"You can't leave. You haven't even seen Mr. Rat." Jake ducked past us into the bedroom.

"Have dinner with us," Tom pleaded. "We'll figure something out. You said yourself that Jake needs schooling, well, couldn't you teach him for a few days? He doesn't like to go to Ms. Tilton's. He says she looks at him funny."

"I don't have any school books," I said, although what I

meant was, I know you don't want me here.

"He hasn't got any books either, except for our mother's bible. But there's a library just eight blocks away. It's a good idea. Every once in awhile I manage to have a good idea."

I couldn't help it, I smiled, and he took it as an assent. I wouldn't sleep under a park bench tonight.

"A couple days here, and you might decide that marrying a rich guy with good genes isn't so bad after all," Tom said.

Jake reappeared with a fat white rat in his hands. He held it up, and the creature just blinked at me, the lazy thing. At least it looked like the sort you'd buy in a pet store, rather than find on a garbage pile.

"Mr. Rat, meet my new friend Anise," said Jake.

I only hoped I'd be a good friend to Jake, and to Tom and the whole family, and they'd not regret taking me in.

Over dinner, a stark beans-and-rice gumbo of which there wasn't enough for anyone, I learned that Honey was not Tom's daughter, as I'd secretly wondered, but his younger sister Julia's.

"Will I meet her soon?" I asked. Jake was trying to get me to take the last of the gumbo, but I refused, and Jake at last took it for himself.

"Julia?" Tom sounded surprised. "No, she took off just after Honey was born. Hitchhiked to California to be an actress. I hope she makes it, too."

Honey gurgled in Tom's arms, her tiny hands clutching her bottle. "If she were mine, I'd never leave her, not for all the starring roles that ever were," I said.

"Me either," Tom said, and he snuggled Honey closer.

It took a few explanations before I understood how everyone was related. Julia was Tom's full sister, Jake his half-brother – their mom had had Tom when she was fifteen, Julia at seventeen, and Jake at twenty-four, just days before she passed away. Tom had been nine years old, the same boyish age Jake was now, but he had managed to bring the family from Cincinnati to Tampa, where Tom's cousin Muriel took them in. She degenerated early, at nineteen, and left behind her own two-year-old twins, Kenny and Kelly.

"So you see," Tom said, "I'm used to getting left with babies. Julia knew I'd take good care of Honey or she wouldn't have left her with me."

"And when Tom passes, it'll be up to me to take care of her," Jake said proudly. It near broke my heart to see Jake brush Honey's golden curls off her face, and give her a gentle kiss.

After dinner, everyone gathered expectantly in the living room. Jake cradled Honey on his lap, as careful as if she were a precious china doll.

"Sit down," Kelly chirped at me.

"It's story-time," Kenny explained, as if I should've known story-time always came after dinner and before bed.

I settled on the worn gray carpet, leaving the couch for the others, but Kelly climbed into my lap, and Kenny just had to sit protectively next to her. Tom sat before us, but there were no storybooks to be seen.

Tom cleared his throat. "Once upon a time, there lived a beautiful princess near a great, gray sea. The princess's name was –"

"Anise," Jake shouted. Honey stirred on his lap, alarmed.

"Kelly," Kenny said, and Kelly giggled.

"Her name was Kelly-rina, and she had the most beautiful dark hair, dark eyes, and flawless face in all the land. Everyone wanted to marry her, but she couldn't be bothered by that. No, what Kelly-rina wanted most was –" He paused, waiting for Kelly's answer.

"Go sailing," she said, her voice full of awe. "In a big pink boat all my own."

"Yes, that's just what Kelly-rina wanted," said Tom. "So Kelly-rina bought herself a great pink boat, no, she bought two of them, because she just couldn't decide between the rosy pink and the pale pink. She sailed out in the rosy pink boat, and she had her lovely maid Honey follow her in the pale pink boat. Dolphins swam before them, and led them to a treasure island with sugar sand and candy bananas. Everyday they sailed to and from the island in their big pink boats, and they were very happy."

We all clapped, Kelly most of all. Tom couldn't give her a

real boat, but he'd given her two imaginary ones, and an island to boot! They might not know it, but they were rich, very rich indeed, in every way that counted. He was brother to Jake, cousin to the twins, and uncle to Honey, but he was more than that. He was father to all of them, and he was a very good father indeed.

Not like my Daddy, I thought, but I pushed that thought away.

"Now do Anise," Jake cried.

Tom looked my way to see if I wanted one, and I nodded. If only Laurice could've been here, she would've loved this.

"Once, in a land far away where the river rocks sing of forgotten battles, there lived a herd of unicorns on a vast, grassy plain. Most of the unicorns were white, but some were green, and a few purple, and, yes, Kelly, some were even the prettiest of pinks, but only one was a rich, marvelous shade of brown, like the color of sunlit earth. Anise was her name, and all the unicorns wanted to give her anything she wanted, but she only wanted one thing." Tom's eyes met mine in an intense look, and I felt my breath catch. "What does Anise want?"

For a moment, I couldn't answer; I knew what I wanted, but it was hard to say it out loud, in front of everyone.

"A brand-new bike?" Jake prompted.

Kelly squirmed around to see my face. "Pink air-o-plane," she said.

"To live forever," Kenny said. Oh, I wished I could give him that.

Tom only looked at me, his eyebrows raised. He must think I could have anything I wanted, rich girl that I was, but it wasn't true.

"Love," I said. "Anise wants someone to love her."

"That shouldn't be difficult to find," Tom said softly. He cleared his throat. "When Anise told the other unicorns that all she wanted was love, they couldn't believe it, because they already loved her so much. But slowly they realized that they weren't doing a good job of showing their love, and so she didn't know, and that's why she drooped her magnificent earth-brown head. So one by one the unicorns brought her things to show their love. They brought her –"

"Chocolate ice cream," Kelly said.

"A baseball bat," Jake said.

"And a giant pink fern from the far side of the plain. Unicorns like to eat pink ferns, but they like chocolate ice cream even more. They formed two baseball teams, and everyone wanted Anise to play on their team so much, she had to play on both, and she knew that she was very loved indeed."

"That was a good story," Jake said.

I thought so too.

Chapter Six

Tom refused to let me sleep on the sofa; he said if there was room for five people in the two bedrooms, there was room for six. Currently Tom, Jake, and Honey shared the big bedroom, and the twins shared the small pink bedroom. After a quick shuffling, Tom, Jake, and Kenny ended up in the smaller, and Kelly, Honey, and I in the other. Boys in one, girls in the other. It seemed a good arrangement.

Honey had fallen asleep in Jake's arms, and Jake tiptoed into the girls' bedroom to lay her in her heavy white crib. It was wooden and very old looking.

"Good night," Jake said. He picked up Mr. Rat's cage and took it out with him.

Tom lingered in the doorway. "I put fresh sheets on the beds for you and Kelly."

"Thank you," I said.

"I'm sure you're used to much softer sheets, and a better bed too."

I glanced at the beds, both of which sagged in the middle beneath faded floral sheets. "I'm fortunate you gave me a place to stay. Sheets and a bed are just icing, Tom, really. Thank you."

Tom went to the boys' bedroom, and I settled myself in. He had thoughtfully left out a t-shirt for me to sleep in. It came down just past my hips. If I were any taller, it wouldn't be decent.

Kelly, wearing a pink pajama dress, came into the room, but she stayed away from the bed. Against her chest, she clutched a one-eared teddy bear.

"What're you doing?" she asked.

I had crossed my legs, sitting on my bed with my hands together. "My mother always prayed when she put us to sleep. I got out of the habit, but I recently picked it up again."

"My Momma died," Kelly said.

I dropped my praying to go to her. I hadn't noticed how scared she looked. I smoothed her hair, and searched for words to comfort her. "Maybe both our Mommas are together in heaven. Maybe they watch us as we sleep, and kiss our dreams."

"I want Kenny to watch over me," Kelly cried, and she ran out of the room.

Soon Tom appeared in the doorway. I hurried back into bed to hide my long bare legs. He waited, then said, "Kelly's never slept without her twin by her side. She's scared to sleep in here, and I don't want to force her."

"No, of course not," I said.

"I'll just grab the pillow and blankets and sleep out on the sofa," Tom said.

I grabbed mine instead.

"Where are you going?" Tom asked.

"To the sofa. I'm not driving you out of your room."

"And I'm not letting a guest sleep on the sofa." He placed his cool hands on my shoulders, and guided me back towards the bed. I resisted. "The sun heats up the living room like an oven, and the twins always play there when they wake up. You don't want to sleep there."

"Neither do you," I said. I felt self-conscious in his thin oversized t-shirt. I'd taken my bra off when I put the t-shirt on, and I was sure that he could tell if he looked, but he kept his gaze firmly on my face.

I thought about him taking care of all these children, and how honorable and responsible he was. He had been very kind to take me in. "Why don't we both sleep in here?" I offered."Would you have a problem with that?" Tom asked.

"I suggested it, didn't I?" That didn't exactly answer his question, but it seemed to satisfy him. He readied himself for bed, but didn't pull off his shirt and trousers until after he was in bed. I wondered what sort of underwear he wore, and then I wondered at myself for wondering.

It took me a long time to fall asleep, but by his shallow breathing, it took him just as long.

The next few days flew by like a dream. I took care of Jake during the days – only Jake, because Tom paid Ms. Tilton forty dollars a week to watch the other three children, and without that money she wouldn't be able to pay the rent.

When Tom came home each day, I had dinner on the table. I'd always helped Marce in the kitchen, and the meals here were extremely simply compared to Marce's entrees. There was only so much that could be done with beans, macaroni, and rice.

Jake grew bored in the apartment, but I had promised Tom that we wouldn't go out in the streets until Saturday, when he could go with us. Tom didn't think it was safe for us out there.

When Saturday rolled around, I woke before Tom. I showered quickly, but managed to drop the soap twice. The twins were playing in the living room, and Kenny assured me that they were hungry, so I started on some pancakes, but the first two burnt. I felt terrible about wasting food, but they were too burnt to be salvaged, and in trying to scrape them off into the garbage, I dropped the pan right on my foot.

In horrible burnt banged pain, I hopped about the kitchen. The children screamed with me. Tom burst out of the bedroom, swooped me up, and doused my foot under running water. It splattered all over my legs, the counter, and the floor. "Kenny, Kelly, don't touch that pan," he shouted.

"I thought you were sleeping," I said, mortified.

"I was," he said, but without blame. He set me down on my good foot, plucked the offending pan off the floor, and doused it too under the water. Jake came into the kitchen with a crying Honey in his arms. My cries had woken her, too.

"Let's get you lying down, and this foot in the air. You'll have to take it easy today," Tom said.

"But we're still going out, aren't we?"

"Not after this," Tom said.

I felt a sudden wave of dizziness. Tom steadied me, but I still needed to sit down, even if it was on the wet kitchen floor. Tom crouched after me, his concern written all over his face. "Do you need me to call a doctor?" He caught my wrist to feel for my pulse, which had to be going ninety miles a minute.

"You can't make plans and then break them," I said in a hushed voice. It was just like Daddy. "You promised we'd go out today, but I didn't know if you kept your promises. It made me worry. That's why I burnt the pancakes, why I dropped the pan."

"I always keep my promises," Tom said.

I cried then, not loud like Honey but softly, silently, the tears rolling down my cheeks one by one as if in steady military progression. I was so dizzy, and my foot throbbed, and Tom brushed away my tears as they fell.

"We can go out even though your foot is hurt," he said. I cried harder. "Or we can stay in," he continued hurriedly, which made me laugh through my tears.

Jake and Tom helped me to the couch, where we propped my foot up; it had swollen up already, and had an ugly red burn coupled with a bruise where the pan had hit. Kelly was assigned to hold an ice-filled cloth on my foot, only her hands grew cold and Kenny quickly took over, while Jake soothed the now-hiccoughing Honey.

"I don't think I should walk on it today," I said.

"I was being overprotective. You and Jake can't stay cooped up here. During the day, the two of you should be fine if you go out together," Tom said. "So you aren't missing out on anything today, you really aren't, because you can go any day."

Oh, he was being so nice, he was going to make me cry again! He didn't understand, either. I told him more about Daddy, about the broken promises and untaken outings. Tom held my hand, and he held it tighter as the story went on. "He's a fool," he said when I was done. "He lost one daughter, and so he should appreciate the other more, not less. You're a good person, just as good as this Laurice could possibly have been."

"Laurice was very good," I said tearfully.

"So is Anise," he said, and for a moment it seemed as if he might kiss me. He leaned closer – and then Honey hiccoughed, and Kelly tugged at his shirt, and he pulled away.

For a moment an awkward silence reigned, and then he asked, "What about your mother? What is she like?"

"She killed herself," I admitted. "She swam away into the bay when I was five. I don't remember her very well."

Kelly was about to ask something, but Tom shushed her. "Do you know why?"

"Why what?" I asked.

"Why she killed herself," he said, seeming embarrassed at having to say the words.

I thought about it for a moment. "I think it's because Daddy didn't love her. He never talks about her."

Tom shook his head. "It's hard for me to understand. As a degen, I'm so aware of the how few years I have left. For someone who has years and years, decades, to just throw them all away? And she had money, and she had you - I'm sorry, I shouldn't be saying all this."

"No, don't apologize," I said. The more I thought about it, it was strange. My mother had been religious. Hadn't she feared that God would disapprove of suicide?

"Maybe it was an accident. Maybe she had just gone swimming," Tom suggested. It would be nice to believe that, but Marce and Daddy had told me enough that I knew otherwise. I knew she had killed herself; I just didn't know why.

Tom and Jake went to the library without me, and he left Honey and the twins at Ms. Tilton's so I could rest. They returned with four books. Jake had a book on baseball heroes and one called, *Everything Your Nine-Year-Old Should Know.* It was quite thick, and Jake dropped it as soon as he got in the door. Tom had chosen a collection of fairy tales and *Dark Highways,* a novel currently on best-seller lists. He'd checked it out for me.

That night at story-time, Tom read "Jack and the Beanstalk," only instead of starring clever Jack it starred our own clever Kenny. We all joined in on the fee, fie, foe, fums. I cradled Honey in my arms, with Jake on my right side and Kenny and Kelly on my left, and I truly felt as if I belonged, as if this were not just Tom's family but mine too.

Honey's rose petal eyelids fluttered close, and she slept in my arms like a soft little angel. We were all tired, but I didn't want the night to end, so I asked, "Can I tell a story?"

"Yes, yes," Jake said, and he took the sleeping Honey from my arms. Tom and I traded spots. I faced the five of them, and saw how they all leaned against each other like branches in a driftwood pile. Together they were strong; together, they were a family.

With a smile, Tom encouraged me to start.

"This is a story about a magic cow," I said, thinking of the fairy tale we'd just heard. "An old man traded a handful of magic beans for this magic cow, and if clever Kenny had known the cow was magic, he might not have traded at all." One of the best part of Tom's stories was how everyone contributed. I wanted my story to be like his. "What was the magic cow's name?"

"Honey," Kelly said, but I couldn't make that sleeping angel into a cow in my story.

"Tom," Kenny said.

"The magic cow was named Thomas. Thomas the Tea-eater because he loved the taste of tea-leaves." Tom smiled at that. He always told the stories, and probably had never had one told of him before. "The old man told Thomas that he intended to set him free, that this was why he'd bought him, because he believed magic creatures should all be free. But Thomas said, in his cowish low, "Being free isn't what I want most. What I really want is – "

Tom stretched one arm around Kenny and Kelly, the other around Jake and Honey. "I have everything I could ever want," he said.

It was a lovely sentiment, but I had no idea how to work it into the story. Laurice could've done it. Laurice was the writer, the storyteller, the poet. My dismay must've shown on my face, because Tom said, "You can do it. You're doing great so far."

He had so much faith in me, I had to have faith, too. I forced my self-consciousness aside. "Thomas the Tea-eater told the old man that he had everything he could possibly want. But if he were set free, then he'd have less, because then he couldn't give his magic milk to the people he liked."

"He ate the tea leaves because their herbs made his milk magic," Tom suggested.

"The old man drank of the milk, and twenty years fell off him. His wrinkles smoothed away, and his back straightened, and he was able once again to work a farm as he had in his youth. He put Thomas the Tea-eater in a big red barn, and planted tealeaves in the pasture. Everyone lived very happily indeed," I finished in a rush.

Poor Honey was woken up by the vigorous clapping. She looked at all of us like we'd gone mad, but Jake just told her, "You missed it, Anise told a great story."

My enjoyment had outweighed my nerves. Of course, Laurice could've told a better story, but at least mine had been well received.

Tom went to lay Honey down, and the children drifted after him. When Tom returned, he sat beside me, and settled his hand casually upon my knee. "Story-telling is a rush, isn't it," he said. "If I lived a thousand years ago, I would've been a story-teller bard. No village, no matter how poor, would've been safe from me."

"You would make a good bard," I said.

"You'd make a better one. Standing on stage, in a medieval peasant dress done up in a bard's bright colors. They'd love you even before you talked, and more afterwards," he said.

I thrilled to imagine it, me a storyteller, before a crowd of peasants who all loved me. I leaned against Tom. "I would like to be loved," I said.

"Your Daddy loves you," Tom said. He studied my face, then said, "I saw the newspaper at the library today. You were on the front page. I never saw a dress with that high of a neck."

I was in the newspaper? I was just a runaway. Why did I warrant the front page? Just because of Daddy's connections, I got more attention than other runaways who were probably in far worse circumstances. And Daddy had sent in a picture of me in that dress, of all things. I didn't even look like myself in it. "Daddy likes that dress because Laurice used to wear it,"

I said.

"The article said he was really worried about you."

"Did it say he'd called off my engagement?"

"No," Tom admitted. "They had a quote from Orson, who hopes you'll be found safely."

"Then I have to keep hiding."

Tom put his arm around me. "That's fine with me."

I studied the gray carpet beneath me, not daring to speak. Tom's embrace felt warm, wonderful. He smelled of musk, like evening dew, a manly smell. It was awhile before he spoke again. "The article had a picture of Orson. He's a good-looking guy. And he's got perfect genes, and he gets to go to college."

He sounded envious. "Do you want to go to college, Tom?"

"No, I suppose not," he said. "I always hated homework. I'm a factory worker, not a college boy. But take little Kenny. He's a thinker, a learner. He'd love college, but he won't get to go, because there's no scholarships for degens. No point in teaching people who are just going to degenerate."

"They're working on a cure," I said.

"How many cancer patients have told themselves that, and how many years have gone by and there's still no cure? I'm a third generation degenerative. How many more generations until there's a cure?" He touched my cheek, turning my face until I looked into his. We were close enough to kiss. "I wasn't truthful during your story. Tom the Tea-eater does want something, and he wants it very badly indeed."

I could barely speak over the thumping of my heart. "What do you want?"

"I want what Orson has. Perfect genes. Ninety-nine point eight five. You only told me once, but I remember that number. I want it for myself, and I want it for my family." His voice hushed. "Jake scored forty-two. He's the lowest of all of us. Kenny and Kelly are forty-eight and fifty-two, and Honey is all the way up at seventy-nine, because Julia got pregnant by the restaurant owner at Groundhogs, where she used to waitress. He was a lifer.

"I'd give them all lifer fathers if I could. Then they'd have scores in the seventies or eighties, where there'd be a chance they'd escape the curse of degeneration. It's all I want, but it's not possible, not even in a story."

"What did you score, Tom?" I had to know. He was so strong and healthy. Surely he'd have a high score.

"Sixty-three point seven," he said. My heart caught. Laurice had scored so close to him. A score in the sixties meant he'd degenerate for certain.

"I'm sorry," I said.

Tom made an effort to smile. "Don't be sorry, unless you caused the degen virus."

"Not many people know, but it came from China," I said.

"Then I blame the Chinese, only you can't really blame someone for getting sick."

"Blame the scientists. Daddy won't tell me one way or the other, because it's all hush-hush, but I think some Chinese scientist tampered with genes, and unleashed this whole nightmare." Oh, Tom's smile was more of a grimace; he didn't want to hear about the Chinese when he'd just shared his pain with me. "If I had some of Thomas Tea-eater's magic milk, I'd give a glass to each of you, and make you live forever."

Tom leaned against me for a while, quiet, thinking. "Jake would make a great old man, hobbling around the baseball bases like you with your hurt foot."

"There's a saying, don't count your blessings before they hatch."

"Don't count your chickens," Tom corrected.

"Well, I'd rather say, don't count your curses before they hatch."

Tom nodded in appreciation.

"Jake might make it to old age. You never know what tomorrow will bring."

"If only tomorrow would bring a cure."

"And I'll have you know that I don't hobble," I said.

Tom shook with laughter. "Yes, you do! Like a duck, with your hurt foot. It's about time for bed. I ought to carry you, I suppose." He placed one arm under my legs, tightened the other around my shoulders, and lifted me off the ground. His musk was stronger from this close, and I could also make out an earthier smell beneath it, the smell of honest sweat. The smell of Tom. I held on around his neck, and I knew he'd never drop me.

He laid me in my bed as if I were as light as Honey, and as precious. "Good night, Anise. Thank you for listening," he said.

"Good night," I said, and I didn't let my disappointment seep into my voice. He'd shared his secret wishes with me, but apparently wishing to kiss me wasn't one of them. When he said he wanted only one thing, I had thought maybe, just maybe, he wanted me.

I waited for him to crawl into his bed, and then I clasped my hands and prayed. I prayed for Tom and his family, but it didn't feel like anyone was up there to hear me.

Chapter Seven

By Tuesday, the bruise on my foot had gone from purple to a green the exact color of a dollar bill. I joked that I should go the grocery store, find the thickest bacon, the freshest Danishes, and then flash my foot at the cashier and walk right on out the door.

Jake laughed, but Tom kept right on eating his grits.

"Something wrong, Tom?" I asked.

He glanced at my foot, then glanced away. "It's not the color of money. It's the color of bad flesh. When a person degenerates, he gets big, green splotches all over. I'm sorry, but it makes me queasy just to look at it." He pushed his grits away.

I knew what he was talking about. Laurice had gotten the green splotches, and we'd hidden them away beneath tan foundation. "It's feeling much better. The green should fade away soon," I said.

"Good." But Tom didn't finish his breakfast, and he soon left for work, stepping heavily on his way out the door.

I finished his bowl of grits; I couldn't throw away food, not when the family never had enough. I'd offered Tom the three hundred dollars I had brought with me, but he refused it, just as he had refused my twenty-dollar bill on the bus. It was a matter of pride to him; this family was his responsibility, and he considered himself enough of a man to handle his responsibilities without help.

"He won't take my money, but if I filled the cupboards with food, he'd accept that, I think," I said, thinking out loud.

"I know where a grocery store is," Jake cried. He always

spoke loudly, as if he had to shout in order to draw attention to himself with so many other children underfoot. Tom gave him plenty of love, but the littler ones needed so much care. I spontaneously hugged Jake, and he hugged back; he needed the attention, and I knew just how he felt.

"Will you take me to the grocery store?" I asked.

"I sure will," Jake said. He immediately began packing Honey's bag – two bottles of milk, four diapers – to get her ready for Ms. Tilton's. The twins weren't even up yet.

I distracted Jake with a game of cards, but when the twins woke up, Jake was as eager as ever. "I never knew a child to get this excited about a grocery store," I said.

Jake grabbed Honey's bag, and ushered me and the twins out the door. "I belong outside, just like a bird. Maybe we can go back to our park and play ball again."

Our park. I liked the sound of that. We'd have to bring the groceries home first, and I promised him that if my foot held up, we'd pick up his equipment and go right back out again. "Just so long as I don't have to run the bases," I said.

"You'd have to hit the ball first," he teased. I swatted at him, and he ran laughing into the hallway.

Ms. Tilton welcomed the children into her small, well-kept apartment. She missed them over the weekends, and always had special treats for them on Mondays and Tuesdays. Ms. Tilton was quite old, sixty-five at least, maybe even seventy. It wasn't just degens that lived in the ghetto; sometimes the very poor, and those who had been abandoned by their families, found shelter here. Ms. Tilton had an old red tricycle out for the twins to play on, and I got the feeling that she'd had a son or daughter of her own who'd once played on that tricycle.

I didn't ask about her past, not wanting to stir up any sadness in the gracious old lady. I just handed over my precious Honey. Ms. Tilton's smile chased her wrinkles away, and as she beamed down at Honey, she looked almost young enough to be the little sweetheart's mother. A child can bring out such goodness in an adult.

Jake tugged on my arm.

"Take care of them," I said.

"I always do," said Ms. Tilton.

"Kelly, Kenny, I'm going to pick up some chocolate ice cream just for you."

Kelly's eyes grew wide, and she clapped her hands to her cheeks. "Chocolate ice cream?" she said, as if it were too good to be believed.

"Or how about Neapolitan ice cream? Then you can have chocolate, vanilla, and pink strawberry, too."

"Kelly likes pink," said Ms. Tilton. She must know our little ones better than I did, she'd been caring for them for so long.

"Can I pick up something for you, Ms. Tilton?" I asked.

She fluttered her thin, veined hands at me, saying, "No, no, get on with you," but she seemed pleased that I had asked.

Jake tugged harder on my arm.

"Bye," I called out. As the door shut, I heard Kelly say, "Choc-o-late ice cream," in an extremely pleased voice.

We left the apartment building behind us, went down the little alleyway – thankfully there were no rats today, although the garbage stank so bad I had to cover my nose to get past. We went out onto East Street, the main throughway. Even the bright Florida sunshine couldn't make this place look anything but dingy. Jake pulled me along at such a brisk pace, I found myself tripping over the cracks in the sidewalk.

"Can we slow down?" I asked.

"Can we run?" he asked back.

We ran. My foot was better, but not completely healed from the pan I'd dropped on it, and I probably shouldn't be running on it, but running brought such a flush to his cheeks. Once again, with that big grin on his face and his hair tangled by the breeze, he looked like Huck Finn in his heyday.

We passed a group of three men, all sprawled on the sidewalk in front of a liquor store. The store wasn't even open this early, but each of the men had a bottle in his hand. They perked up as we passed. The biggest of the men leered at me. He was the ugliest man I'd ever seen, with grimy blond hair, a squashed nose and a tattoo of a naked fat woman on his cheek. With a twist of a smile, he said, "Them breasts look like they wanna jump right out of your shirt."

I was too shocked to answer, and I put on a burst of speed. Maybe my breasts were bouncing, and maybe speeding up made them bounce more, because the men roared with laughter. Catcalls followed us down the street. I felt dirty, even though I hadn't meant to bring their cruel attention to me.

Jake stopped suddenly. "This is it," he said triumphantly. Behind us, I still heard catcalls. I hurried Jake into the store. I felt safer as soon as we were off the street.

The Dewdrop supermarket was poorly lit, and the aisles needed to be swept, but there were tons of groceries crowding the shelves and the refrigerated areas. Jake wanted to push the cart, and he exclaimed every time I put something into it. I picked out fresh bread, and steak for dinner, and green beans and broccoli and fresh carrots, good healthy foods to help the children grow. I had two choices for Neapolitan ice cream, and I chose the one that had on its box a little girl with a big ice cream cone. Jake wanted the largest bottle of orange juice I'd ever seen.

"Are you sure we can drink all that?"

His voice got hushed, his eyes big. "I never get orange juice. It's my favorite. Please, Anise?"

How could I say no to that? We filled up the cart, so much so that the young clerk looked surprised when we wheeled it up. "You need any cigarettes or lottery tickets today?" he asked.

I assured him I didn't smoke and I didn't gamble.

"Then you don't fit in around here," he said. "We take cash and check. Have you got the money for this?"

"I've got cash," I said.

The total came to fifty-nine dollars and fifteen cents. The clerk closely examined my hundred-dollar bill before accepting it. The twenties he gave back were greasy and torn.

"Have a nice day," he said, a dismissal if ever I heard one. We even had to bag our own groceries. We'd bought too much, and it was a struggle to fit it all into four grocery bags, the most that we could carry. We couldn't take the cart with us; it had a sign attached to it that said, *This cart does not leave the store. Violators will be prosecuted.* Beneath it, *Screw You* was scrawled.

I gave Jake the lighter two bags. The little bell dinged as we left the store. The transition from poorly lit store to bright Florida sunshine was too much for my eyes; I could barely see.

Very close to my ear, someone catcalled.

I blinked, catching bright glimpses of the men leering at me from where they leaned against the side of the grocery store. They'd followed us. Beside me, Jake whimpered. He hadn't paid attention to them before, he'd been so focused on getting us to the grocery store, but it was impossible to miss them now.

"Did you pick up anything for us?" said the scrawniest of the three. He had a nose ring, deep-set eyes, and a scar that ran across his upper lip.

The big man with the tattoo on his cheek was silent. The third guy coughed, wiped his nose with the backside of his hand. He had bloodshot eyes and a full beard. "What'd you bring? We're real hungry. Haven't had anything but drink all morning, right, Al?"

"Shut up, Sicko," said the big man. He seemed to be the leader, the one to worry most about. He grinned, a big dangerous grin that distorted the tattoo on his cheek. "Hello, ma'am," he said. "Hello, little boy."

"Hello," Jake said hesitantly. Scar-lip and Sicko thought that was real funny, but Al just kept looking at me with that dangerous grin on his face.

"Run," I said to Jake.

"Don't run," said Al. "I got something to show you, ma'am. And you've got something to show me, although you started the show early. I ain't complaining." He dropped his stare to my chest. "I ain't complaining at all, am I boys?"

"Run," I said to Jake, and this time I gave him a push. He dropped his bags, and glass shattered. Orange juice leaked through the bag. Jake did not run.

I shoved my bags at Al, caught Jake's hands, and dragged him along. A hand seized the back of my t-shirt, and I heard it tear. "Run, Jake, for my sake, please run," I cried. I was pulled down roughly onto the sidewalk. Jake hesitated, and Sicko grabbed his neck, oh, the hand he'd wiped his nose with was around Jake's neck, and now Jake couldn't run. Neither could I. Trapped against the cement, I felt Al's heavy weight on my back. I wriggled, helpless to get away, like a fish out of water, like a fool who'd thought she'd be safe on ghetto streets.

"The store clerk's watching, Al," said Scar-lip.

"He's no dummy. He won't interfere," Al said. He placed both hands through the tear in my shirt, and ripped it all the way apart. I had worn my burgundy satin bra today, the one that made me feel pretty. Al ran his hand along the bra strap.

"Umn," Sicko said. He licked his lips, and then had to wipe his nose again.

Al unsnapped my bra. My breasts fell free.

"Let me go," I cried.

"Or you'll do what?" Al said.

"Let Jake go," I begged.

"He's old enough to learn what women are for," Al said. He gently pulled the bra straps down my arms. "And you are definitely a woman." He turned me around, still trapping me with his body weight. My shirt and bra came free, and I was naked down to the waist. Al grabbed my breasts, squeezing hard, and I cried out in pain.

"You like that, do you," Al said, and he squeezed harder. His fingernails cut into my breasts.

"Help me, someone," I screamed. Back at the grocery store, the clerk stood in the window. "Help me." He caught my eyes, and then turned away. Maybe he was going back to call the police. Maybe. He hadn't looked like he was in a hurry. He had looked guilty.

"Jake, shut your eyes, shut your eyes and wait for this to be over," I cried.

Scar-lip tore the diamond ring from my hand. "This ain't real, is it? No degen would have a rock this big."

"Give me that," Al said.

"Shouldn't we take her off the streets?" Sicko sounded worried. "Someone might come by."

"Help me," I screamed. Al took his hand off my breast to slap me, hard. I tasted blood. My own bra was shoved into my mouth. My own t-shirt, wrapped around my eyes to blind me. Al's weight left me. I flailed about in darkness, hitting my hand against cement, against the wet grocery bag. They laughed at my helplessness. I was breathing heavily, my chest in constant motion.

"The alleyway," Al said. "Let's see what else she has to show us."

Sweaty hands grabbed my waist, tried to lift. I resisted, flailing, knocking over the grocery bag nearest me. I was instantly punished, slapped hard across the face, my head driven against the cement. My t-shirt fell off my eyes, and I could see again. A broken jar had fallen out of the grocery bag. The orange juice bottle. A weapon. I seized it, stabbed upwards. Scar-lip was on top of me, and I gave him another scar, right across his cheek. It would've been his eye if I'd hit higher. He seized my hand, driving the glass into me, cutting me. My hand curled protectively in, around the glass. Blood ran through my fingers.

"My wrist," I cried. "You've slit my wrist, you've killed me."

Scar-lip, Al, and Sicko went completely still. My wrist was not cut, only my hand was, but they didn't know it. So much blood.

"The store clerk," Sicko said. "He saw everything."

"He won't talk," Al said, but his cheek twitched, making his tattoo jump.

"My wrist," I cried, deliberately fainter than before.

Al and Scar-lip turned and ran up the street. Sicko shoved Jake aside and took off after them. I fell back, covering my breasts with my good hand. My breaths caught in a sob.

"Don't die, please don't die," Jake said. He knelt beside me, he was only a nine-year-old boy, he didn't know what to do. I had to protect him. I had to get us out of here before they came back.

I sat up, forced myself to open my hand. The glass was stuck against the flat of my palm, cutting into me. I pried it loose, felt a wave of dizziness. Jake was depending on me. I tied my torn shirt around my hand. It blossomed red.

"Give me your shirt," I said. It was too small, but it covered me. "Do you know a back way home?"

"Yes," he said, a very small voice.

"It'll be okay," I said. "We just need to get home, and then it'll be okay." Jake helped me to my feet. I was shaky, barely able to stand. I needed Jake's help to take a step. Our groceries were scattered all over the cement. Kelly's ice cream was among them.

"I promised her ice cream," I said. "She'll cry if I don't

have ice cream." And something broke within me, and I cried myself, my whole body shaking with it, my breasts loose beneath Jake's too-tight shirt. I had promised her ice cream.

"It's still good. It didn't break. See?" Jake picked up the ice cream. He was crying too now. I had to be responsible for him. I had to get him home safely. I put a hand on Jake's shoulder, and he put an arm around my waist, and we walked toward home.

Chapter Eight

Jake proved himself to be as much a man as Tom was. He found a back route home, and he peeked around into each street before we took it. He had been as scared as I, but he seemed to be getting stronger now that it was behind us. I was getting weaker. I trembled so much, I could barely walk. The cuts in my chest smarted. My head spun, and I wondered if I had a concussion. Concussion had been Laurice's word, for when I hit balls into the bay. Giving the fish concussions.

"I can't take you to the park," I said.

"We're almost home," Jake said.

"I can't play baseball with you today. I'm sorry. Jake, I'm so sorry."

Jake led me into the apartment complex, up the stairs, not to our own apartment but to Ms. Tilton's. As soon as she answered the door, her face went very gray.

"Give Kelly her ice cream," I said to Jake, and then my legs gave out, and I slid down the door to the ground. Ms. Tilton tried to lift me, her hands on my waist. Just as Scar-lip had done. I shuddered away from her. "Don't touch me," I begged.

Ms. Tilton drew back at once. "Jake, bring the children into my bedroom. There's games in there for you to play. Anise, whatever happened, you're safe now. I want to get you inside, out of the hallway. Can you come inside?"

I crawled through the doorway. She shut the door behind me. Honey had made her look young, but I made her look very old indeed. "Let's get you onto the couch," she said. I let her take me there.

She brought me a glass of iced tea and a wet rag for my

forehead. She seemed to be spinning, the whole room was spinning. I shut my eyes.

"You've hit your head," she said. "I can't allow you to go to sleep."

"I might have a concussion," I said.

"That's right."

"Just like the fishes."

She looked worried. "Fishes? Are you seeing things? How many fingers am I holding up?"

"Three fingers," I told her. It didn't reassure her. I counted again. "I mean four. Four fingers."

She got out a first aid kit. She cleaned and bandaged first my hand, then my forehead, then the scrapes along my legs. She lifted up a corner of my shirt, and I jerked away.

"Are you hurt under there?" she asked.

"No," I lied.

"Okay, then. Your hand's badly cut. I'd like you to move each of your fingers, to make sure the nerves aren't cut."

She seemed to know just what to do. "Did you used to be a nurse?"

"I used to be a mom."

"You aren't anymore?"

"Please move your fingers, dear. Now's not the time for my sad story."

I moved my fingers, one at a time. Everything worked. Spots of blood appeared in the bandage, my cuts reopened by my movements.

"You're going to be just fine." Ms. Tilton handed my the iced tea, and I took a sip. It tasted bitter. I drank more. "Can you tell me what happened?" Ms. Tilton asked.

I discovered that yes, I could talk about it. The words rushed out of me, undeterred by the bitter taste in my mouth. It was as if I was reliving the whole nightmare – Al, Scar-lip, Sicko – but this time I knew how it turned out. It was horrible, it was humiliating, but I got away, and I never saw what Al had planned for me in the alley.

I had just finished when Tom arrived. He rushed to my side. "Are you all right?" he asked.

"She will heal," Ms. Tilton said. "She'll be well again in no time." That was a discreet way of saying that I wasn't all right, not at all, not yet.

"You're supposed to be at work," I said to Tom.

"I called him, when I got the tea," Ms. Tilton said.

"She has my number in case of emergencies. This is an emergency. And it's all my fault. I should've known better than to let you go out alone. I should've taken better care of you."

"It's not your fault, Tom." It was my fault. Or it was the fault of the men who attacked me. Not Tom's. He shook his head. He wanted to take all the responsibility, all the blame.

"Check on Jake, please, Tom? It was horrible for him," I said.

"Horrible for you, too," Tom said, his voice wracked with guilt. He went into the bedroom, came back out. Jake had fallen asleep. Kelly and Kenny had eaten most of the ice cream and were sticky and sick to their stomachs. Ms. Tilton hurried in to them. Tom knelt beside my sofa.

"I promise I'll never let anything bad happen to you again." He kissed my forehead, my hand, my legs, next to each and every bandage. There were many bandages. "I promise that Jake, Kenny, Kelly, Honey, and I will take good care of you. It'll be like this never happened."

I reached out with my good hand, ran my fingers through his hair, pulled him close. He needed comforting almost as much as I did. We held each other for long minutes. He peppered my face with kisses, and then he lingered, his lips just barely touching mine.

"I'll take care of you," he whispered, his breath hot on my lips. He kissed me, deeply, gently. My head swam. My eyes fluttered closed. When our kiss was done, I fell back on the sofa, my hand to my chest.

"Was that okay?" he asked.

"Yes," I said. His kiss had been so gentle. I'd wanted him to kiss me, but after what had happened today, I wasn't able to think straight. "Will you take me home?"

Ms. Tilton agreed to watch the children for longer, and Tom lifted me easily. I clung one-handed to his shoulder. He was so strong. He took me to his apartment, and laid me on my bed. It creaked beneath my weight. He turned to leave, and I caught his arm. "Don't go," I said.

He sat on the edge of the bed. "I thought maybe you should rest."

"I'm not supposed to sleep, in case I've got a concussion."

Tom nodded. "A concussion. Yes. We wouldn't want you to get a concussion."

He didn't know what the word meant. But he'd said himself, he was a factory worker, not a scholar. The concern on his face was what mattered. I was in good hands. "Tom? Tell me a story."

"I don't think I can today. It'd be a story about myself, and how I screwed up, and how you got hurt. That's the only story I can think about."

"I don't want that one." The cuts on my chest seemed to smart more than ever, now that the others were all treated and bandaged. "Tom, did Ms. Tilton tell you everything that happened?"

"When she called, all she knew was that you'd shown up on her doorstep, very hurt. I guessed the rest, that some guy must have attacked you."

"Three guys," I said.

"If you want me to find them and hurt them, I'll do that for you, Anise. Just tell me what they looked like."

"No," I said. I couldn't have Tom get hurt. He thought it was his fault, but I was responsible for my own actions. I'd chosen to go out, even though I knew the ghetto was dangerous. "There is something I want, though."

"What does Anise want?" he asked. It was the line from our stories.

"They took my shirt off. My bra too," I said. "I'm cut on my chest, but I didn't want Ms. Tilton to treat it. I didn't want her to touch me. But I think I'd be okay if you treated it. Will you do that for me?"

"Of course I will." He went to get the first aid kit. I pulled off my t-shirt. Long scrapes ran down the far sides of my breasts, all from Al's fingernails. It looked worse than it felt. I hid myself beneath the covers before Tom came back. He could tell at a glance that I was worried.

"Lean back against your pillow and close your eyes," he said. "And remember that it's me, and I'd never do anything to hurt you."

I leaned against the pillow, but I kept my eyes open, just a crack. He rolled the covers down, and he gasped when he saw my breasts. Oh, I knew they looked awful.

"I'm going to clean the cuts first," he said, warning me before he brought the stinging iodine to my chest. His hands moved very gently, cleaning first the big scrapes, then all the little ones across both breasts. He put the bandages in place, and they pushed my breasts up from both sides like some strange fluffy cotton bra. Tom had a flush to his face, as if he'd been working out. "All done," he said, and his voice was tender.

"Thank you." I didn't move to cover myself, and his attention returned to my breasts. He brought his fingers down, running them lightly from one breast to the other, around the nipples, down the valley between them. "Is this okay?" he asked, even as he brought his lips down to kiss next to each of the bandages on my chest.

I didn't answer. I didn't know what I wanted. What the men had done to me today had been wrong, and it made me feel dirtied. Tom was cleansing that away with each kiss. And yet, there was such an intensity to his movements now, to his kisses, his touches. Everything was going too fast. He brought his head up to kiss me on the lips, a hard kiss, and his hand slid down to the rim of my jean shorts. He was unbuttoning them.

"No," I moaned.

He withdrew his hand at once. "I didn't mean to do that," he said, sounding as dazed as I felt. "After what you've gone through today." The flush fell from his cheeks. He brought me a t-shirt, one of his oversized ones, for me to cover myself. "I won't take advantage of you again. It was horrible of me."

"Where are you going?" I cried. He was leaving me. I hadn't meant for him to leave.

"I need to recover myself," he said.

A few minutes later, I heard him leave the apartment. He returned with the children, and he brought Honey in for me to hold. He sat next to us on the edge of my bed, his face very solemn. "I'm going to be honest with you," he said. "You've been here, what, eight days? I barely know you. And I can't stop thinking about you. Especially with us sleeping in the same bedroom. Late at night, I listen to you breathing, and I think. . ."

I'd lain awake at night, listening to him breathe too. "What do you think about?"

"No, I won't say, because I'm not going to act on my thoughts. You deserve better than me."

But he was wonderful. Didn't he know how wonderful he was? "I've never met anyone like you before," I said.

"Your Daddy would know what I mean. If you hadn't stopped me, I would've kept going. I would've made love to you, Anise, right here, right now. You deserve better. You deserve someone who will be there to hold you on your fiftieth wedding anniversary. I can't even promise you tomorrow."

"I'm not asking you to," I said.

"I won't do that to you." He put out his finger for Honey to play with, and she grabbed on with both hands. "I won't begin something with you, because it's obvious that I wouldn't be able to stop myself. I would make love to you if you didn't stop me. And if I put a baby in you, I couldn't live with myself. It would ruin your life, and it would ruin the baby's life too. You know, I look at Honey, and my heart breaks. She deserves a long, full life." He broke away suddenly from my bed. Honey stretched out her arms after him. "I won't touch you again. You've got my promise," he said, and he hurried out of the room.

Chapter Nine

Tom moved out of our bedroom that very night. Jake moved in. He brought with him his bible, his rat, and his book on baseball heroes. "I brought this for you," he said shyly, handing over the baseball book.

"Thank you," I said. "I wish I had something for you."

"I don't need anything."

"Maybe I could get Tom to pick up some orange juice for you tomorrow. I know you wanted –"

"I don't ever want orange juice again," he said angrily.

Oh, the poor kid. I had such a troubled little boy before me, and I barely had the resources to deal with my own pain.

"Today was awful, wasn't it," I said.

Jake nodded, less angry, more solemn.

"We're going to take care that it doesn't happen again. Tom's going to take care of all of us. You're safe now," I said.

"I'm going to grow up big," Jake vowed. "I won't ever let anyone hurt you, or Kelly, or Honey."

I had so many protectors. "Thank you." I hugged him tight. My arms fit around him easily. He was just a kid. "It's over now. It's over and you're safe."

"I'm still scared," he said.

"Sleep in my bed tonight. I'm scared too."

There was just enough room for both of us. Despite his earlier nap, Jake fell asleep easily. Tom, as thoughtful as ever, had left the hallway light on for us, and I watched Jake sleep. I thought of his poor mother, who'd only known him as a little baby, not as the responsible young man he was fast becoming. And I thought of my own mother. She'd taken care of me until I was five, until I was enrolled in school and didn't need her – but of course I had still needed her, I needed her so much, and she had swum away forever. She would never know the woman I was becoming. Unlike Jake's mother, my mother had chosen not to know me.

I was angry at her. I was angry at Daddy, for loving Laurice and not loving me. I was angry at Tom; he should be in here to comfort me, he'd promised to take care of me and where was he? My anger ate away in my stomach, and I knew I was really angry at myself. I hadn't been smart enough; I laid myself open to Al, Sicko, and Scar-lip to attack me. What if, when I passed them the first time, I'd told them to back off, instead of running and letting my breasts bounce and intriguing them more? What if, when we emerged from the grocery store, I had heard the catcall and ducked back inside? I could've saved myself this trauma, and saved Jake from it too.

Tom might think it was all his fault, but the truth was, it was mine.

Jake came down with a cold. Sicko's cold. He spent most of the week in bed, miserable. I spent the week out of bed, miserable. I couldn't sleep. Every time I slept, I had nightmares. First I was watching from the grocery store, and it was Laurice pinned down in the street, and Al on top of her, and Laurice screamed for me to help, but I couldn't move. Then I'd be the one trapped, naked, terrified. I'd wake up, a stifled scream trapped in my throat, and wish that Tom were in the room to comfort me.

I fastidiously cleaned the apartment. Tom said he'd never seen the apartment look so good, but he didn't say anything about how I looked, because I looked terrible. Dark circles lingered under my eyes. My cuts were beginning to heal, which meant they itched terribly, and my bruises went the shade of green that I knew Tom hated. I felt so alone. I prayed, as I knew my mother would have done, but I couldn't keep the anger out of my prayer. Where had God been when I needed him? Where was he now?

But there was one person who was always there for me.

Each day, I wrote in Laurice's diary. Each day, I imagined Laurice up in heaven, getting the diary entries. I addressed them as if they were letters. I imagined that she wanted to write back, but there weren't any pens in heaven, and that made me cry. A poet like Laurice needed pen and paper, and I had pen and paper, and I couldn't give it to her. She was gone.

June 2, 2050

Dear Laurice,

I feel like my breasts aren't mine anymore. Like Al and Sicko and Scar-lip, or whatever their real names are, stole my breasts and left me with these lumps that are no good to anyone. No good to me; I can't look at them without thinking of my burgundy bra torn off, my breasts open to the world. No good to Tom. He doesn't want me. I thought he was my Jimmy, but now I think I don't deserve a Jimmy.

Yours, Anise

June 7, 2050

Jake laughed today. It's the first time he's laughed since the attack. His cold is almost gone, and he's eating again. I told him he needed to eat if he was going to get big and strong like he said he would. I don't know if he'll ever look at food again without remembering our full grocery bags, crashing to the streets. But I was going to tell you about the happy part of the day, not the sad parts. Jake was reading aloud from his *Everything A Nine-Year-Old Should Know* book. He was getting real frustrated, because there's so much that's new to him, and it's hard to take it all in. He asked me, "How come they don't ask about baseball players? I know them all, major league and minor. How come they don't ask about the stuff a nine-year-old actually knows?"

"Well," I said, "What do you know?" And he had so much to tell me. How to whistle, and which beaches have the best fishing, and how to look real cute when you get in trouble, so that you don't get in trouble. "I'm going to tell Tom about that trick," I said, and Jake laughed, he even surprised himself with the laugh, and he definitely surprised me.

We gave up on the books for the day. He seemed to know enough.

Love, Anise

June 12, 2050

Dear Laurice,

How would you have answered the question, "What do you want?" Tom tells these stories, and the kids have no trouble coming up with what they want, and in the story, they get whatever it is they wanted.

I know how Daddy would answer. He'd want you back. Not me, no, he'd want his Laurice. If he had you, he wouldn't care if I stayed run away forever. But I don't know what you would've wanted. You had it all, didn't you?

Love, Anise

As the days passed, I began to feel better despite myself. It felt good, the day I removed my bandages and saw the new pink skin beneath. New skin, new life. They'd done me no permanent damage. Jake and I caught the bus with Tom one morning, all the way out to the baseball park, and although I was scared, nothing bad happened all day.

Story-time remained a highlight for all of us. I told more stories. With Tom's encouragement, and the children's eager faces, it was easy to spin tales of Kenny the goat-herder and Kelly the straw-spinner, Jake the baseball king and Honey the queen of all hearts. I began to think that everything was going to be okay, my Daddy was never going to find me here, and I would live with this loving family for as long as they would have me, which Tom assured me was just as long as I wanted to stay.

One day, as I changed Honey's diaper and Tom and Kenny were tending to Kelly, who'd hurt her knee, Honey wriggled free from me. As I tried to get her back into position, she rolled over all on her own. Even Kelly stopped bawling to come admire Honey, who seemed very proud of herself.

"They grow so fast," Tom said, close to my ear. "I can

remember when Jake first sat up, when Kenny first walked, when Kelly first spoke. Honey's on her way."

He loved the children so much, it seemed to me that he would want to have children of his own, but he'd made it clear that he didn't. His genes had brought him only suffering, and he didn't want a child of his to suffer.

"Children are amazing," I said. "I hadn't thought I wanted to have children. I thought they were so difficult to raise, so easy to hurt, just because Daddy hurt me so. But they're not difficult at all. Just sprinkle them with love, and stand back and watch them grow."

Honey cooed happily. Jake held her arms, and pretended to dance.

"That's just the problem for a degen. We don't live long enough to watch our children grow."

I hated to hear the sorrow in his voice. He was the sort of guy who was meant to be a father and a husband. He was responsible and loving and always knew how to make the children happy, and he knew how to make me happy too. When I closed my eyes, I could still feel his kisses on my chest. I didn't want to give up on him, just because he'd given up on himself. "Didn't you say yourself that degens appreciated life more because they had less of it?"

"That's true," Tom said. "We've definitely got less life."

He'd turned into a pessimist the day I got attacked. That was weeks ago. It was in the past now. We had to live for the present. I thought about Laurice and her Jimmy. They'd only had a short time, but they'd filled it with several lifetimes worth of love. "Did I ever tell you about Laurice's boyfriend?"

"Please don't," Tom said. "I know what you're getting at. It hurts me just to think about. If I let myself be your boyfriend, I wouldn't be the man I think I am." He caught Honey, finished her diapering, and held her to him. "You've got to think about the future. You've got a future."

"So do you. You're not dead yet," I said, only I said it too loud, and poor Kelly burst into tears.

Chapter Ten

In the days that followed, I caught Tom watching me when he thought I wasn't looking. When I'd look his way, he'd look away real quick. He dressed nicer than he had when we first met, and he asked me one day if I'd be willing to cut his hair.

We found a pair of scissors, and Tom sat on the arm of the couch while I stood behind. Sometimes, when I breathed in, my chest brushed against his back. It made it hard to focus on his haircut. I'd never cut hair before. I couldn't tame his thick curls, but I trimmed them back, and did my best to make an even hairline in back.

"My turn next," Jake called.

Tom slipped away from me as soon as I was done. Jake took his place. He had the same curls as Tom, the wild dark Huck Finn curls. "What would you like?"

"I want to look like Tom," he said.

I trimmed Jake's hair more quickly than I had Tom's. I was nearly done, with just the patch behind his ear to take care of, when I saw a small green splotch. It was the size of a dime, just behind his ear lobe. As green as a dollar bill. Jake's hair had been covering it, but I'd trimmed that away. It was small, but that didn't matter. I knew the course of degeneration. Laurice's splotches had started out small, but they multiplied, and they grew inside her too, on her organs. I dropped the scissors. Tom came running to my side, he clutched my shoulders, he asked, "What's wrong?"

"Nothing," I lied. "You're done now, Jake."

Jake ran off to study the math book Tom had gotten him.

He liked math.

"You're shaking," Tom said. He turned me to face him, studied my face. "You're not blinking, either."

I blinked. I couldn't tell Tom here, not where Jake could hear.

"Blink again," Tom said. "Once isn't enough." He hesitated, then held me close. "Anise, I know something is wrong, I just can't imagine what. You were fine a moment ago."

"Come into the bedroom with me," I said.

He backed away as if I were on fire. Did he think I was coming onto him? I laughed, and my laughter had a hysterical edge that must have convinced Tom, because he took my hand and led me to the bedroom. I sat on one corner of the bed, and he sat on the other, far away from me.

"When I was cutting Jake's hair, I saw –" I began, but I had trouble continuing. The bed creaked beneath us as Tom reached across the great divide to catch my hand. "Right behind his ear. He's got a green spot."

"No," Tom said. "No, he's only nine."

"His birthday is next month. He might make it to ten, before –" I couldn't finish my sentence. I couldn't stand thinking about what was to come.

"I need to see it. Maybe you were mistaken," Tom rose to go, but I held on to his hand. He stared down at me, not seeing me, his eyes wild.

"Don't tell him. He doesn't need to know yet. Pretend you're checking out his haircut."

Tom did as I asked. When he returned, he threw himself onto his bed, his hands pressed hard against his eyes. It was as if he thought that if he pressed hard enough, he'd grind away the image of that small green splotch. The same image floated before my eyes, every time I blinked.

"You aren't hurting yourself, are you?" I asked.

"I would, if it'd do any good." But he lowered his fists. They lay helplessly on his lap. We were both helpless.

"It's not fair," I said.

"We'll take him on extra trips. He likes to go to the beach. He fishes with that old net I found." Tom stood up suddenly, fists clenched. It seemed as if he might hit himself, but he hit the wall instead.

"They'll hear," I said. The children were all in the living room.

"You're thinking of them. That's good. I can only seem to think of myself. What I'll do with Jake gone. How he cried when Momma died, and I didn't know how to take care of him. I couldn't even get his diapers on without poking him." Tom hit the bed, again, again. It frightened me, to see a man so worked up, so violent, and yet I went to him anyway. He embraced me, his face pressed to my chest. "He's like my own son," he said, and he shook with sobs.

"We'll get through this. Maybe it'll go away," I said. I knew it wouldn't go away, and he knew it wouldn't, but it was some comfort to imagine that it would, to imagine Jake growing up, his shoulders broadened, his voice deeper, his resemblance to Huck Finn fading as the boy became a man.

When Tom was able, we went back out to the living room, and we pretended that nothing, nothing at all, was wrong. "I think it'd be fun to go fishing tomorrow," I said as casually as I could.

"That'd be the best," Jake cried. "I never had this much fun before you came to live with us." He dropped his books and threw himself into my arms. I held him too tightly, and he squirmed to get away.

"I love you, Jake." I let him go, ruffling his hair as he raced back to where Kenny was playing with old Matchbox cars.

"Love you too," Jake called, and he immersed himself in play.

Fishing. Games of tag. A weekend trip to the Everglades, just me, Tom, and Jake. Jake loved to spot the alligators. We went to the beach, to the children's exhibits at the art museum, to the baseball park where I'd met Jake. Tom accepted fifty dollars from me at last, and we went to see the Florida Marlins take on the Toronto Blue Jays, and we even had hot dogs and popcorn. At the end of the game, after we filed out of the stadium into the cool night air, Jake stopped us for a moment.

"I'm dying, aren't I," he said.

Tom and I were struck dumb. People pushed past us, happy baseball fans in their team hats and jersey shorts. The Marlins had won tonight. A bird screeched overhead. Jake looked up, and Tom and I looked at each other. Tom nodded.

"I should've known you were too smart for us," Tom said.

"You've been awfully nice to me. And the twins and Honey keep getting left behind. I figured it had to be something big." Jake smiled. Even in this, he was proud of what he'd figured out. Even this. "Do you think we could go to Busch Gardens before I die? I'm tall enough for the rides, I think. I've never been on a roller coaster."

"We can go," I said. "We can go anywhere you'd like."

"What does Jake want?" Jake said. He looked down for a moment. "No, I guess I don't want to waste a day on a theme park, not if I haven't got many days left. I guess what I'd want most is to get up every day and go play ball in our park."

"I'm sure Anise would love that," Tom said. I couldn't trust myself to talk. I was fighting back the tears. Laurice had lived long enough to find her Jimmy. Jake had found himself in baseball. It was a good thing, I tried to tell myself, but I just kept picturing Jake on a high school baseball team. Jake playing with the Marlins in the stadium behind us. Jake, teaching his own son to play baseball. It'd never happen now. It wasn't fair.

We got up early every day. Tom went to work, and Jake and I went to our baseball park. On the weekend, the whole family joined us, and Jake tried to teach Kenny to hit the ball. "He's not as good as me," he told me later. "I'm the best at baseball."

The green splotches appeared elsewhere on him. They were soft to the touch. The day came when he didn't feel like getting up to go play baseball. I left him in bed. He didn't get up until noon, and he went back to bed before Tom got home. I paced the apartment like a caged lion, nothing I could do, no way to save him. I prayed to God, take it away from Jake, let him grow up, but every day the splotches grew worse.

"I've got to do something," I said to Tom one evening. "I want to bring him to my Daddy's Institute. They might be able to help him."

"Nothing can help a person once he starts to degenerate,"

Tom said.

"Maybe they can make the pain less." Whatever was happening inside of Jake was hurting him, constant hurt, and aspirin and hot pads and kisses couldn't make it go away. He groaned now, sometimes all night long, and when he did sleep, it was in exhaustion. Sometimes his body dripped with sweat, and sometimes he turned nearly blue with cold. Laurice had never gotten this bad.

"What if your father sees you?" Tom wanted to know.

"It's worth the risk," I said. "I can't sit still, knowing that he's hurting."

"I'll go with you," Tom said.

He took the next day off of work. His boss was happy to give it to him, because Tom had always been a good worker, and everyone at work knew how much stress he was under right now. Watching a loved one suffer is the hardest thing in the world.

We bundled Jake up in the nicest blanket we had, the soft pink one that was normally Kelly's. Ms. Tilton took the little ones, and she squeezed my hand when I turned to go. "The Lord calls all his children home," she said. "I don't tell people about this, because it hurts too much, but He took my boy, Andrew, when he was no older than Jake. The Lord loves the little children. They play by his feet, and braid flowers into his hair. I know they do. I've dreamed about it, and my Andrew waves to me, and Jesus softly smiles."

I hugged her, whispered how sorry I was to hear of her loss.

"It's been fifty years, but a mother never recovers. You've been a mother to Jake this past month. You'll know what I mean."

I knew already. Jake lay listless in Tom's arms. A green splotch was growing across his face, from left to right. Every day this week, it had advanced. He had a fever, and shivered within his pink blanket. "Ms. Tilton loves you," I told him. He managed a smile. "I love you," I added.

He tried to respond, but a coughing fit seized him, and when it was done he lay weakly in Tom's arms, too weak to speak.

We caught the bus. Tom expertly slid his card through the slot, once, twice, three times. The bus driver was about to stop

Tom from bringing Jake on the bus until Tom said, "It's not contagious." Tom showed him Jake's face.

"My condolences," the bus driver said. He looked no older than eighteen himself. Probably he was a degen too. Most service jobs were held by degens. The sort of jobs you didn't have to train long to do. Because you never knew when a degen might degenerate.

"Thank you," I said. I boarded the bus, even though I felt like grabbing Jake and bolting back to the apartment where I would make him some hot soup, bring him a rag for his forehead, tell him a bedtime story. But soup and a story were not what Jake needed. This had been my idea. I remembered something Orson had said, a lifetime ago, in my father's office. *It was the right thing to do.* I was trying to do the right thing for Jake, even though I wanted him home with me.

The bus jerked forward. "Hurts," Jake moaned.

"Would you like a story?" I asked.

Jake's face tightened in pain. Had this boy ever resembled Huck Finn? He looked more like a Holocaust survivor now, gaunt face, haunting eyes. Huck Finn had been carefree, Huck Finn didn't know pain except for the crack of a whip on his bottom when he'd gotten in trouble – and he was always getting in trouble. "This is a story about Jake Finn," I said. "He lived by a big river, and he went fishing every day. He didn't have any parents, but he figured he made out well enough without having someone tell him what to do and what not to do and when to get it done by." I tried to brush Jake's sweat-soaked hair back, and a small clump came off in my fingers. Tom kissed the spot where it had been. "Jake Finn had most everything a boy could want, long days and plenty to fill them with, but he wasn't satisfied. He wanted something more."

"What did Jake want?" Tom asked softly.

Jake thought long and hard, his face puckering every time the bus hit a bump. "A Momma," he said at last.

I pressed a hand to my mouth, as if that could keep my sorrow in. Tom picked up the story. "Once Jake had a Momma. She was a beautiful woman, graceful, with laughter like a river and eyes the color of heaven. She loved Jake's father very much, and together they decided to have a child, so the world would have something to remember their love.

"Jake's Daddy passed away before he was born, and Momma got sick too, not degenerating but sick of heart. She slipped further away from life every day, but she had to hold on, because she had a baby in her that she needed to bring into the world. She wouldn't let that baby down. She had a name picked out for him and everything, and she knit soft blue booties so his feet wouldn't get cold when she was gone.

"When Jake was born, his Momma didn't have eyes for anyone but him. Jake had an older sister, and she got jealous, but he also had an older brother, and the brother knew how much joy this baby had brought to Momma. He was a very special baby indeed, and Momma made the brother swear –" Tom brushed at his eyes, but tears kept sneaking out. "Momma made me swear to take good care of him and to raise him to be a good man just like his Daddy. I don't know how much I had to do with it, but you turned out just as fine a man as Momma hoped for. She's in heaven right now, and you and her have nine years to catch up on, so don't you be afraid of anything. Don't you forget that you have a Momma, and she was the best Momma anyone ever had."

"Love," Jake said. He loved us. Oh, how I loved him, and Tom, and how helpless I was to take away their pain. Tom held Jake close, and I sat beside them. It seemed as if that bus ride would never end, but it did, all too soon. All things come to an end. All things.

Chapter Eleven

I had come to the Degen Institute often when it was first built, the year after Laurice died. I came less often as the years passed. I had grown to resent this innocent-looking building, with its white columns and bright red roof. It stole my Daddy from me, every day.

"Where to?" Tom asked, as I tucked Jake's blanket tighter around him. I led the way to the admissions room. Painted on the walls were palm trees, and the tiles were a textured sandy gold. Daddy had wanted this room to be cheerful.

"Oh, he doesn't look too good," said the clerk behind the counter. "I'll get a room cleared." She left us with a stack of forms in every hue. Tom filled them out slowly, determinedly.

I divided my attention between watching Jake, who was doing better now that he wasn't being moved, and watching the door for my Daddy. He worked every day, all day. He was, without doubt, in this very building.

It made me weak in the knees just to think about Daddy. If he walked into this room, smiling like the president of the United States, could I raise my voice and refuse to go with him? Tell him that I wouldn't marry Orson, wouldn't be a dutiful wife, dutiful daughter? Or would my resolve melt away in the heat of Daddy's presence?

I didn't want to see him, because I didn't know. It seemed I could be swept back into Daddy's orbit, if he came to this door and said, "Anise, dear Anise, I've missed you." Could I refuse his hugs, his kisses, even knowing that I was to be delivered to Orson like a piece of freight, sign here, she's all yours? Daddy had such force of will that mine was weakening just being in the same building as him.

Jake's room was painted a sunny yellow, with a large picture window opening up to the gardens below. Tom had refused the gurney and carried Jake in with his own arms, and he lovingly laid him onto the enormous white bed. A boy could drown in all that white. We buried him under the thick white coverlet, so that just his face stuck out, wide eyes, sweating brow.

"Cold," he said. I spread the pink blanket atop the bed as well.

The clerk took Tom's forms, and asked him about his employer's health insurance. I sat with Jake, talking of the fun we'd had this past month, all the games played, all the balls hit. One day, not more than a week ago, Jake had knocked the ball so far back it had taken an hour to find it. And not five minutes after we found it, I sent the ball into a tree and scared a bird right out of it; when we'd climbed, we found a nest of birdlings, four of them, all hungry and naked pink.

Tom returned with a nurse, who took Jake's blood pressure, and then a doctor, who took one look at Jake and frowned. "He's far along," the doctor said. He listened to Jake's heartbeat, and frowned, and he pressed his long fingers against Jake's stomach, and frowned. When he took Tom and me aside, I knew what he was going to say. Just like when Laurice degenerated, there was nothing anyone could do.

"I'm putting him on morphine to ease the pain. He's in a lot of pain. He's degenerating inside. I'm sorry."

"How long does he have?" I asked.

He avoided my eyes. "I really can't say. We'll see how he gets through the night."

The nurse came with a syringe, and once the medicine was in him, Jake's pain lessened, and he slept. Tom sat on one side of the bed, I on the other. The grief on Tom's face was reflected on my own, I knew. Jake's birthday was the day after tomorrow, and there was no knowing if he'd make it that long.

When Jake woke, his eyes were brighter than they'd been in several days. He beamed up at Tom and me, and said, "I get a whole room to myself?"

"Yes," I said. I blinked back tears. I had given up on hearing his boyish voice ever again, except in those one-word sentences that had been all he could do through the pain.

"I've never had my own room before. This is like a hotel room, isn't it? It's even got a TV." He grinned. He didn't look like a dying boy anymore. It was just the medicine, masking his pain, and it didn't change anything, I knew that. But I hoped anyway. Miracles sometimes happened. Jake could live to see his tenth birthday, and his twentieth.

"Can we see what's on TV.?" Jake asked.

Tom found the remote, and we flipped from station to station. They had cable here. Daddy had asked himself what Laurice had enjoyed whenever she went to the hospital, and he'd put everything in here. He had thought of so much, even teddy bears free for every child. They hadn't brought Jake's yet.

Last night's game, the Marlins against the Braves, was being rebroadcast. Jake cheered at first, but grew tired as the game went on.

"We should let you rest," Tom said.

"I don't want to sleep. What if I don't wake up?" Jake huddled deeper in his blankets. "Anise, you'll watch out for Mr. Rat for me, won't you? He knows I gotta leave him. I told him yesterday."

"I will," I said.

"Tom, you'll make sure that Honey remembers me?"

"Of course she'll remember you," Tom said. "I'll tell her stories about you every day."

"I'm scared," Jake said.

"I am, too," I said.

"Crawl in bed with me," he pleaded.

It was a big bed, big enough for five Jakes. I crawled in on one side, and Tom on the other. Jake cuddled close in between.

"Got all I want, just like Tom," Jake said. He yawned, and just like that, he slept. I kissed his hot forehead before I slipped out of bed.

When he woke, hours later, he was groggy, disoriented. "Where's Momma?" he yelled, even though he'd never known his Momma. He thrashed within his big bed, and he hit his arm against the bedside railing, and the large green splotch on his arm split neatly open. No pus oozed out, no blood, nothing. It was as if his arm wasn't alive, wasn't human, not where that splotch was. I caught his other arm, kept him from hurting himself. At last the nurses arrived with a medicinal.

He slept. Tom and I clung to each other, and outside the day turned to night, but inside nothing changed. Jake was dying. His sleep, at first disturbed, grew softer, and his mouth fell slack to reveal his tongue, swollen, green-tinged as if moss had found a shady spot there. A sour odor filled the room. The degeneration was speeding up. It's like that, slow at first, barely noticeable, just a splotch behind the ear, but just like biking up a hill, once you reach the top, everything speeds up. It may take forever to crest the hill, but once you do, you coast down, faster than the breeze can catch you, and you hit the bottom in no time.

I listened to Jake's soft breaths, in and out, and the time came when he breathed out, and did not breathe in. Tom rang for the nurse. She came, pronounced him dead, offered her condolences. She never had brought his teddy bear.

I kissed Jake's forehead good-bye, and I stumbled with Tom out of the room. Tom had taken care of all the paperwork already. Jake was to be cremated, and we could pick up his ashes the following day. Oh, God, his ashes.

It seemed we could only walk if our arms were tightly wrapped around each other. I supported Tom, he supported me. Neither of us were strong enough on our own. We'd come with Jake, and we were leaving without him.

Out on the building steps, I thought I heard my name called. I looked around. It was dark. I didn't see anyone.

"Anise, wait right there." I heard it faintly, coming from above. I looked up and there was Daddy, staring down. He wore a shirt and tie. He was working late tonight, that was all I could think; my mind was full of cotton. Daddy vanished from the window, and just like that, he fell from my mind. I continued slowly down the steps, but Tom had seemed to wake up when Daddy called my name. He dragged me faster, faster, down the steps. He waved for a passing taxi. It didn't stop. The next one did. The doors burst open behind us, and as Tom bundled me into the taxi, my Daddy screamed, "Kidnapper! Let my daughter go!"

"East Street," Tom told the driver.

We pulled away. Daddy chased us down the street, his hands waving for us to stop. I waved a sad good-bye to him, and to Jake, as the taxi carried us far away from them both.

Chapter Twelve

I automatically went to Ms. Tilton's door when we got back to the apartment complex. Pull the family together, that was what I thought we should do. Grief is lessened if shared.

Tom disagreed. "They're already asleep in there," he said. "Let them rest tonight, and I'll tell them in the morning."

"We'll tell them together," I said. He wasn't in this alone. "Oh, Tom, he went so fast."

Tom took my hand, entwined his fingers through mine, and squeezed so tight it hurt, but I didn't let go. Sometimes love hurt. Sometimes little boys didn't make it to their tenth birthdays.

Our apartment was dark, and empty; it was like entering a cave, where a bear growled from the dark depths. There was pain, now, in this apartment that had been so joy-filled. By the sofa, Jake's math book was left open, face-down, waiting for Jake to come back to turn the page that would never be turned. I checked on Mr. Rat, and he lay so still that I feared he had died along with his master, but when I poked him, he stirred, and he blinked his dull pink eyes uncomprehendingly at me. *Jake never disturbed my rest,* that was what Mr. Rat was saying. *Jake was a great friend, but he had to leave me, he told me so yesterday.*

"Anise." Tom startled me, coming up from behind, wrapping his arms around me. I'd only left him for a moment, but he must have felt abandoned out alone in the living room. "Don't leave me, it hurts to be alone."

"I know," I said. Only he and I could know. Only we understood what a gift to the world Jake had been. "Who knows what would've happened to me if Jake hadn't brought me home with him like a stray cat?"

"Or like a stray rat," Tom said. "Did you know? Jake found Mr. Rat abandoned in his cage, out behind the liquor store. Mr. Rat's water bottle had been filled with alcohol. People are awfully mean sometimes. Jake saved him."

"The day I got attacked, Jake refused to run. He could've gotten away, but he wouldn't leave me."

"He looked up to me. He wanted to dress like me, act like me. I let him down. I let him die."

"Tom, you're not God, you didn't let him die."

Tom twisted away from me, crossed to Jake's nightstand, pulled out Jake's Bible. Tom considered the worn, old book, considered it for a long moment, and then he threw it on the ground, and he spat on it.

"No, Tom, no," I cried, too late. Jake had treasured that Bible. It had been their mother's.

"If it's God who let Jake die, then he is no God to me."

I wiped the book clean, replaced it on Jake's nightstand. "This was your mother's bible. You spit on it, you spit on her. It's wrong, Tom."

"I loved my Momma," Tom said. "But she made me swear to take care of Jake. I swore on that very Bible. And I failed her." He trembled, and I didn't want to see him cry again, couldn't bear it if he cried. I ran my hands along his face, but I couldn't smooth away the pain. His legs seemed to give out under him, as if they couldn't bear the weight of his grief, and he sat down, hard, on his bed. He dropped his head into his hands, and his whole body shook. Like a palm tree in a hurricane, violent shaking, as if the very air in this room attacked him. He hit himself on the knees with his fist, again, and again. I caught his fist.

"Let me go," he said.

"Never," I said. I brought his fist to my lips and kissed each tightened knuckle. Slowly his hand relaxed, and I kissed his fingernails as they escaped his palm. Bloody half-moons showed where they had been. His knees had flared a violent red where he had hit. "Jake would not want you to hurt yourself."

"I failed him," Tom said. "I failed Momma, I failed myself.

If you don't go, I'll fail you too. I'm just that way. I can't hold on to those I love."

"Not true." I joined him on Jake's bed, and brought Tom's head to rest against my shoulder. "You've got Honey, and Kelly, and Kenny, and me."

"But not Jake," Tom said.

"And Jake in heaven, and your Momma in heaven. That's six people who love you, who'd never leave you of their own free will. That's more than I'll probably ever have."

"I love you," Tom said. "You don't have to worry about love. Anyone who gets to know you will love you, and your Daddy's a damn fool if he doesn't."

"Don't swear," I said.

"A damn fool," he said. "There's no way around it. Did you hear him call me a kidnapper? As if you didn't have any choice in anything you did, and so if you were going with me, you were surely being kidnapped. You have choices, Anise. You are your own person, a fine person, and your Daddy's a damn fool for not recognizing that."

He slipped away from my shoulder, for I had begun to shake in my own, private hurricane. The world was not as it should be. Daddies shouldn't be fools. Nine-year-old boys shouldn't die. Tom wrapped his arms around me, pulled me down on the bed with him, held me close. His lips flutter-kissed across my face, like a butterfly unsure of where to rest. "Your Daddy's a fool, but I'm not," he said, and the butterfly found its resting place; his lips pressed against mine, a deep kiss, a hard kiss. A storm roared through me, awakening my body, pushing back my grief. I kissed Tom back, hard, as hard as I could. Sometimes love hurt. The kiss broke, and Tom hesitated, and my grief threatened to swamp me. Oh, that grief, I could be dragged under and drowned just by the thought of Jake.

"Comfort me," I said to Tom. "Let me comfort you."

He kissed me again, gently this time. Love didn't always have to hurt. He pulled off his shirt, and then my own. I looked down at my breasts, framed as they were by my pink lace bra. "Are they ugly?" I asked.

"Ugly like a sunset, or a child's smile," Tom said.

"They look like lumps to me. They didn't used to, not

before the day I was attacked. I once thought that they were beautiful, especially in my burgundy bra, the one that pushed them up so they looked fuller."

"They're beautiful now, just as they are." Tom unbuttoned my bra, freed my breasts. Under his soft kisses, his questing tongue, my nipples grew painfully hard. I wanted to pull him away, to take a moment to breathe, but I couldn't do that to him. Our grief waited for both of us, just beyond this respite that we had made for ourselves.

He flutter-kissed down my stomach, past my belly button, and onto the thick denim of my jeans. No one had ever touched me there. No one, besides Tom, had ever touched me anywhere, not this way. It felt so good, better than I'd imagined. Laurice had been fortunate, to know love like this before she died.

When Tom unbuttoned my jeans, stripped them from me, I welcomed him. I welcomed his hardness. He pressed into me, but it hurt, it tore me inside, and I cried out.

"I'm sorry," he said at once, and he pulled himself from me.

I looked into his brown eyes, his flushed face. I reached up, touched his freckles as if I were connecting the stars in a constellation. The Thomas Constellation, in the shape of a giant heart, filled with love for the children, and love for me. I wanted to give him my body. He had given me so much.

I ran my fingers from his face, down his chest, to his hardness itself, so hot, so needing. I could satisfy his need. I could comfort him. I pulled him into me. He moved slowly, even though I could feel his legs tensed to do more, to go wild. He moved slowly, and slowly the hurt faded, and the heat built, as if the sun itself had come to live between my legs. He seemed to know when to go faster, and when to slow down, so that I was brought to the edge of the sea, brought back, brought to the edge again, until at last the waves crashed through me, and I was the sea, I was the sun, I was everything. I was caught in a moment that lasted forever, and nothing existed except Tom and me and the sun exploding between my legs.

All things end, even this, even though it felt as if it never would. Tom's hardness shrank away, and when I looked down

I saw no blinding sun between my legs, only my small patch of black hair pressed wetly against me.

Neither Tom nor I spoke, for we didn't have to. Our bodies had said all that could ever be said. We lay together, legs entwined, and after a short while, we slept.

Chapter Thirteen

Tom's arms were still wrapped around me when I woke the next morning. His body was warm and naked against me. He didn't wake when I kissed his chest, but when I ran my hand down beneath the sheets, his eyes flew open, and he sat bolt upright. I reached for his waist, meaning to draw him to me. He flinched away from my touch.

"What's wrong?" I asked. My heart seized tight within me. This wasn't what I had imagined him doing. He had loved me last night. Did he love me today?

"I didn't, did I? Tell me it was all a dream, a nightmare. Tell me you didn't let me do that to you."

"It happened," I cried. I reached for his hand, but he kept it limp within mine. He had called our love a nightmare. He regretted what we had done. Oh, I couldn't deal with this, not after Jake's death. I trapped my ears behind my hands, for I would not hear any more, I would not let him speak these words that stung.

"We weren't in control of ourselves," he said. Oh, I could still hear him, even with my ears trapped, even with my heart breaking. "One time can be forgiven. But if we do it again, I'm lost. Anise, listen to me."

"I'm listening," I said. I kept my hands clamped as they were, but I couldn't block out his words. They were so sharp, they darted between my fingers to plunge into my ears. His words, his rejection, it was like a physical thing and I took it inside of me, and it hurt worse than anything had ever, ever hurt. As sure as I had been of his love, I now was sure of the opposite: he had never loved me. He had used me, taken what

I had to give, and now he cast me aside.

"Never again," he was saying. "I will never kiss you, I will never touch you, I will never dream of a future that cannot be. I was weak last night, I'm still weak, but I will be strong, for your sake. Never again."

"Then I've lost everything," I heard myself say, as if from far away. "I've lost everyone." He tried to speak, but I left him, and I ran to the other bedroom, and closed the door tight behind me, and I slid the dresser in front of it, so it could not be opened. He didn't try. I heard him in the bathroom, and then the kitchen, and then he went out the door.

Never again would I be touched, never again kissed? Never to feel Tom's arms around me, never to feel the sun trapped between my legs. It was too much to bear. I thought I would break under the strain of it, under the weight of my own grief. The hours slipped away. Somehow I rode them out, I did not break, and at last I was drained enough to leave my room, and shower, and bring the children home from Ms. Tilton's. Only three children, when there had once been four.

Tom returned late in the afternoon. In his arms he carried a small stone urn. Jake's ashes. I couldn't look at it, just as Tom couldn't look at me. He glanced toward Kenny and Kelly, who were playing leapfrog, Kenny over Kelly, Kelly over Kenny. "Have you told them?" he asked. I had not. He wanted me to take the urn, but I could not touch it. Its stone was too slick, too cool. Too lifeless, to contain my lively Jake. Tom set the urn respectfully on the kitchen table. Then he gathered Kenny and Kelly in his arms, and sat on the sofa, and I brought out Honey. She needed to hear this too.

"Story-time?" Kenny asked. It was early for story-time.

"Yes," Tom said.

"Story 'bout Kelly," Kelly begged.

"No, this is a story about Jake," Tom said. "Jake, who began as a kiss between his mother and his father, and who represented their love in this world, for they had loved each other very much. Jake, who I raised, and who was like my son, and like your brother. We wanted him to stay with us forever, but his Momma in heaven wanted him too."

"What does Jake want?" Kelly lounged her head back,

hanging dizzily over Tom's arm. She didn't understand yet. Tom kissed her nose, and she giggled.

"Where's Jake?" Kenny asked. His little face was furrowed in thought. He knew something was wrong.

"I've told you how we're different from other people. You know how Ms. Tilton's old, gray-haired, wrinkly? Kelly here will never get that funny looking. We're degens, and it's not a slang word, no matter how you hear people say it. It just means that we don't live to be old." He drew a deep breath, exhaled slowly. "Jake died last night. That means he won't come back to live with us. He's gone to be with his Momma in heaven."

"Died?" Kelly asked. Kenny let go of Tom so that he could hold Kelly's hands. He understood, he was only five but he understood, and Kelly did not.

"Everyone dies sooner or later," Tom said softly.

"My mommy died," Kelly said. Her chin begin to quiver. Tom tightened his hold on her.

"I know, honey. And it's not fair. Your momma was a wonderful person. She took me and Jake in, after our own momma died. She loved us. But people aren't born equal. Some are rich, some poor, some black, some white. That makes sense, right?"

"Yes," Kenny said.

"We're degens. It's who we were born to be, and we have to accept what it means. Even though it hurts. Even though it's horrible."

"Where's Jake?" Kelly asked. She looked from Tom, to Kenny, to me and Honey. "I want Jake," she cried, but we all remained where we were, helpless to give her Jake. We wanted him too. Tom's hands clasped into fists, and he looked imploringly up at me. But what had I to say? Kelly's big child's eyes were welling up with tears. She didn't understand death. She was only five.

"A story," I said at last. "That's what we need. A story starring Kelly."

"Me?" Kelly's lower lip trembled, out of control. I knew just how she felt. I was there too.

Tom spun the story, and sure enough, it starred Kelly. She wanted nothing so much as a big pink airplane, and she used it to fly to heaven, and bring back her loved ones.

There was even room on the plane for Laurice.

But even though we'd grieved together, after that evening Tom kept me at a distance. If it weren't for the children, I would have lost my mind. Tom did not talk to me. My heart caught in my throat whenever he entered the room, and I would open my mouth, ready to pour my feelings out to him – and then he'd look at me, and look quickly away, and I knew he did not want to hear of my feelings, for he had no feelings for me.

I wrote in Laurice's diary of how mistaken I had been. Of course Tom did not love me. I was unlovable. It was not my breasts that were unshapen lumps, it was my whole body, my whole self. I was nothing, and Tom knew it.

The empty bed in my bedroom was a constant reminder of how I'd lost Jake, and lost Tom. I ceased to tell stories at story-time. Without Jake, I couldn't. Tom returned Jake's library books. I used to spend the days teaching Jake, and playing with him, but now there was no use for me. I couldn't bear the echoes of the empty apartment. I slipped across to Ms. Tilton's, and spent the days with her and the children. Jake's death had hit her especially hard. Her Andrew had been the same age. She told me about the car that had struck him on his way to school, how it had been a Dodge Dakota, and the driver had been drinking. She opened the locket around her neck to show me his picture. Blond, willowy, he looked nothing at all like our Jake, except for his smile. He smiled as if the world was his to conquer.

We mourned together, Ms. Tilton and I, and the days trickled past. Jake's birthday came and went without any mention, not by me, not by Tom, not by the twins. Tom came home late each night, and I learned that he was working overtime; his employer's health insurance would pay only half of Jake's hospital bill. The Degen Institute had not been a network provider, even though it was the only hospital in the city to specialize in degeneration. Daddy worked so hard to provide a good hospital, and do good research. It was wrong of the insurance company to undermine Daddy's efforts. Tom didn't want to talk with me about it. Tom didn't want anything to do with me.

One week after Jake's death, Tom left for work in the morning as usual, but he returned not ten minutes later, dozens of bright pink sheets clutched in his hands.

Kelly clapped her hands in excitement. "For me?" Anything that was pink was Kelly's. Tom handed her all but one of the sheets. Kelly dropped them on the carpet, and ran to get her coloring crayons. Tom held the remaining sheet out to me.

I took it, not wanting to look but looking all the same. My own face smiled up from the front of the sheet. *Have you seen this girl? $15,000 reward!* was printed in big block letters across the top. Five foot eight, brown hair, brown eyes, 135 pounds. I had never weighed 135 pounds, not ever. I weighed 125. But Daddy didn't know that, Daddy didn't know anything about me; I was lucky he'd gotten the color of my hair and eyes right.

"Where did you find these?" I asked.

"On East Street, plastered all over. He knows because of the pawn shop."

"The pawn shop?" I asked, confused.

"Read the rest," Tom said.

Beneath my picture and the misinformed statistics, a thick paragraph stated, *Anise Hunt was at the East Street U-Pawn on June 5th. She may still be in the area. She was last seen in the company of a young man, age 18-20, dark curls, muscular. Please call if you have seen her. I miss my daughter very much.*

"Notice he doesn't say which daughter he misses," I said. I was angry at Daddy. If I was worth fifteen thousand dollars, why hadn't he treated me better? Why hadn't he had time for me?

"When were you at the U-Pawn?" Tom asked.

"Never," I said. "I don't know how he found me."

"We've got to get you out of here."

"Unless –" The memory flashed through my mind – Al holding me down, Scar-lip tearing my ring off my finger. I forced the thought away, and unclenched my fingers. My ring finger had been bare for this past month. I had counted myself lucky to lose only the ring, and not my life. "They stole my ring, that day. That horrible day. They must've pawned it."

"Why didn't you tell me?" Tom demanded.

"I forgot," I said. "I've tried to forget everything about that day, but I can't."

Instantly Tom backed down. "I'm sorry."

"It's okay," I said, although it wasn't. He had yelled at me. He didn't love me. Nothing was ever going to be okay.

"I don't think we can afford to lose time. You need to pack and catch a bus out of here. California. Georgia. Anywhere. You should have gone long ago."

I left him, went into the bedroom, took Honey from her playing. When I brought her back out, Tom frowned.

"Did Julia love Honey?" I asked.

"We don't have time for this," he said.

"Because Julia should've loved Honey, and she should've stayed, or else brought Honey with her." I hesitated. I knew Tom didn't want to hear about my feelings, but he had to know, had to understand why I would rather die than go. "I love you," I said. "I gave myself to you the night Jake died. You see, don't you? Why I can't leave? It was wrong for Julia to leave her Honey, and it would be wrong for me to leave my Tom."

Tom breathed deeply, seeming to steel himself. He did not meet my eyes. "I don't love you," he said, all in a rush. "You've got to go."

"No, Tom, no. There's hope for us. You don't mean what you're saying."

"I'm lying? Even if I am, if I don't want you here, you have to go. You need to go where you'll be safe, where your Daddy won't find you. He's hurt you more than I ever could."

"Daddy never gave me his love. You gave me love, Tom, and then you took it away. What do you think hurt more?" Honey stirred unhappily in my arms. I kissed her forehead, smoothed her soft blonde hair into place. "The children just lost Jake. It's too soon for them to lose me too."

"They've got me," Tom said. "They don't need you."

How could he be so hurtful? If he was trying to make me cry, it had worked; my sorrow rolled down my face and onto

Honey's. She rubbed the wetness away with her dear little hand.

Tom was at my side at once. "Don't cry. The children love you. We both know that. I'd say anything to get you to go." He crumpled up the flyer in his hand, threw it aside. "A $15,000 reward, Anise. The people around here, they'd betray their own mother for that. Think about the children, and how scary it would be to see you dragged out of here by the police. Think about me. I'd feel so guilty if you lost your freedom because you made the mistake of loving me."

"Tell me the truth," I begged. "You don't love me? Oh, if you don't love me, if you never did, I'll go, right this minute."

He dropped his gaze. "I never loved you," he said.

My tears blinded me. As I cried, as I rocked Honey and cried, Tom went to my bedroom, packed my things into my backpack. He wanted me gone, right this minute. He had never loved me.

I took my backpack, and I kissed Honey, Kelly, and Kenny good-bye. I brought Mr. Rat with me, because I had promised Jake to watch over him. Tom held the door open for me, and I stepped through. The hallway was dimly lit. The apartment across from Tom's was empty, and its door had been kicked in.

"Let me walk you to the bus stop," he said.

"No," I said. I didn't care if I was attacked again. I didn't want him doing anything out of pity for me. "No, you're rid of me."

He caught my arm, stopping me, nearly knocking Mr. Rat's cage to the floor. A driver's license and a bus card were in his hands. "Take these. Julia knew she'd need a new driver's license out in California, so she left her Florida one behind. Don't use your name, use hers. The bus card has seventeen credits left in it. That should get you anywhere, anywhere at all." He slid the cards into my back pocket. The touch of his hand against my jeans sent shock shivers through me.

"Let me go," I cried, and I broke free from his grasp. When I reached the stairway, I couldn't help myself, and I glanced back. Tom watched me from where I'd left him. When he saw me looking, he closed his eyes. A tear spilled free, coursing down his cheek, glistening in the dim light of the hallway.

"You're crying," I said.

He stepped back into the apartment, and shut his door.

I stepped into the stairway, and the door banged shut behind me.

I will never see Tom again, I thought. What might've been, will never be.

Somehow I managed not to fall down the steps, not to break my neck in my flight from Tom's closed door. Somehow I managed to make it to the bus stop, and get on a bus, the first bus that pulled up. It was the very bus I'd come in on with Tom and Jake. I rode out of the degen ghetto, and I saw the clean, tree-lined Koontz Street, the beginning of the eastern suburbs. I did not get off. The bus went further east, to the very edges of Tampa, and then it turned and followed its route back into the degen ghetto. I did not get off. I waited until I reached the baseball park. There I got off. I curled up under the bleachers where Jake had first found me, and I waited to die, or for Daddy to capture me, whichever came first.

Chapter Fourteen

It rained that night. The raindrops drummed against the metal bleachers, as if God felt sorry for what he'd put me through and sought to cheer with this wet melody. I listened through my sorrow, and it sounded just as lovely as Laurice's piano playing, long ago. I didn't mind the cold, or the wet, or the sand that turned to mud beneath me. My suffering came from within, not without.

In the morning, despite my exhaustion, I crawled out from under the bleachers. I had not died. Daddy had yet to find me. I had just enough energy to press on, and so I had to do so. Anything less would be giving in.

I cleaned up in the park's restroom. Inside my backpack, I found the clothes that Tom had carefully folded. Such care taken, for someone he despised. I pulled on a white t-shirt and damp khaki shorts. I looked almost normal, if you didn't look too closely. I left the restroom behind, and wandered through the park, knowing I had to leave but not wanting to, not yet. This park held such bittersweet memories. Behind third base, a tall oak tree stood sentry over the baseball diamond. I stopped beneath it, and listened for the chittering of baby birds. Yes, they were still up there. I climbed, my bare legs scraping against the bark, and I saw again the nest that had once amazed Jake and me. The birds had grown feathers, and now looked like tiny versions of their mother. She called angrily from above the tree. I whispered to the baby birds, "Someday you'll ride the air. Someday you'll soar. Your life awaits."

Back on the ground, I wondered – would I ever soar again?

What life awaited me? Tom had claimed I could make my own choices. The choice I wanted to make was to go back to him, but he did not want me. His choice for me was to run far, far away, but that was his choice. Not mine. I didn't want to be that far away from him. Even if I never saw him again, I could not be the one to sever our chances to reunite. I could not go. And if Daddy was looking for me in the ghetto, then perhaps he wouldn't look for me here in the rich part of the city. I just needed to get off the streets. I needed a job, and a place to stay.

With my backpack slung over my shoulder and Mr. Rat's cage in my arms, I headed down the street in search of an employment office.

Everyone knew that temp services were for degens; they were temporary people, after all. So when Ms. Hamilton, the recruiting agent, asked if I was a degen, I said yes. I was Julia Conroy, seventeen years old, degenerative, looking for a decent job with decent pay.

"Do you not have a place to stay?" she asked, eyeing the rat cage I'd hauled in with me. Mr. Rat snoozed in the corner of the cage.

"No," I admitted. "My boyfriend threw me out yesterday. I slept at a park last night."

Ms. Hamilton softened immediately. She had daughters of her own, two smiling blond girls in a frame on her desk. She was too old to be a degen. "How awful of him. It's not safe out there, not for a pretty young woman like yourself." Ms. Hamilton was homely, but well kept. Her clothes were clearly tailored to hide her hips. "I had thought to put you in a business setting, you speak very clearly. But if you need a place to stay, then it's best to go with one of the servant jobs. I've got a few listings that offer onsite living." She took a moment to call them up on the computer, and printed them off. "You could be a maid, or a cook's assistant. Or how about this one? Do you have a driver's license?"

I handed her Julia's license.

"This is a wealthy family, very degen friendly, that's looking for a chauffeur. Sometimes employers fire degens when they start degenerating, and then the poor souls have no health insurance. This family never does that. We placed their former employee, and he was very happy with them. Poor Juande has passed on now, I'm sad to say." She handed me the job listing. "It pays well, and there's a nice servants' quarters attached to the main house. You'd be sharing it with Bonita Nierve, the maid. We placed her too. She's a friendly girl."

"Is it hard to drive a limo?" I asked.

"I'm sure it's a challenge at first, but you'll get used to it. Does that mean you want the job?"

I wanted it. She made a few calls, copied my driver's license, and had me fill out a tax form. I didn't know Julia's social security number, so I left that blank, and she didn't object. Maybe she didn't care if I was a citizen or not. Ever since the degen virus hit, there'd been more refugees than ever trying to seek opportunity in America.

"I told them you'd like to start immediately, so they'll be expecting you this afternoon. Find a better boyfriend next time, okay? We don't want you to end up back on the streets."

"Thank you," I said. I took the job listing and the sheet of directions. "Am I dressed okay?"

She pursed her lips. "Dress slacks would make a better impression than shorts."

I'd been thinking the same. I had a few hours, and I still had most of the money I'd originally brought from home. I bought a pair of sand-colored rayon slacks and a dress shirt to match, and a pair of black slacks and a light blue shirt. If I interchanged all of them, I'd have four days worth of outfits. I also needed a haircut, and since my new employer's house was on the key just north of my Daddy's house, I decided to lighten my hair as well. It would be my disguise.

My new look was quite startling. My clothes looked much more grown-up than the dresses and jeans I normally favored. My thick hair was cut at a slant, angling down toward my chin. I'd never had short hair before. The blonde highlights made me look as if I'd spent months lounging in the sun, carefree and happy. No one could tell by looking at me that I was no longer a virgin, or that my heart had been broken.

It was only an illusion, a way to hide my soul from prying eyes, but it was exactly what I needed. I could grieve inside, and smile on the outside, and no one would be the wiser.

I caught the bus to Weston key, and walked the few blocks to my new employer's house. I had never had a job before, and I found myself hesitating, nervous, just outside their gates. This was an even bigger mansion than my Daddy's. Shrubs lined the front drive like little button dots, each the exact same distance from each other, the same height, the same everything. Whoever lived here liked things to be extremely precise. What if I wasn't precise enough for them? What if I hit the curbs, or turned too wide, or didn't drive fast enough?

The intercom gave a burst of static, and I jumped. The gate swung open. It was too late to turn back now. I calmed myself, said a quick prayer, and walked in. Mr. Rat yawned from within his cage. "Glad to see you're taking it easy," I whispered to him. My heart was pounding.

I passed each of the button shrubs, my feet hitting heavily on the stone walkway. In no time at all, I reached the front of the drive, where a man stood within the shadows of the entranceway. He coughed, a horrible deep-lung cough.

"Welcome," he said, and I stepped up next to him. He reached to take the cage from me, and I got a good look at his face. I knew him. Oh, God, I knew him, he was Orson's father. In my shock I let go of Mr. Rat's cage, and it crashed to the ground. The glass broke, and a tinkling shower of glass shards sprayed against my feet. Mr. Rat crouched where he landed, his tail straight out. I scooped him up, and he seemed fine, just fine, only he was more alert than I'd ever seen him.

"I can't believe I dropped that," Mr. Denvers said. He turned to the door behind him and yelled, "Bonita! Bring bandages and a broom, quick!" His attention was turned from me. If I wanted to run, if I wanted to fight this, now was the time. But I couldn't rouse myself to care what happened to me. I had been so sure that Tom loved me, and I had been wrong; maybe I was wrong about everything. Maybe it didn't matter who I married, because no one could love me.

Mr. Denvers turned back to me, and my chance for flight was lost. He bent, brushed the glass fragments from my feet, turned each one this way and that. Satisfied that I wasn't hurt, he rose to look at Mr. Rat, who also checked out fine. "That's a relief," he said. "Come on in. I'm Jonathon Denvers."

"Hello, Mr. Denvers," I said.

"Am I too old to call by my first name?" He winked at me, which made me uncomfortable. He was a married man, and he was my fiancé's father. He'd been a handsome man once – he had strong features, a thick shock of blond hair, and deep blue eyes.

"I'm Julia Conroy," I said. He nodded. He believed I was who I said I was. "I'm your new chauffeur."

"Of course you are," he said. With a smile, as if he knew a joke and I didn't, he ushered me over the remains of Mr. Rat's cage and into the house. Mr. Rat was already settling down in my hands, falling asleep again, the lazy thing.

Hurrying past the richly decorated main rooms, Mr. Denvers showed me to the servants' quarters. Bonita and I both had very large bedrooms, with full bathrooms coming off of them, and a living room to share between us.

"Do you like it?" Mr. Denvers asked.

"I love it," I said. The king-size bed, draped in a thick yellow comforter, looked so appealing to me. Much better than sleeping under park bleachers. Mr. Denvers followed my gaze to the bed and smiled.

"I'm an architect and designer by trade. I wanted this room to be a happy place. I've always believed that a man who treats his employees well will be repaid in kind." He crossed to the window, drew open the yellow and blue curtains. "You've got a view of the gardens. This is the same view as my wife and I have in our bedroom, right above this room."

"It's lovely," I said.

"Let me give you a quick tour of the house, and introduce you to the two Mrs. Denvers."

"Two?"

"My wife Sandra and my mother Roberta. But you better stick to calling my mother Mrs. Denvers. She's an opinionated woman, and she is of the opinion that formality must be maintained between one's servants and one's self." He glanced down at Mr. Rat, now sleeping in my hand. "Let's leave him here, shall we? Neither of the Mrs. Denvers take kindly to rats."

With Mr. Denvers' approval, I made him a makeshift home for him in a dresser drawer. I laid my backpack on the dresser, and I was all moved in.

Bonita caught us on our way out of the servants' quarters. She looked about my age, but with very delicate cheeks, eyes, and nose, and very light Hispanic skin tones. She wore a tight black dress with a white apron around her waist. "The bandages?"

"Won't be needing them, thank goodness. What we need now is a rat cage and all the accessories."

Oh, that wasn't necessary. "I can buy –"

"But I dropped the cage. I insist."

"Jonathon is very good to servants," Bonita said. "You will like it here."

Mr. Denvers led me through the main hall, the parlor, and the dining room, then out to the extensive gardens that led down to the beach. Rows of lilies and hyacinths swayed in the saltwater breeze. Everything bloomed with color, even the paths of crushed pink stone. If Kelly were here, she'd run down every path, and claim them as her own.

"I thought we'd find my wife out here. She must have gone for a walk."

"Who does your gardening? He must be very talented," I said. I knew how tough the salt air was on plants.

Mr. Denvers looked pleased. "Mrs. Denvers does it all. She often plans the grounds for the houses that I design, but I can never convince her to go into business for herself."

"She doesn't work?"

"She's a mother. That's enough of a job for anyone." He led me back into the house, up the staircase, and into a darker hallway lined with doors. "This is my son's room. He's attending a summer session at Harvard now." I peeked in, and what I saw just reinforced my impression of Orson. His room was unerringly neat, undecorated but for a wall of books – and no fiction books among those, but all heavy tomes on business and politics. The shades were pulled down over the window, and the walls were painted a gloomy blue. I couldn't imagine anyone choosing to live in this room, and choosing to keep it so void of personality.

Mr. Denvers erupted into another coughing fit. I clapped him on the back, which he seemed to appreciate, and when he was done we moved on. At the end of the hallway was an ornate, ruby-red door. It fit with the heavier feel of the upstairs rooms, as opposed to the airiness of the downstairs. "This is my mother's room. Brace yourself. She has back pain, and it's worse today." With that, not even giving me time to brace myself, he swung open the ornate door. A gigantic bed dominated the room, and an old woman lay in the bed. When we entered, she pulled herself upright.

"Stay comfortable, Momma. This is our new chauffeur, Julia."

"If you'd wanted me comfortable, you would have knocked, as is only proper, and I would have told you I was in no mood for company." She had pale blonde hair, just like Mr. Denvers, and the same aristocratic nose, but on her it looked too masculine, just as her hair looked too thin in its sharp bun. She looked me over, from head to toe, and I was glad I'd spent such effort on my appearance. "Well, my son certainly chooses the pretty ones. I'll have you know that my grandson is engaged, so don't entertain any thoughts of social climbing. In this house, we work hard, and we don't complain. Is that understood?"

"Yes, ma'am," I said.

"My son insists upon hiring degens as a form of charity. Well, I don't believe in charity. I believe in hard work, and if you are unable to do that, you won't last out the week."

"Mother, it's her first day, why not go easy on her? A new job can be very emotional," Mr. Denvers cut in.

"Emotions, Jonathon? You know how I feel about emotions. They weaken a person. I will not tolerate a weak employee, or a weak son."

"Yes, Mother," Mr. Denvers said, although his face flushed angrily.

"Now leave," she said. "You should have known better than to come in at all."

Mr. Denvers obediently led me out of the room. Instead of continuing the tour, however, he pulled a cigarette from his shirt pocket in one quick motion, like a magician pulling a coin from behind an ear. He looked away from me, apologetically.

"If you need a cigarette, I understand," I said.

"Thank you," he said softly. "And perhaps you need a nap, on your new yellow bed? I saw how you looked at it."

"I slept poorly last night," I admitted.

"Because your boyfriend threw you out, that dog. The temp service told me about it." He stretched his arm around my shoulders. "If you want to talk about him, or about anything at all, I would be honored if you turned to me. Even if there are emotions involved," he said. "Especially if there are emotions."

"You've done enough for me already," I said.

"Well, then, we're off to a fine start."

He went outside for his cigarette, and I went back to my new room, and lay down on my new bed. As soon as I closed my eyes, sleep claimed me, and I did not wake until the morning.

I had needed the rest, and now I was able to marvel at this coincidence. I tried to remember what the Denvers' former chauffeur had looked like, from the day of my party, but all I could see was that green splotch that had stretched across his face. I knew his name now. Juande. Daddy had said he wouldn't live much longer, and of course Daddy had been right; that was how degeneration went, no matter how many prayers one said.

Mr. Denvers had not recognized me, but Mrs. Denvers might. She had been very kind to me at the party. And if Orson had studied my face with anywhere near the scrutiny I gave to him, a haircut and change of clothes wouldn't disguise me. Oh, it was foolish, it was mad, but I wanted to stay. This big room and this yellow bed, they comforted me. Mr. Denvers was right, this was a happy place, and I was so sad inside.

Even the audacity of the plan appealed to me. I was hiding from Daddy not only in his own neighborhood, but also in the house of my fiancé. It was either brilliant, or insane, and I didn't let myself stop to ponder which one it was.

I found Bonita's note on the sofa in our shared living room. Her handwriting was large and childish. *Today is day off for you. Mr. Denvers says to take it easy. I am gone grocery shopping. I look forward to knowing you better.*

A day off already? I hadn't even had a day on yet. That was generous. I returned to my room, and crawled back into bed. Between the sunshine coming in through the bay window and the bright yellow bed cover, the room seemed to glow. There was more than enough light to read by, and for a time I lost myself in Elizabeth Bennett's well-ordered world.

When I set down the book, after Mr. Collins' proposal but before Mr. Darcy's, the sun was higher, and there was someone in the garden outside my window. I slipped out of bed and pulled my clothes on, but I needn't have worried. The person in the garden was Mrs. Denvers. Even with her back to me, she was clearly recognizable by the grace of her stature and the golden sweep of her elegant hair. She moved through the garden like a fairy nymph, checking the undersides of leaves and nipping away unwanted buds. I watched, enthralled. Had I chosen differently, she would have been my mother-in-law, my second mother. She knelt on the pink path to tend to a sagging azalea bush. Her quick fingers broke away the excess branches, and tenderly packed the soil into place. So tender. She would've been a good mother to me.

She turned to check the red rose bushes on the other side of the path, and her gaze met mine. Startled, I stepped back from the window. I felt instantly guilty. I hadn't meant to spy on her, and now I didn't know what to do. I couldn't go out there and further intrude on her privacy. I nodded at her, and moved to shut the curtains. She raised her fingers, clad in well-worn brown leather gloves, and gestured for me to come to her. Flecks of dirt fell from the gloves as she gestured, and more so as she pulled off the gloves to wipe her sweatless forehead. She was too elegant to sweat. She was perfect.

I didn't want to go to her, but I had no choice. She was my employer, at least until she saw through my disguise and sent me straight home to Daddy. Oh, I was so foolish. I should've been gone by now. I should've run away from here. I was playing a childish catch-me game, when my future was at stake. Tom was right. I ought to be in California by now. Except that wasn't right, because Tom was here in Tampa, and I longed to be with him. As I found my way through the Denvers' house to the French doors that opened onto the gardens, as I stepped out into the dazzling sun, I thought of Tom's strong arms, Tom's full heart. It gave me strength. It wasn't just for myself that I wanted Tom's love, he needed somebody too, somebody to be a mother to the children and a wife to the man.

Mrs. Denvers had knelt beside the rose bushes. She was inspecting the soil near the roots. "I nearly lost this one last spring. Aphids. She's fully recovered now." She hadn't replaced her gloves, and the dirt had gotten beneath her manicured fingernails. She held her hand out to shake, then realized how dirty it was, and tried to pull back. I shook before she could. I didn't want her to feel ashamed of the dirt.

"Julia," I said.

"Sandy," she said. "But I suppose you better call me Sandra, or even Mrs. Denvers, or else I'll hear about it from my mother-in-law. You're the new chauffeur?" She looked me over closely, and suddenly her arched eyebrows came together. I stammered out a yes. Had she recognized me? Her eyebrows remained concentrated, but she spoke lightly. "Where are you from?"

"Here," I said. "Not right here, of course, but the other side of Tampa. The poor side." Oh, I wasn't any good at lying! I couldn't meet her eyes. "I'll do my best to be a good chauffeur, so that you never regret hiring me. I didn't have any place to live."

"I'm glad, then. Julia. To be able to do this for you. If I can do anything more, just ask."

"Everything's perfect," I said.

"Yes, it is," she said. "It's perfect now, isn't it? Will you help me garden?"

I didn't know how to garden, but she directed me to the plants that needed extra water, or the buds that, having bloomed and withered, now needed nipping. We worked side by side. The feel of the dirt and the leaves reminded me how alive I was. The sunshine on my shoulders reminded me of Tom's hands there, spreading warmth from his touch. I knew why Mrs. Denvers liked the garden. I liked it too. It was a place where you could forget yourself. After an hour, even Mrs. Denvers had broken a sweat. She leaned back on her heels, not so elegant now but still beautiful. The work had brought a flush to her cheeks.

"My garden is what I live for," she said in a confiding tone. "My garden, my son, and my husband. But Orson's away at school now – although he'll be home on break soon," she added quickly. "And my husband. . ."

"Yes?" I prompted.

"Never mind my husband. This garden is always here for me. And you're welcome to join me here, anytime." She rose suddenly, and headed along the pink path back toward the house. Her posture was as elegant as ever, but this time I noticed the vulnerability in the way she held herself.

Chapter Fifteen

Soon after I woke the next morning, Bonita knocked on my door. She must have heard me stirring. "Jonathon will wait for you at nine o'clock, to take him to his office," she said. She had such a pretty, lilting accent. She'd had a full day of work yesterday, and so we hadn't gotten to talk. Today she wore a lavender dress, even tighter than before, with a deep blue apron around her waist. "Until he has your uniforms made, I will share mine."

"That's very kind." She handed me a pale green dress, with its matching dark green apron. It didn't seem like enough material to make a dress for a child like Kelly, let alone me. "Do you think it'll fit?"

Bonita smiled comfortingly. "Even if it doesn't, Jonathon won't mind. He is very nice to us."

When I went in to shower, I found a shower basket waiting for me: vanilla soap, expensive shampoo, and several vials of vanilla bubble bath. Yesterday I had made do with the hand soap. I had time, and so I took a bath, and pretended my troubles were soaking right out of me. I had to admit, I'd missed the small luxuries like a hot bath, and sweet-smelling soap. The bathtub was so large, it could fit two people, and it had small jets that made the most magnificent, foamy bubbles. I hadn't had this nice of a bathtub back at Daddy's house.

Once I dried myself off, I pulled on Bonita's green dress. It barely made it over my chest, and then stuck again at my hips; I forced it on, but it was far too tight. When I pulled it down, trying to make it a decent length, my chest threatened to tumble out of the swooping neckline. I was embarrassed to step out into our small living room, but I had to see if Bonita had any larger dresses.

"You look nice," Bonita said, and she looked down at her own chest. "I wish I looked as nice as you."

"I feel naked," I said. My heart pounded. The dress didn't come high enough to cover my chest, nor go low enough to reach anywhere near my knees. I thought of Al, Sicko, and Scar-lip. In this dress, my breasts would bounce when I walked, and everyone would see. "Don't you have any others?"

But Bonita had turned, and curtsied to Mr. Denvers, who had entered our quarters without knocking. I blushed crimson; I felt my blush on my cheeks, and saw it on my chest. If I curtsied, I'd fall right out, I knew I would.

"Is it nine o'clock? Am I late?" I asked.

Mr. Denvers smiled reassuringly. "I'm early. Just wanted to see how things were going. That dress doesn't quite fit you, does it? We'll get you measured for your own uniforms, but that will have to do for now. Mrs. Denvers insists that the servants wear uniforms."

"Yes, Mr. Denvers," I said. I knew he meant his mother, not his wife. His wife was kind, but his mother was heartless, just like Orson.

"Do you notice anything?" he asked, smiling. Bonita gestured toward my bedroom.

A giant cage with a yellow bow sat on my bed. Mr. Denvers must've brought it in while I was in my bath. "You didn't have to do that. My rat won't know what to do with that much space."

"I want to spoil you. I never had my own daughters, but if I did, I'd want them to grow to be fine young women like yourselves. I hope you don't mind."

"No, it's very kind," I said. I hoped he wouldn't mind if I waited until he left before I introduced Mr. Rat to his new cage. I didn't want to have to lean over, in this dress, in front of anyone, and certainly not in front of my fiancé's father.

"All right then," he said, lingered for another moment, and then left the servants' quarters.

Bonita watched, wide-eyed, as I spread the litter in the new cage, and then lifted Mr. Rat from his slumber. "Are you not afraid he will bite you?"

"He doesn't bite. Here, hold him," I said, but Bonita shrank back. She really was afraid of him. "I knew someone who once claimed that girls don't like rats. I guess he was right."

"A special someone?" Bonita asked. She stretched out a finger, ran it quickly along Mr. Rat's back, and drew back shivering.

"Yes," I admitted.

"Is he young, and handsome?" she asked.

"Yes," I said. "Yes, he was everything I ever wanted in a man."

"A good lover?" she asked.

I was too embarrassed to answer.

"I did not mean to pry," she said quickly. "I have a special someone too. We are lovers."

"Are you happy?" I asked.

"Yes," she said simply. "You should make love, if you have not already. You have not lived, if you have not loved."

"I made love to Tom, just once," I said. "He didn't want me afterwards. He was terrified of getting me pregnant, and he admitted that he never loved me."

"Oh, my lover does not love me." Bonita sighed. "American girls expect so much, you set yourselves up for hurt. Where I come from, things are more casual."

"Do you come from Spain?"

"Brazil," she said. "But my father was an American, and he brought me here before he died. I have been poor all my life, but in this house, I feel rich. You'll see. It is very nice here." She led me out to a tray of strawberries and bagels, left for us on the coffee table. "Jonathon is very nice," she said, and she nibbled on a strawberry.

I took one myself, and it was delicious, but I limited myself to one. In this dress, I had no room to spare for strawberries.

The limo was longer than I'd expected. I tried not to let Mr. Denvers see how nervous I was, but I couldn't imagine how I would control this black beast. When I climbed into the driver's seat, the seat was set so far back, I couldn't even reach the pedals. It was as if I were a child, pretending to drive Daddy's car. Mr. Denvers crawled into the passenger seat next to me. "I'll sit up here today, to help you learn. First, it looks like that seat needs adjusting." Before I could do it myself, he reached under my seat, his arm brushing against my bare legs. As soon as the seat was positioned, he withdrew.

"What now?" I asked.

"Why don't you drive around the front circle here? You can get a feel of how the limo turns."

I turned the keys, and the limo buzzed to life, but I hesitated.

"Remember, unlike my mother, I care about your emotions. You're nervous, aren't you?" Mr. Denvers asked.

"Yes," I admitted. "I've never had a job before."

"I want you to be happy," he said.

"My life hasn't been very happy up to now. Every one I care about has either rejected me or passed away."

"I'm very sad to hear that," Mr. Denvers said. His coughs overcame him for a moment, and I had a nightmare image of him sloping to the floor of the limo, dying right here, right now, and God whispering to me, that's what I do to people who are nice to you, remember this, Anise.

"Are you all right?" I asked, panicked. Mr. Denvers waved my concern aside, and his coughs gradually subdued.

"Go ahead, drive. Be brave. You've met my mother, so you know that I know what it feels like to be scolded. I'm not like her. You could knock out all these button shrubs, and the palm trees too, and I wouldn't scold you. That's a promise."

"Do you keep your promises, Mr. Denvers?"

"What a funny question," he said. "They wouldn't be promises if I didn't keep them."

I thought of Daddy, and all his unkept promises. Mr. Denvers had signed the promise contract with Daddy, pledging Orson and me to a marriage without love. "A person should keep all the promises he makes," I said. I moved the limo forward, and crept around the circular drive. "But what if someone makes a promise for someone else? Do you think that's fair?"

Mr. Denvers looked at me with interest, which at least kept his attention away from my driving. The back of the limo fell off the pavement, and I jerked it back on, but he took no notice. "Can a person make a promise for someone else? That's a question I've spent a great deal of time on. Several weeks ago, I made a promise contract for my son."

"You did?" I asked, feigning surprise. I sped up to twenty miles per hour, which was as fast as I could go on the driveway circle.

"Go on out to Onassis Avenue. You're doing well. And yes, as I was saying, I made a promise for my son. He's twenty-one years old. He could've had several children by now, but he hadn't even considered marriage. I spent years introducing him to eligible young ladies, but he always managed to scare them off. He hasn't much social tact, I'm afraid."

"No, he hasn't," I said.

"Have you met?"

With my attention split between the discussion and my maneuvers to get the limo out of the driveway, I had blundered. "Of course not, no, but just from how you describe him, I imagine he would scare me too," I said.

Mr. Denvers nodded. "I don't know what to do with him. He's even scared his fiancée away. She looked rather like you, actually, only younger and with radiant dark hair."

I glanced at my face in the side mirror, trying to see if my sorrow had aged me. Perhaps it was this dress, that accented my chest and legs, so that no one could look at me and see a child.

"Sometimes I think degens are the lucky ones," Mr. Denvers said. "They don't have to worry about the survival of the species, and they can marry and make love for their pleasure only." My attention was on the road, but out of the corner of my eye, I saw Mr. Denvers lick the corner of his lips. His head jerked up when he saw me looking. Had he been looking down my dress?

"Turn right at Tamiami," he said, suddenly businesslike. Surely I had been mistaken. Mr. Denvers was in his forties, and wouldn't be interested in a young girl like me.

It took me long minutes to merge onto Tamiami through the rush hour traffic. Mr. Denvers directed me to a tall, mirror-plated building. I couldn't look at it directly, not with the sun reflected out of all those mirrored windows. It stretched skyward like a pillar of fire. "That's where I work," he said. I started to turn in, but he waved me to go forward. He had plenty of time, and I needed more practice. I kept my attention on the road, and Mr. Denvers kept his on me. I took us down Tamiami, onto the back streets, back up Tamiami, back to the Denvers' house, and from there back to the pillar of fire where Mr. Denvers worked, reaching it right at the stroke of ten o'clock. I was to return to pick him up at four o'clock.

If only Daddy worked such short hours, maybe he would have had time for me.

Mrs. Denvers waited for me in the parlor, but her smile fell away when Bonita showed me in. I curtsied, and she looked away. "Did my husband dress you?" she asked sadly.

"Jonathon told me to share my uniforms." Bonita spoke softly, but defiantly. I expected Mrs. Denvers to scold her, or me, but she only sighed.

"He's going to have uniforms made to fit me," I said.

"I'm sure he will. I'm sure he'll be in to take your measurements before the sun sets," she said. "Bonita, bring us some tea. Julia, please sit. It isn't your fault that my husband is who he is."

When I sat on the plush couch, my skirt rose even higher. "And who is he?" I asked.

"No, my dear, I'd rather discuss who you are."

My heart stopped beating. She recognized me, surely she recognized me. "I can explain," I cried.

She leaned forward. In her ivory silk blouse and pants, she looked so elegant, especially compared to my tart little get-up. "Explain what?"

I couldn't speak. Bonita returned with the tea, and Mrs. Denvers took a sip. Her gaze encompassed us both. "Are you honorable? Are you trustworthy? That's all I need to know. I only ask one thing of my servants: do not accept favors from my husband. You'll learn soon enough how things are between Mr. Denvers and myself. Please, please, do not do anything in my house that you would not want done in yours."

"Yes, ma'am." Bonita dropped a short curtsy, and left with the tray.

"He's given me a rat cage," I said. "And in my bathroom, I found a basket of soaps and lotions."

"Yes, you smell of vanilla."

"I won't accept anything more, I promise," I said.

"You know, I believe you," she said. A kind, sad smile crept across her face. She sipped her tea, and I sipped mine. I felt like crying for her. How humiliating, to have to ask her servants for help in such a private matter. "I won't bring this up again," she said, and I knew it had been hard for her.

"You won't have to." I stretched out my teacup, and she clinked hers against mine, and it was agreed. The very air around us seemed to warm. This was how it had been in the garden.

"Maybe you'll be a breath of life for this house," she said. "God knows we need it. You've met my mother-in-law?"

"Yes," I said.

"Then you know how difficult she is. This weekend you'll meet my son," she said. "I hope you'll look past his gruffness and see the man inside."

Gruffness, that was what she called it? I called it meanness. "I'll try."

"He needs people to try. He throws himself into his studies, and he doesn't admit that he's very alone. Just as alone as I am," she said.

"But you have a husband," I said.

"And I'm more alone with him than I ever could have been on my own." She looked at my tight dress once more. I wished I could comfort her, but her sadness seemed to come from deep within her soul. "Don't ever marry except for love," she said. "And even then, beware."

Chapter Sixteen

Every night that week, I woke to the sounds of Bonita and her lover. The walls were not thick, and I heard every gasp, every cry, every cough. Sometimes their lovemaking would stop, and the man would cough as if he were dying, and then their loving would resume.

Friday morning, I opened my door to our little living room and there they were, Bonita and Mr. Denvers, naked, entwined on the couch. Her lithe brownness looked out of place against his thick white body. They seemed to sleep, but as soon as I shut the door I heard him rise, and when I next peeked out the living room was empty.

I writhed into my dress. It was ivory, with a soft yellow apron. I chose an ivory scarf from the array that Mrs. Denvers had provided for me. My chest was not public property for everyone to see, not once I tucked the scarf around my neck. If only Bonita would do the same.

As if to trumpet her adultery, Bonita wore a brazenly red dress, with a stark white apron. She had painted her lips red, her cheeks pink. "How did you sleep?" she asked.

"More innocently than you," I said, and at least she had the grace to bow her head. I brushed past her, leaving her behind as I emerged into the main rooms. I wanted to flee this house, to separate myself from their evil, but I couldn't leave Mrs. Denvers. They had treated her so poorly. She needed someone, and there was only me.

I drove Mr. Denvers to his office, but I did not return his conversational parlays, and he soon lapsed into thoughtful silence. I turned up the air conditioning, as if to drive home the point that it was cold in here, cold in his heart. In his thick suit, I doubt he even felt the breeze.

After Mr. Denvers was done, I took Mrs. Denvers on her errands. Mrs. Denvers' excitement over her son's homecoming that evening was contagious. She insisted that I help her pick out a gift for Orson, and when I suggested books, she clapped her gloved hands. "That's just what he would like!" Oh, all her elegance was just a front, a mask; this was who she really was. She was vulnerable. How could I tell her what I knew?

Once we got to the bookstore, Mrs. Denvers stared at all the books in dismay. "There's too many of them," she whispered to me. She was not a reader. She preferred music, and old motion pictures, and live theater. Sometimes Mr. Denvers took her out, and they had lovely evenings together, she told me wistfully.

Does he take Bonita out too, I wanted to ask, but of course I couldn't. I gathered a handful of the dry political books, and drier business books, that reminded me of the ones I had seen in Orson's room, but I couldn't resist slipping a copy of *Pride and Prejudice* into the pile as well. If anyone needed to read a romance, it was Orson.

Several times that afternoon, I tried to bring up my discovery of Bonita and Mr. Denvers. Each time, Mrs. Denvers shifted the conversation onto safer waters. We picked Mr. Denvers up at two o'clock, and he slid in next to his wife, and she lay her head on his shoulder. She loved him. I couldn't bear to uproot that love. She needed to know of her husband's adultery, but it should be him to tell her, not me.

The Denvers had an afternoon tea scheduled at the Nolan's estate, after which I would drive them to the airport to pick up Orson. Mr. Denvers handed me an envelope just before he left the limo, and told me to have some fun during the three hours they would be at the tea. When I opened the envelope, a thousand dollars slid out onto my palm. I knew what this was. Hush money. How could Mr. Denvers be so coarse?

I waited, fully intending to return the money and tell Mrs. Denvers the truth as soon as they came back from the tea. I waited, but the money on the seat called to me. It would be wrong to accept it. I closed my eyes, and imagined a new pink dress for Kelly, and a college fund for Kenny. Until I lived with them, I had never known what it felt like to want for money. A college fund for Kenny. It was nothing more than he deserved.

It took a half hour, but my conscience won out over the money. I tucked it back inside its envelope, and lay it on the seat behind me. I would not sell my soul, just because Mr. Denvers had offered to buy it.

Over an hour remained before the Denvers would be done with the tea. The money wouldn't have tempted me so sorely, if not for the added lure of seeing Tom again, and helping his family. I could still go to see Tom, even if I didn't bring him the thousand dollars. Maybe he would accept some of my earnings, or maybe he'd be so glad to see me, it wouldn't matter if I came empty-handed. Surely his body ached for me, just as mine did for him.

My mind decided, I pulled the limo out of the drive, and set my course for the furniture factory where Tom worked.

A group of men sat outside the squat warehouse. A late-day break. I strained to catch a glimpse of Tom among them, and I accidentally ran the limo up on the curb, and fell off again. The men hooted at my mistake, and hooted more when I stepped out. I had forgotten how tight this dress was. I tensed, ready to dart back inside the limo; there were ten of them, and only one of me, and I was half-naked already in this dress. Then Tom stepped forward from the group, and my fears fell away. He looked as handsome as ever.

"Anise." He savored my name. "I thought I'd never see you again."

"I couldn't leave you." I joined him on his side of the limo, and his coworkers hooted louder than ever. One of them yelled, "I'll take her if you don't want her."

I flinched back. "He's only joking. I know these guys, they're good men," Tom said.

"Can we talk in the limo?" I asked.

Tom crawled in after me, and we shut the doors behind us.

I hadn't been in the back of the limo before. The bench seats were plush, and the windows darkened. Tom sat beside me, and my pulse quickened. "What does Anise want," I whispered.

"What's that?" Tom leaned closer, all the better to hear me.

Oh, how I longed to say, *I want you, only you.* But Tom didn't want to hear that. I studied his kind face, his dark unruly hair, and I said, "I want to help out. I've got a job."

"You're a chauffeur." He nodded appreciatively. "I saw you hit that curb, you know."

"I almost hit a stop sign yesterday," I confessed. "But they pay me well, and I don't need the money."

"You need it to travel to California, and make a new life for yourself."

"I'm not going anywhere," I said.

"Of course you are. You have to go." He ran his hands through my hair, so changed from just a week before. "What have you done to my Anise?"

"I'm Julia now. They don't recognize me."

"I'd recognize you even if you cut it all off. Even if I was blindfolded." He caressed down my cheek, to the swell of my lips. I kissed his fingers, and he jumped back, as if my kiss had burned. "You torture me," he said.

I leaned back against the plush seat. If he wanted me, we could make love right here. No one could see in. "Do you want me?" I asked.

"I can't answer that."

"Of course you can."

"It's too complicated. You torture me, you know you do. Why do you come in that dress, in this limo? Why, if not to tempt me, when you know that we can't be together?" Tom clenched his eyes shut, as if to block out the very sight of me.

"I came to offer you my earnings, for a college fund for Kenny. Any temptation you feel, I feel it too, right here." I caught up his hand, pressed it to my chest. Surely he could feel how my heart pounded. Surely he could hear the very beat of my love for him.

He tore his hand away, gripped the seat beneath him. "You mustn't come again. I can't bear this. I'll quit my job, if that's what it takes, to save you from yourself. To save you from me." He fumbled for the door handle.

"Don't go, not yet. Please tell me, how is Honey? And Kenny, and Kelly?"

"They cry," he said. "They cry for Jake, and they cry for you. Honey cries all night long, and neither of us sleep."

"Let me visit them. Please, Tom."

"No," he said. "Everyone in the degen dungeon knows your name, your face. Everyone is looking for you. You're like a walking lottery ticket." Outside, a bell rang, and his coworkers filed back into the building. "I've got to get back to work."

"Can I visit you again?"

"Please don't," Tom said. "For both our sakes, please don't." He jerked open the limo door. I reached for him, one last touch, but he moved too quickly; within seconds, he had fled into his workplace. He was gone.

In a daze, I drove back to the Nolan's estate. It seemed that God must have guided the wheel, for when I arrived I had no memory of the trip, and only wondered how I had not hit any cars, or trees, or pedestrians. *Can I visit,* I had asked, and Tom had said, *please don't.* He couldn't be any clearer than that. I had to respect his wishes, and ignore my own.

The tea eventually let out, and the Denvers boarded the limo. Mr. Denvers raised an eyebrow at the discarded envelope, but he tucked it inside his suit jacket without a word. He met my eyes in the rear view mirror, and he gave a respectful nod. He knew that I could not be bought. "To the airport," he said.

"To my son," Mrs. Denvers said.

To my wretched fiancé, I thought. I had no choice but to pull forward, even though Orson was the last person on earth I wanted to see right now. I couldn't have a man like Tom, an honorable deep-hearted man, but I could have a cad like Orson. My misery twisted in my stomach, and I found myself hoping Orson would recognize me, so that I would have an excuse to run away, plunge into the bay and swim far out to sea, just as my mother had done. Far, far out to sea, away from all my troubles. Better to die young, as Laurice had, as Jake had. Better to die, than to live the life my Daddy had planned for me.

Chapter Seventeen

I saw him, striding purposefully down the gangway, long before he saw us. He wore a pale blue polo shirt that didn't match his maroon shorts. Mrs. Denvers waved excitedly to him, but when he caught sight of her, no emotion crossed his face. No emotion at all! I, who would've dropped and kissed the grimy carpet if my Daddy showed me love, watched in horror as Mrs. Denvers threw her arms around her son, and he shrugged neatly out of the hug. He ran a cursory glance down my body, not even looking at my face, and said to Mr. Denvers, "Did Juande die?"

"A week ago Tuesday," Mr. Denvers said.

"We didn't want to bother you with that, dear, not while you had your studies," Mrs. Denvers said.

"How about Bonita? She kick off yet?" He directed the question at Mr. Denvers, who hotly replied, "You will not speak so disrespectfully. Not everyone is as fortunate as you."

Orson bowed to me. "Welcome to the family," he said dryly, and took off towards the baggage claim.

Although I was the servant, neither of the men allowed me to carry even one of the four bags that Orson brought home with him. All I was good for was to hold the limo doors open while they loaded the bags in. Oh, and to look sexy in this dress, I was good for that. Orson shot several glances at my chest. At least he wasn't looking too closely at my face.

I drove them home, and opened the doors for them, and followed them into the house. The elder Mrs. Denvers waited for the family in the parlor. As I headed away from them, to the safety of my room, I heard Orson declare, "Good to see you haven't died, Grandmother. You could've been three months buried before anyone bothered to let me know."

He was just as callous as I remembered. His good looks couldn't cancel out his bad manners. I found myself feeling sorry for whoever he did end up marrying; the poor girl would think she was getting a prince, when all she'd have was an Orson.

The next morning, Orson desired a ride to the beach, where he planned to read the new books Mrs. Denvers had given him. I was to drive him. He deigned to allow that I could bring a swimsuit as well, and take the morning off, as he would be there for several hours.

I didn't have a suit, but Bonita offered me one of hers, and she hurriedly brought me the selection: a red triangle bikini, a black triangle bikini, or a floral patterned triangle bikini. The floral one had a thong bottom, which I couldn't imagine myself wearing in public. "You may wear any of them. I consider you my friend," she said.

I chose the black triangle bikini, since it seemed the fullest cut, but Bonita's sharing didn't change anything between her and me. She was a friendly girl, but she was sleeping with a married man, and I couldn't condone that.

"If you really want to be my friend, give up your lover. It's not fair to Mrs. Denvers," I said.

"It would not be fair to Jonathon to turn him away now. I am not the cause of their problems. Jonathon tells me I am his solace. Would you have me say, no, I will not solace you?"

"That's exactly what you should say."

Bonita would not have it. "I need solace too. Who knows when I will die? Making love is a good thing, and I will have good things while I live."

Bonita was furiously cleaning when I left with Orson. At least I had upset her, and maybe when she thought it over, she would come to see that what she did was wrong.

Orson made no conversation, only sat in the back seat and stared moodily out while I drove to private Turtle Bay Beach. It took me several minutes to find a parking spot that would fit the limo. Orson looked up when I turned off the car. "You drive well, for a girl," he said.

Inwardly I riled against him. For a girl? I hated that phrase.

It sounded like a compliment, but really it was an insult, every time, because good for a girl still meant that a guy would have done it better. "I'll get the cooler from the trunk," I said.

"No, I can," he said.

I beat him to it. Bonita had loaded the cooler down with sodas, and sandwiches, and whatever else the little master might desire, but I took effort to show that I could carry it with ease. Orson followed me with his beach bag, and my own. "You'll sit with me," he said.

"Is that an order?"

He only laughed, and spread his towel out on the sand, and after a moment I did the same. It looked to be a beautiful day; the water was calm, disrupted only by the occasional pelican diving down to catch a fish. Perhaps this was the beach where Laurice had made love to her Jimmy. It was certainly deserted enough; but for the pelicans, we were the only creatures here.

Orson stripped down to his bright blue bathing trunks; at least, with only one article of clothing on, he couldn't clash. I went into the rest rooms to change into Bonita's bikini. The bottoms fit nicely, but the top left most of my breasts uncovered. Bonita was small chested, and I was not. My heart pounded as I went out into the sunshine to join Orson. He lay on his back, but he sat up as I approached. I quickly crossed my arms over my chest.

"Don't hide them. They're practically mine, after all."

My breath caught. "What do you mean?"

"I played along at first, because I thought it might be some strange joke of my parents, but they really don't recognize you. It's a very brazen plan, although I don't quite catch the logic." He patted the towel next to him. He'd opened up a Coke, even though it was hours until noon. He smelled of sunscreen. I turned away from him, facing the deep blue of the ocean. The waves were light today. They would not fight me, and I could swim far, far out to sea, as far as my mother had gone.

"I'm tired," I said.

"Did you really think you could fool me? They engaged me to you. I studied your face, your body. You've got a great body, by the way. Procreation wouldn't be at all unpleasant."

He reached out, ran his fingers along my legs. That got me walking, down toward the water. Orson leapt up and followed. If he followed me all the way out to sea, he could drown too, and the world would be a better place.

"Have you slept with my father?" he asked. That shocked me to a stop, right on the water's edge.

"Of course not," I said. "How could you think such a thing? I wouldn't do that to your mother."

"Your future mother-in-law."

"No. I would rather die than marry you."

"To each his own," Orson said. "Although I do think there are some in-between options. Why not tell your father that you won't have me? A promise contract is just that, a promise, nothing more. It can be dissolved. He can't make you marry me."

The water lapped against my toes. "I tried to tell him."

"You must not have tried too hard."

I ignored him, and thought of Tom. If I were going to do this, if I was about to swim out of existence, I didn't want my last thoughts to be of Orson. But all I could see of Tom was his back as he left me.

"I won't tell anyone, you know. If you want to work as a servant, then by God, work away. You can even polish my shoes if you like."

I studied his face, his indifferent eyes, the half-smile on his lips. "Do you promise?" I asked.

"Yes, I promise I'll let you polish all my shoes."

"Promise that you won't tell."

"Oh, is that what you meant?" He mocked me.

"I couldn't believe a promise of yours anyway, could I?"

He jerked me by the shoulders to face him. My breasts nearly escaped my bikini, which no doubt would have rewarded him for his violence. I struggled to break free of his grip, but he held on tightly. "Don't call me a liar. My promise is good, and you have it. I don't know why you're hiding in my house, it makes no sense to me, but I will tell no one that our maid Julia is no maid, no degen, but my unwilling fiancée. You have what you want." He dropped me then, and strode back up the beach.

I sank down, into the sand, into the ocean's steady embraces. If Orson would keep my secret, then I would struggle on. I stared out at the vast expanse of blue, at the tiny dots that were faraway boats, and whispered, "Not today, mother." *Not today, I will not join you today, but someday I will be with you again, and you will love me. I know you will.*

Sunday afternoon, just to torment me, Orson made me a gift of a window box herb garden, since I had such a sunny room, so he said. Five plants grew, all the same herb: flowering anise. One of them had come to seed, and the seedpods looked like tiny stars. Mrs. Denvers saw the gift, and began to tell me about Orson's fiancée, that poor little rich girl Anise. "She had such a sadness about her," Mrs. Denvers said, while Orson watched me. A smile danced on his lips.

"Did she," I said, without much enthusiasm.

"I do hope she's somewhere safe and warm, although I think my Orson could've been good for her. And her for him. Orson takes after his grandmother too much, sometimes."

"Don't talk about me like I'm not here," Orson said, his smile dropped now that the conversation had turned to him. He enjoyed talking about me in front of me, but we couldn't talk of him, now?

"I think the young master needs a woman who won't stand for his gruffness," I said.

"We're of the same mind exactly," Mrs. Denvers declared. "Orson needs a smart, heartful young woman, and Anise seemed like just the thing."

"I shall leave you to your gossip." Orson made a show of sweeping out of the room, to both Mrs. Denvers and my enjoyment.

"He pretends to be light-hearted, but really he takes everything far too seriously," Mrs. Denvers said, once he was gone. "If I ever teach him to laugh at himself, I'll consider myself a success as a mother."

That evening, Bonita recruited me to help serve the dinner. The Denvers' regular cook had not been trusted to prepare a meal worthy of Orson's home-coming; a Parisian chef had been brought in, and prepared course after course of all the most elaborate meals, replete with tomato roses and decorative sauces. As I served, Orson did not speak to me, nor even meet my eyes as I exchanged one plate for another.

The elder Mrs. Denvers normally took her meals in her room, but she had come down for this event, and she dominated the dinner conversation. She criticized the Waldorf salad and the French duck, and according to her the Tianellan wine was undrinkable swill, although the rest of the family drained their glasses easily enough. As I brought out the chef's final number, a caramel crème brulee that had my mouth watering, the elder Mrs. Denvers said to Orson, "Don't you love crème brulee?"

"No, I don't," he said.

"Nor do I, it's far too sweet. You're too clever for my trap, dear boy. They're teaching you well at Harvard."

"I happen to love crème brulee," Mrs. Denvers asserted. She wore a lovely blue satin evening gown, with a diamond choke in her soft blonde hair. Mr. Denvers had complimented her several times that evening, and her son's presence enlivened her, and so she must be feeling brave.

The elder Mrs. Denvers pointed her sharp forefinger at the lovely Mrs. Denvers and said, "Not so clever as your son, are you? Perhaps you like crème brulee, perhaps you enjoy the sweet smoothness, but to say you love it? Such intense emotion, applied to a mere food? Ridiculous. Jonathon, you married a fool."

I set Mr. Denvers' dessert sharply before him. He looked from his mother to his wife, and stretched an arm around his wife to comfort her. The elder Mrs. Denvers only frowned. "Orson, if you ever do manage to secure a bride, I hope you won't constantly disgust your relations with excessive affection." I plunked her dessert down in front of her, but she did not stop. "When your parents first married, they were always kissing and giggling and pinching each other's privates, right out in front of me and your grandfather, God bless his soul. Just think how that would've impacted your growing up, if I hadn't commanded them to stop."

"Or just think what all that affection would've done to their marriage," Orson said. Bonita had brought out a pitcher of coffee, and Orson looked meaningfully, meanly, from her to Mr. Denvers.

Mr. Denvers withdrew his arm from his wife. Mrs. Denvers pushed her crème brulee away without a single bite of its sweetness. I slammed Orson's dessert down in front of him so hard, some of the crème brulee splattered onto the table. He wiped it away without even looking at me. "When I marry, my wife will know her place. Not below me, nor above me," he said.

"Don't be vulgar," Mr. Denvers said.

"I'm not talking about sex, I'm talking place. A man and his wife should be equals. If one isn't on the same mental, or physical, or spiritual level as the other, they'll both be miserable."

"My marriage is a happy one," Mrs. Denvers said, but the tremor in her voice betrayed her.

"Mother, I never implied otherwise."

"Oh, such a delight to have you back," the elder Mrs. Denvers said. She stood up, shakily, and Orson hurried to assist her from the table. I began to clear the plates, and saw Mr. Denvers raise Mrs. Denvers' hand, and kiss it very delicately, before she fled to the sanctuary of her gardens.

Only he and I were left, and he raised his gaze to meet mine, and said, "Did you think that the rich had it easy? That our lives were as smooth as this crème brulee?"

"No one has it easy," I said.

"No one does," he agreed. "Although I've often thought that degeneratives are as much blessed as cursed by their short lives. They die idealists, and romantics, and all the things that I was at age twenty that I am not at age forty-three."

I thought of Laurice, and Jake, and what they could've done with an added twenty years. "Mr. Denvers, you know not of what you speak."

"No," he said, "You know not of what I speak. Age has its disappointments. Life brings you places very different than you imagined, when you were young and foolish."

I cleared away the uneaten desserts. When I returned from the kitchen, Mr. Denvers had gone outside for a cigarette. Where would life take me, I wondered, and would I accept it as wearily as Mr. Denvers did, or as bitterly as the elder Mrs. Denvers? Age had its disappointments, but so did youth.

Between Tom, and Daddy, and Orson, it seemed as if a maze of misery lay between me and happiness. Thus far, I had found only dead ends, and there was no guarantee, no guarantee at all, that I would ever find more.

I wrote of the dinner conversation in our diary (for I now thought of it not as Laurice's diary, or as mine, but as ours both):

> Dear Laurice,
>
> I no longer wonder why Orson is so heartless. With a grandmother like that, and a father who seems more a whipping boy than a man, Orson could hardly be expected to turn out well. I wish I could help Mrs. Denvers, but I don't know how. You would figure something out, wouldn't you, Laurice? I try to be as kind and insightful as you were, but as Daddy has known all along, I'm no Laurice. Nowhere close.
>
> Anise

Chapter Eighteen

That night Bonita and Mr. Denvers made love again, shortly after midnight. Their bed squeaked its protests, and they moved to Bonita's Jacuzzi bath, where the sounds of the jets and bubbles combined with Bonita's pleasure to make a strange, wet musical. I was their captive, unhappy audience. I fell asleep before they finished, and I dreamed of Tom and me, making love on the edge of the ocean, only his eyes were blue instead of brown.

I woke sweating, aroused, my body longing for the touch that Tom would never again give me. Instead I touched myself, and pretended that it was Tom's fingers and not my own that brushed across my nipples, down my stomach, to the wet longing between my legs. I could not fool myself, no matter how tender my strokes. My desires weren't satiated, and a long hot bath did little to drain them away.

After my bath, I wrapped my sunny yellow towel around me, and waited for Bonita to come with whichever of her dresses she would lend me today. I had not waited long before the knock came, and I threw open the door. Mr. Denvers stood before me.

"Good morning," he said. I clutched my towel closer. My nipples showed through the towel, their two hard little points unmistakable atop the greater swell of my breasts. I tried to think them away, tried to convince the hard little pebbles to become the softest sand, but my body would not cooperate. Oh, if only I could believe that Mr. Denvers did not see, but he smiled brightly, too brightly, with his eyes too fixed upon my face, which I knew he had surveyed all, and approved the lay of the land.

He wore a full suit, complete with tie and watch. The bulge in his pocket was not what I first imagined; he withdrew a bright yellow tape measurer, and stretched it open before me. "Orson asked why I had not yet gotten you measured for a proper uniform, and I had no answer to give him." From his other pocket he withdrew a small notepad and pencil. "Orson suggests a long black skirt, coupled with a suit jacket, all very similar to what Juande wore, only feminized, of course. Just putting you into a suit would feminize it."

Oh, what a relief it would be to have my own clothes, properly fitted, that covered my chest and my legs. "I'll measure myself at once," I said, reaching for the tape measurer with one hand, holding up my towel with the other.

Mr. Denvers did not give it to me. "It would be difficult, wouldn't it, to take your own measurements? And if you get them wrong, than anything made from them will be worthless. These uniforms will not be cheap, and I'd like to get you several of them, so you can alternate from day to day."

My body ached to be touched, but not by him. "Bonita can take my measurements," I said.

"I gave Bonita the day off, and she's left the grounds."

"Mrs. Denvers –"

"My dear wife is in bed with a headache and chills." He smiled, almost fatherly. I backed away, but was stopped by my bed, and he closed the gap that I had made. "Don't be afraid. This will only take a few minutes, and then you'll have nice new uniforms, in all the best fabrics."

I clutched my towel, but he was stronger than I, and he pulled my towel from me. "No," I said, but his hands were already on me. He measured the distance from shoulder to shoulder, and from arm to wrist, and around my neck. I shut my eyes and prayed for this to be over. His hands found my breasts, and he held the end of the measuring tape against my traitorously hard left nipple, stretched it around my back, and across my right breast, right nipple, until the circle was complete.

"So lovely," he murmured, and measured me just beneath my breasts, and then my waist near my belly button, and then the length of my body from my shoulders down. Crouched on the ground before me, his breaths coming heavily, he measured around my hips. Then he placed the end of the measuring tape down by my foot to measure the inside of my leg, and he brought his hand up past my knee, past my inner thigh, to the very core of me.

The measuring tape fell to the ground, but his hand remained, and with one finger he moved against me on the outside, sending sharp hot shocks through me, and another finger plunged into my wetness. His body came forward, and he knocked me down onto the bed, trapping me beneath him, his hand working me, playing me; I tried to tell him no, but his mouth came down on mine, and his fingers moved faster than before, and he stole my breath with his hard, heavy kiss.

When his kiss broke, his mouth remained close to mine, his breath steaming against my cheek, and I couldn't protest, I couldn't scream, because my breath came in short, hot gasps. Between my legs, his fingers stirred me hotter and hotter. An orgasm ripped through me with its violent burning thrusting waves, and as soon as it was done he withdrew his hand, and I lay weakly shivering on the bed. He cupped my breasts with eager hands, and he traced the sweat that trickled down them both. Then he stepped back, gathered his notepad and measuring tape, and covered me with my yellow towel. Without a word, without an apology, he left me there, quivering crying on the bed.

The door clicked shut behind him. I bound the towel around myself, tighter and tighter, but no matter how hard I squeezed I couldn't expunge the looseness from my legs, or the heat from inside of me. I buried myself beneath the thick yellow covers of my bed. I was too shamed to leave it. I had let him touch me, touch inside of me. My body had betrayed me, and welcomed his knowing hands. I was not the person I thought I was. I wasn't worthy of Tom, no, I wasn't even worthy of Orson. I cried at the loss of myself, and when the tears were gone, I shook, and I shivered, and I begged God to strike me dead where I lay.

Hours passed like minutes, or minutes like hours, I had no sense of time, but at last a knock came at the door. I cried out, afraid that Mr. Denvers had returned. Orson stepped into the room – perhaps he'd heard my cry as a welcome. He hurried to the side of my bed. My breasts showed beneath my tear-streaked face, but it didn't matter if he saw my breasts, it didn't matter if anyone did; they were public property after all, they were hideous hurtful lumps that I had no power to keep unseen.

Orson tucked the blanket over me, and wiped my face with the edge of it, but my ability to cry had recovered, and more tears came to wet the blanket, until Orson gave up the effort. "My father did this," he said. I made no answer, but he seemed to need none. His face stony, emotionless, he said, "I'll kill him."

"No," I cried. "No, Mrs. Denvers loves him, and you mustn't hurt Mrs. Denvers, because everyone hurts her. Everyone does."

"It's you who've been hurt," he said.

"Will you hold me?" I hated to ask it of him, him of all people, but I was shaking again, and he sat on the edge of my bed and embraced me; for as long as I needed him, he embraced me. My breasts had fallen free again, but he paid them no mind, swollen disgusting lumps that they were.

"You're a minor, we can put him in jail."

"He didn't rape me," I said. "He only touched."

"He touched you against your will," Orson said. "That's illegal. You don't want him touching other girls, raping other girls, do you?"

It was too much to think about, and I buried myself beneath my covers again. Orson brushed his fingers through my hair, untangling some of the mess. "I'll call you a doctor."

"Please, no," I begged. I couldn't bear to have someone else touch me. "No, I'll be all right. Maybe some aspirin, or a bath, will make me feel better."

"I'll get you both," he said.

Along with the two aspirin, he brought a glass of cool water, and I drank it down fast, and was about to ask for more when I spit it all back up again, including the aspirin. "That's okay," he said, wiping me dry, wiping away my renewed helpless tears. He helped me out of bed, and held my towel around me, and brought me to the bath. The smell of vanilla filled the room. I stepped into the water, and it was nicely hot, but not hot enough to cleanse away Mr. Denvers' touch. I turned it hotter, boiling hot, but Orson was quick to turn it down.

He stayed with me, and after several minutes my body had relaxed, and my mind grown sleepy, and he helped me from the tub again, back into bed. He found a white nightgown of mine, made of innocent cotton, and he pulled it over me, and he even brought me a pair of white panties that I slipped into beneath the covers. "Sleep, now, I won't leave your side, you'll be safe," he said, and I felt safe, and I allowed sleep to sweep me under its protective curtain.

I woke, and for a moment I remembered nothing, and then I saw the shape of a person in the plush yellow chair by the drawn curtains. The room was dark, and I remembered menace, Mr. Denvers and his unwelcome touch, and I screamed; with all the breath my lungs could hold, with all the air the room could give, I screamed.

The intruder left the chair to hurry to my side, and I saw that it was Orson, and still I screamed, as I should have screamed that morning, and I battled away Orson's hands, as I should've battled Mr. Denvers.

"You're safe, you're safe," Orson was saying, again and again. "You're safe, you're safe now, shush."

"Is he gone?" I said, too loud, too frantic.

The door to my room opened, and I screamed again, but it was only Bonita; she brought me a hot washcloth to cleanse my face, and a tray of food that I had no interest in.

"He left on his own, but I'm having the locks changed," Orson said.

"No," I cried. "No, Mrs. Denvers mustn't know, she loves him."

"Things have gotten worse while you slept," Orson said.

Bonita sat on the foot of the bed, peering worriedly up at me. Her blue dress revealed what cleavage she had, just as Mr. Denvers liked. "You are okay?" she asked.

I bit my lips to stop any more screams from coming. That I was not okay should have been obvious to anyone who saw me. Orson, crouched close alongside me, said, "There's a doctor waiting to see you. A female doctor, but you don't have to see her yet, or not at all if you don't want to."

"She is nice," Bonita said.

"I said I didn't want to see a doctor."

"I know," Orson said. "And you don't have to. She's just here if you want her."

"She has been here all day," Bonita said. "She gave me an exam, and she was very nice."

"I don't want to see her. You shouldn't have gotten her when I said I didn't want her."

Orson and Bonita exchanged glances, and Bonita blushed. "I am glad she came," Bonita said. "For the last two months, I have not bled. I told Dr. Rollins, and she tested me. Be happy for me. I am going to be a mother." She lay her hands on the curve of her stomach, and she blushed a pretty pink.

"Oh, poor Mrs. Denvers," I said.

"My father thought it best to take a short business trip to Miami. Mrs. Denvers is very emotional right now. I'm surprised you slept through it."

"Very emotional? That's all you can say?" I struggled to get out of bed, but Orson single-handedly kept me down. "I've got to go to her."

"She knows that her husband got Bonita pregnant. She doesn't know what he did to you. Do you want her to know?"

I lay back, momentarily unsure what to do.

"The elder Mrs. Denvers is with her, trying to get her to put her emotions aside and deal with the situation."

"No, that's no good," I said. "Your grandmother is too harsh, she'll just make things worse."

"Can you make things any better?"

"Yes, I can." I slid past his arm, out of bed. As soon as I stood, dizziness swept through me, but I clutched my dresser, and rummaged for my clothes. I found the slacks and shirts, never worn, that I had bought to wear as work clothes. I ripped off the tags with a vengeance.

"You're in no shape to help anyone," Orson said.

"Some son you are!" I cried. "Why aren't you by her side?"

"Because I promised I'd stay by yours," he said. For the first time, I noticed how distraught he looked. His hair was in complete disarray, his fists clenched. He did not look like the Orson I was used to.

"Thank you for staying." I pulled out my slacks, and pulled them on under my cotton nightgown. Orson turned to face the other way.

"I can get you one of my dresses," Bonita said. As if I would ever wear one of those rape-me dresses again. I hid my unsightly breasts behind a pretty white bra, and buttoned my black shirt all the way up to the top button. The rayon shirt fell lightly against my chest, but still the rise of my breasts could be seen. I longed to hide them away beneath a sweat-shirt, or a parka, but it was too hot for that.

"She's outside in her gardens." Orson followed me out my door, out of the servants' quarters. Bonita stayed behind.

"Brace yourself for what you'll see, or what she'll say," Orson warned. "There's darker depths to my parents' relationship that you can possibly imagine."

Chapter Nineteen

The sun soaked the gardens with its furious light. I hurried down the crushed pink path, drawn by the sound of the elder Mrs. Denvers' voice. Her tone, so sharp and cruel, reminded me of the whacks of a butcher's knife. "If the marriage bed were welcoming, Jonathon wouldn't have turned to Bonita. It's as simple as that. Your hysterics waste time and energy better spent on him."

Mrs. Denvers knelt before a half-emptied bed of lilies. One by one she yanked the beauties out of the ground. The path was littered with flowers. "Mrs. Denvers, you're hurting them," I said. She tossed a lily at my feet, its roots pitifully broken.

"She's hysterical. I always told her to keep her emotions in check. I told her –"

"I'd like to talk to Mrs. Denvers alone," I said.

"And I'd like it if the servants around here knew their place. Bonita is the maid, not the mistress. You are the chauffeur. Go drive somewhere."

"Grandmother," Orson said. He'd only just caught up to us. "You've had plenty of time to talk with Mother. If anything, she's gotten worse." Mrs. Denvers cleared the final lily, and crawled right through the dirt to attack the peonies on the other side. Her ivory slacks and silk shirt were completely ruined.

"Oh, yes, by all means, everyone indulge the woman. Reward her for her lack of self-control." Despite her cruel words, the elder Mrs. Denvers accepted Orson's arm, and let us be. I waited until they were out of hearing, and then I joined Mrs. Denvers among the peonies. They were intricately crisscrossed with ferns.

"You don't have to destroy this beautiful garden, just because Mr. Denvers did something ugly," I said. If she even heard me, she showed no sign of slowing. Her beautiful blond hair, clumped with dirt, fell before her face; she might not even be seeing the flowers, but she deftly wrapped her fingers around them, pulled, discarded, again and again. Nothing I could say would help her; the elder Mrs. Denvers had already said too much. I would have to show my concern through actions, not words.

I crouched down next to her, as mindless of my clothes as Mrs. Denvers was of hers, and I ripped an innocent fern from the earth. I threw it aside, and felt on my shoulders the sunshine that would quickly shrivel these poor uprooted plants. I pulled another, and another, letting my anger escape me too; I imagined each fern to be Mr. Denvers throat that I wrapped my fingers around, and I imagined each peony to be his manhood, uprooted, discarded. I tore up a bright red peony, and flung it as far as I could; I hoped it would catch the wind and be carried out to sea, never to be a threat to me or Mrs. Denvers again, but it landed in the next bed over. Roses. Their thorns would hurt when we pulled.

Mrs. Denvers slowed, now that I was helping, and when we cleared the last of the ferns and peonies, she lay her dirty hand on mind. I drew her into an embrace, and we held each other for long minutes, the sun burning down on us, the sweet smell of flowers competing with the smells of earth and sweat. At last we separated. Mrs. Denvers surveyed the ravaged garden beds, and she slowly began to gather the discarded flowers.

"These are my babies," she said.

I added a handful of drooping peonies to her growing pile. "I'll help you replant them."

"Replant," she said, her head drooped just like the peonies. "That's what everyone always says. 'Try again, you can have another one, forget this baby and try again.' As if my babies weren't real, weren't individuals, as if I had only wanted any old baby. I wanted my babies." She hit the pile of flowers, scattering them across the path. "And now Bonita is having the baby that should have been mine. My baby, not hers."

"It's awful," I said.

"You don't even know. I've had fourteen miscarriages in the last twenty years. I am the mother of fourteen babies, but I never held a single one of them. And now Bonita, she gets my husband's baby, and I get nothing." She plucked the rose buds from their bushes, one by one, shredding the petals onto the ground. I watched helplessly. It would hurt terribly to lose any child, but to lose fourteen of them, before she even knew them? I couldn't even imagine that much pain.

"Orson was a true miracle baby, then," I said.

She tried to tear the rose bush from the ground, but it held fast. "The miracles of science. Sperm meets egg in lab, grows in another woman's womb. Not my womb, not my egg. Not my child. I wasn't woman enough. Even the maid is more woman than me." Her hands quivering, she abandoned the roses. I took her hands in mine. Droplets of blood formed in her palms, from where the thorns had cut her. And there was nothing I could do. Her grief went so deep, there were no words that could comfort her, no sayings that wouldn't be as trite as the ones offered to me when Laurice died. *At least she's in heaven now. God must have wanted her. I know just how you feel. I'm so sorry for you.* Words like those only made me want to cry out, you can't know how I feel, I'm so alone in this.

I held Mrs. Denvers' hands, and it seemed to be enough. Her strength left her, and she sank down, mindless of the rose thorns behind her that snagged her silk shirt. "I named them all," she said. "I sprinkled their ashes here in this garden, and I planted lilies, and roses, and allamanda, whatever their namesake was. Three of them were so little, they had no ashes. Meredith, named after the ocean. Coral. Robin." She pointed to the robin's nest, up in the tallest oak tree. "They're here with me in spirit. I imagine them, fourteen happy children, running through this garden. I come here to be with them."

"Should I leave you alone?" I asked.

"No, please stay," she said. "My Lily would have been your age now. I like to think she would've been like you, so beautiful, so kind."

I stayed, and I told her about the sister I'd lost, and she

told me about her fourteen pregnancies, and how hopeful she'd been each time, and how awful it was to leave the hospital with empty hands, and an empty womb, time after time. We talked, and we cried, and, somewhere deep inside, we began to heal.

Orson, true to his word, had the locks changed that very day, but Mr. Denvers did not return to test the doors. I regretted that I had ever thought him charming, or believed Bonita when she called him kind. Of anyone, he knew how Mrs. Denvers would take this – he had been at her side for each of her miscarriages – yet now, when she needed him and might have been able to forgive him, he was absent. The days passed, and he did not call.

Mrs. Denvers gave me a pitifully large stack of pregnancy books, which I passed on to Bonita. Pregnancy suited Bonita; she was prettier than ever, and her stomach was just beginning to show. She examined her breasts daily to see if they'd grown bigger yet. She had always wanted large breasts. She even confided that she had secretly hoped Mr. Denvers would get her pregnant, because his good genes meant her baby might not be a degen. "I am sorry for Mrs. Denvers, but I am happy for my baby," she said, and that was the closest to an apology she ever came.

Despite her general happiness, however, she accepted the pregnancy books with a frown. "I am not a good reader," she said. "What if I am too dumb to be a good mother?" She ran her hands over her stomach, and she looked so worried, I couldn't keep up my anger.

Bonita was on light duty around the house, and wasn't allowed to do any heavy lifting or chemical cleaning, so she had plenty of time to study. She despaired a thousand times, but I wouldn't give up on her, and together we made it through the first of the books.

Orson acted cooler than ever. He treated me as if I truly were just a chauffeur, a nobody, a no-good degenerative. When he looked at me, he seemed to look right through me, as if I weren't even there. And I didn't know why.

Mr. Denvers had not returned from his so-called business vacation, nor had he called. Mrs. Denvers was still in low spirits. She had hired a gardener to tend the gardens, instead of doing it herself as she had always done. I offered her my pot of anise herbs, but she only examined them, told me to keep them out of direct sunlight, and handed the pot back. Orson gave her his unread copy of *Pride and Prejudice*, and Mrs. Denvers and I spent a few afternoons reading in the parlor. She had never read any Jane Austen novels before, and she seemed to think *Pride and Prejudice* was a tragedy, because of how poorly Mr. Bennet treated Mrs. Bennet. I tried to interest her in something else, but Orson had given her the book, beloved Orson, and she read it to the end. She didn't recognize it as the book she had bought for Orson, but thought it a true gift. When she finished the book, she caught Orson in the hallway and thanked him profusely.

"Thank yourself, you're the one who bought the book. It certainly wasn't something I was likely to read," he said. Mrs. Denvers didn't know what to say, and Orson brushed past her. How could he treat his own mother so callously? I knew he could be kind.

I followed him upstairs to his room, firmly shutting the door behind us. Orson started to sit on the clunky black bed, then changed his mind and took his computer chair instead. "You look angry," he said, without emotion, as if he couldn't care less if I were angry or not.

I sat on the bed, tried to contain my anger. I knew he could be kind. He'd taken such good care of me the day Mr. Denvers left. "Why do you treat her like that?" I asked. "She's your mother. This is a horrible time for her."

"She brought it on herself," he said. Oh, how I wished I could slap that smug smile off his face! He was being awful, just awful. "She told you about her miscarriages, did she? But she didn't tell you about the abortion that began them all. Her womb worked fine until the doctors went in there for a little cutting and killing."

"Oh, poor Mrs. Denvers."

"No, not poor Mrs. Denvers! She chose. She chose to let my licentious father have his way with her, not two weeks after they'd met, and she chose to do away with the inconvenience of an out-of-wedlock baby."

"That doesn't sound like her," I said.

"She regrets it," he said, with a casual air, but his hands tightly gripped the handles of his chair. This was not as easy a conversation for him as he would have me believe. "She pours on the charm to me, wants me to love her like a true mother, but it's not me she wants. She wants the baby she killed. She pours on the love, and it's all false love, it's not for me."

"It could be, if you would take it," I said.

"I don't want her love," he said coldly.

"Then you're more screwed up than I am. At least I know what I want," I yelled. My heat only made him colder.

"If you knew what you wanted, why are you still here? You've got enough money. Go away." He swiveled in his chair, turned on his cold gray computer. Go away. Run away. That was my usual way, wasn't it?

"No," I said. "Mrs. Denvers needs me here." And, I added silently, I needed her. She was a daughterless mother, I was a motherless daughter. We fit.

"Then go to her," Orson said, and he started up his computer, and ignored me completely. The endless clack-clack of his typing chased me from his room. He could have his computer, and his calculated business books, and his emotionless, humanless world. I would take the love his mother had to offer, and build my own world.

Chapter Twenty

For a time, we were happy. The more Orson emphasized my servant role, and had me drive him here and there in complete silence, the more Mrs. Denvers treated me not like a servant at all, but like a daughter. We shopped together, and I helped her pick out fashionable new clothes, lighter jewelry, new lipstick, all the things that gave a woman confidence in her appearance. *The Phantom of the Opera* came to town, and she got front row tickets for Orson, herself, and me. Both Mrs. Denvers and I wept near the end, and Orson in his stiff black suit leaned away from us, distancing himself from our womanly tears.

Mr. Denvers returned to Tampa, taking a residence at the Hilton Towers Hotel, and I drove Mrs. Denvers to occasional lunches and dinner dates with him. I refused to drive Bonita to see him, and so he sent a cab for her, every Tuesday, and she came back all rosy and garrulous. The third Tuesday, she did not come back at all, and Mr. Denvers sent word that he'd established her in a house of her own, for her peace of mind and ours. It was a small house, only two bedrooms, one for Bonita, one for the baby. Mrs. Denvers went white when she heard. She wanted to reconcile with him, I knew she did, but his buying a house for Bonita made it too real.

I thought of Tom and his family, in their even smaller living quarters. Honey was two months older now. Would she be sitting up? I pulled open one of Bonita's baby books, and looked up Honey's age. Yes, she might well be sitting up, and smiling, too. I missed her, and Tom, and the twins, but it was a nostalgic missing, a longing for what I knew I could not have back. Life in the degen ghetto seemed almost like a book I had once read, one that I wanted to reread but couldn't. The evenings we'd spent, gathered in the living room, telling stories – those evenings were too perfect to exist outside of a storybook, too perfect to be a part of my life. I treasured my memories, but I left the book on the shelf; I knew where Tom worked, I knew where they lived, but I did not attempt to cross back into that magical land. He did not want me.

One hot July afternoon, after dropping Orson off at a local university lecture, I returned to the house. Somewhere in the bathroom drawers, I knew I had a hair tie. The heat made me want to pull my hair out by its roots, which were coming in brown again, but I'd have to settle for binding it up. I didn't find the hair tie, because I found a dusty box of tampons first, and I sat down hard on the toilet. If it had been open instead of closed, there might've been a splash, and I doubt I would have noticed.

Despite all this talk of pregnancies, and miscarriages, I had never once thought about my own cycle. My last period had been at Tom's apartment, and I had craved chocolate even more than little Kelly, even though there had been no chocolate to be had. That had been weeks ago. Weeks and weeks. I wiped the dust from the bright blue of the box. I stared up at the mirror, and the frightened girl stared back at me. I did not look pregnant. I did not feel pregnant. Surely it was stress that had pushed my cycle so far out of whack. I shoved the tampon box back into its drawer, yet I couldn't shove the thought from my mind.

If I was pregnant, it was Tom's baby. Oh, the thought gave me joy and pain, both at once, both as sharp as nails. To have a living testament to our love! To have a baby with Tom's eyes, Tom's smile. But then, to lose that baby, like I'd lost Jake, because of the cold reality of his degen genes. I longed to go to Tom, to tell him, but I couldn't bear to imagine the pain that he would surely suffer. He hadn't wanted to pass on his genes. He hadn't wanted me.

And perhaps I was getting ahead of myself. I needed to pick up Orson from his lecture, but first I stopped at a drugstore. Next to the contraceptives, and the mounds of feminine supplies that I would, perhaps, not need for the next several months, lay the delicate boxes with their pictures of smiling children and promises of pink pluses or minuses, ones or zeroes, pregnant or not pregnant. Such a little box to contain my whole future.

I parked in the visitors lot at the University of Tampa, and I walked determinedly to the women's bathroom. The lecture had just gotten out, and a pair of giggling co-eds waited in line before me. The bathroom was brightly lit, and smelled of bleach. The girls in front of me debated whether the Japanese lecturer had looked more like singer Lerome Hones or sitcom star Palada. Had I ever been that concerned about singing groups and cute boys? Had I ever been a normal girl, like those two, with their self-assured chatter, their easy assumption that the world revolved around them and their favorite stars? The answer came easily: no, I had never been normal, not after Laurice died. And now, if I was pregnant, I never would have a normal life. I had wanted to attend college, I had wanted to learn Spanish, but now the only foreign language I would learn was baby-babble.

I was getting ahead of myself. First I had to take the pregnancy test. The girls went into the stalls, chatting even from their separate privacies, and then my turn came. I followed the instructions, and I waited. The smell of bleach was stronger here, strong enough that my eyes watered.

The line appeared, a vivid bold pink. *This is my baby's first announcement,* I thought. *This is my baby saying, look out world, I'm on my way.*

I tucked the test into my purse, and I stumbled from the bathroom. The sunshine was too bright, the world too real, when all I wanted was to dwell within my thoughts. I was going to have a baby. I was going to be a mother.

Orson had found the limo, and waited impatiently by its locked doors. I let him in, and he looked at me curiously, but if he noticed anything unusual in my appearance, he kept it to himself.

"Did you enjoy the lecture?" I asked, feigning normalcy.

He warmed to the subject. "Definitely thought-provoking. Did you know that hundreds of Japanese degens kill themselves every year? They consider themselves a drain on society, and they put society's needs before their own."

"That's horrible," I said.

"You would say that. I think it's rather noble, although sterilization would be a simpler solution."

"How can you say that? Every one has a right to live, and a right to have children," I cried. This conversation hit too close to home, knowing as I did that a degen baby nested within my womb. "Would you sterilize America's degens? Or maybe just send them to concentration camps, and be done with it?"

"You're acting like I'm Hitler," Orson said.

"No, *you* are acting like you're Hitler." I pressed hard on the accelerator, and the limo screeched as I pulled out of the parking lot. Orson fell back against the seat cushions. "Where to?" I demanded.

"The Oceanview Plaza," he said. "I made reservations for two for dinner, because I thought you might be a good conversation partner to discuss Wohniko's ideas on degeneration. Should I cancel?"

His tone enraged me. It was as if he were saying he'd thought me an adult, but now suspected I was a child, incapable of intelligent discourse. "I know more about degeneration than you do," I hotly said.

"I'm sure you do."

I didn't want to dine out, not today. I wanted to go home and read Bonita's pregnancy books – my pregnancy books, now. But I couldn't turn him down, because that would be saying I was a child. He would think I was afraid of his intellect. He would think I was afraid of him. I turned off onto Seashell Trail.

"There's a good girl," he said.

The Oceanview Plaza, hidden away on the tip of Weston Key, was the most expensive restaurant in Tampa. The food was good, but what you really paid for was the atmosphere. Long, gleaming windows stretched from the opal-dusted floor to the soaring arched ceiling. The maitre d' greeted Orson by name – "Good evening, Mr. Denvers, right this way" – and led us to a table situated right by the windows, with a glorious view of the ocean.

Orson did not even glance at the view, but picked up his menu at once. No matter what the maitre d' thought, it wasn't evening yet; the sun was still high above the waves. As always, at the sight of that infinite blueness, I thought of my mother, and of Laurice, and of death that separated me from them; if they were on the far side of the ocean, on the edge of the world, I could still go to them, but death kept them further away than any mere ocean's span.

I settled into my chair, and accidentally bumped against the table; instinctively I wrapped my arm forward, cradling my stomach, cradling the child inside. Here I was thinking about death, when life had formed inside of me. A new soul waited to be born.

"The cod's delicious here," Orson said.

I looked at the menu, but I couldn't concentrate. What would I name my child? Where would we live? "What did you say?"

"I said, the cod's delicious."

"I'll have that, then," I said, and set the menu down. It had been seven weeks since Tom and I had made love. My baby had been with me for seven weeks, and I hadn't even known. *I'll make up for the lost time,* I told him – or her. Oh, imagine a child that looked like Tom and Jake, imagine another bright-eyed, curly-haired, Huck Finnish little boy. Or imagine a girl, as beautiful as her aunt Laurice, with Laurice's easy-going air, her grace, her laughter.

Our waiter arrived, sleek and only slightly pretentious in his spotless black suit. Orson ordered the steak, medium rare, and a bottle of house wine. "And for the lady?" asked the waiter.

"I can't drink wine," I said, startled, one arm across my stomach as if to protect my baby.

"She'll have the cod," Orson said. The waiter leaned past me to light the two candles.

"I won't drink the wine."

"We can walk it off before you drive. Don't worry," Orson said.

"Don't bring me any wine, I'm not old enough," I told the

waiter. He nodded, and quickly withdrew; he didn't want to be in the middle of our dispute. Orson and I couldn't even have a dinner without arguing. How ridiculous to think Daddy had wanted us to spend a lifetime together. "Tell me about the lecturer," I said, forestalling any more discussion of the wine.

Orson leaned forward, suddenly animated. "According to Wohniko, Japan's economy improved because of the reduction in degens."

"Their suicides, you mean."

"Here in the U.S., society is stratified. Degens don't live long enough to produce wealth, and each generation brings them further into poverty. We're rich, they're poor, and the divide grows every year. You should see the statistics."

"You sound excited." I made no effort to hide my distaste. Orson never hid his, after all. "Is that all people are to you? Statistics?"

"You've got to look at the numbers if you want to look for a solution. Here, each degen woman has an average of three children. Regular women, despite their longer lifespans, only have two. We need to turn that around."

"Have you thought about why degen women might be having so many babies?"

"Lack of education, I suspect," Orson said.

"Think about it harder," I snapped. Harvard-educated or not, he should do better than this. "Degens live such short lives. The only way for them to touch the future is through their children."

"Oh, please. That's so idealist."

"Yes. Degens are idealist. A degen pregnancy is, by definition, usually a teenage pregnancy. Either it's a slip-up, which can happen to anyone, or it's a chosen pregnancy. If it's chosen, it's because they're in love, because they want a child."

"Then why don't they go on down to the sperm bank, or your own father's Institute, and ensure that their child has a future? Artificial insemination is free and easy."

"And cold. And heartless. Orson, don't you know anything about love? Can't you see why two people, degens or not, would want to have their own children?"

"No, I can't," he said.

"Then you're wasting your education. You might as well go get that job you were so afraid of. They're hiring here, I think." As if on cue, the waiter arrived with our meal. "You could wait tables, or wash dishes, and keep all your awful opinions to yourself."

"The wine, sir?" The waiter spoke respectfully.

Orson held out his glass. As soon as it was filled, he took several sips. The waiter placed our entrees before us, then hurried away before he could hear more of our charming conversation. To him, we must seem like spoiled rich kids, not even able to enjoy the fine atmosphere or food here, and not caring if we made a spectacle of ourselves.

I made an effort to calm myself. "Is the steak good?" I asked.

"Delicious," he said. "And the cod?"

I took a bite. "Slightly overcooked, but still good."

We ate in silence, until Orson capped the meal with the rest of his wine and said, "I intend to have a career in politics, you know, after I go to graduate school."

"I didn't know that," I said.

"I want to make a difference. I want to turn our society around, make things good again. It's why I study so hard. The solution is out there, and maybe I'll be the one to find it."

"Do you really think you'll find it in a book?" I asked.

"Maybe," he said. "Or maybe I'll find it in a dinner conversation, or, God forbid, in a stack of statistics." He smiled, and I found myself smiling back. This was just like him. He could be so hateful, and then so nice; it was impossible to understand who he really was. "I've enjoyed our dinner, Anise. Are you sure you won't toast with me?"

"I can't," I said.

"All right, then I'll toast to both of us. May we find our way in this world, and may we live up to our talents, whatever they may be." He clinked his wine glass against my water glass, and drank to us.

Chapter Twenty-One

I almost told Orson about my pregnancy, that late afternoon as we strolled down the beach after our fancy dinner. He seemed so friendly, and he repeatedly told me that even though we'd disagreed about degens, we'd had a good discussion, and that was all that mattered. Maybe that's how college students thought. I knew better. He had been wrong to think of degens as statistics. If he wanted a career in politics, he needed to see the faces of the people.

But I kept my thoughts inside, and perhaps he did too, and we walked comfortably down the beach. With each step, the sand pulled my feet down, and wrapped around them like a blanket around a newborn. Sandpipers raced to and fro, in rhythm with the waves, and I closed my eyes and pictured a little girl, twirling her baton, learning to walk in rhythm. Or a boy, all grown up, dressed in army garb, ready to take his part in the liberty march.

My mind elsewhere, I stumbled on the sand; if Orson hadn't caught me, I would have fallen. "Thank you," I said, and then I caught the way he was looking at me, and I pulled myself free of his arms.

"My mother rejected me before I ever rejected her," he said softly. "I thought you should know that. She built it into my name. Orson. What does it rhyme with? Your son."

"That's crazy."

"I heard her say so. She and my dad were fighting. She said she named me Orson because I was his son, not hers."

"Even if she did, that was years ago. It's time to forgive her."

"I know."

We walked in silence then, until Orson found a pretty purple shell, and handed it to me. "I leave this Friday. Back to school already, and normally I'd be thrilled for it." He glanced at me, then glanced away. "Think anyone's going to miss me?"

"Your mother has talked of little else, this past week."

"I wasn't asking about my mother," he said.

I was glad for the shell he had given me; I rubbed the sand from it, kept my hands busy. "Do you want me to be honest?" I asked.

"Didn't I say so the first day we met?"

I couldn't remember if he had or not. The sun on the ocean was glaring, but I kept my gaze there, and not on Orson. "You take me out for a fancy dinner, and now a walk along the beach. I think you want to romance me, but not because I'm me. I think it's because I'm here, and our fathers chose us for each other, and it's easy."

"That's not exactly how I'd put it," Orson said.

"You deserve to know that I love someone else."

We walked in silence for a time, and then Orson said, "Who's the lucky guy?"

"His name is Tom."

"Tell Tom I concede. I'll have my father dissolve our promise contract. You can be with him tomorrow."

"I wish it were that easy," I said. "But my father would just promise me to someone else. As would your father. It's our sacred duty to repopulate the earth with healthy-gened children, and all that." I kicked at the sand before me, and scared away the sandpipers. "As long as you're promised to me, and I'm in hiding, your father isn't going to cut off your education, right?"

"So it seems," Orson said.

"Then at least one of us gets what he wants." I turned abruptly; I'd had enough of walking. What does Orson want? A big pink boat. No, that wasn't it. A college education. A life in politics. "You've got the good looks for politics. People will look up to you for that alone, and for your score on the degen measure. Coupled with years of study, and heart, you really could have something. You could be a governor. A president."

Under his breath, barely audible over the soft ocean waves, Orson said, "Since when do I have heart?"

I didn't think I was supposed to hear that, but I answered anyway. "You've got a heart in there. It's just a little dusty, and out of shape. Maybe in your house, your grandmother comes down on anyone who shows affection, but that's not how the world works."

"Sage advice, from the worldly seventeen-year-old," Orson said, but he smiled kindly.

"Seventeen years and three months," I corrected.

"If you love this Tom, you shouldn't be wasting your time here."

"So now it's your turn to give advice?"

"I'm an opinionated guy," he said, as if I hadn't learned that the first day I met him.

"Things with Tom are complicated. I don't know if we'll ever be together," I said.

"I feel for you," he said, with a straight face, but a moment later, we both broke out laughing. I had never seen him laugh before, except in cool sarcasm; his mirth made him look younger, and more good-looking than any man had a right to be. If Mr. Denvers had looked like Orson, no wonder he turned into a womanizer. And if Orson loosened up at school, he could have any woman he wanted.

"Race you to the limo," I said, and if he thought me childish, that didn't stop him from outrunning me through the heavy sand.

Over the next few days, Mrs. Denvers followed Orson from room to room, everywhere he went, almost as if he were the parent and she a timid two-year-old. Any mention of Harvard, or Friday's plane, and Mrs. Denvers fell terribly silent. She missed him already, and he wasn't even gone yet. I thought it was sweet of her, but Orson chafed under all the attention.

Even so, the evening before he left, he presented her with a leather-bound collection of all six Jane Austen novels. She broke down into tears, and he winked at me over her head. He knew how to please her, when he chose to do so.

She cried more the next morning, and even more at the airport itself, until Orson broke away from her hugs and practically ran down the gangway. She called after him, "I'll write you every day, Orson, I love you," and even with his back to us, I saw him flinch. He had confided in me that morning that he hated airport good-byes, that they always turned into dreadful spectacles. He was right; all the tourists were staring. Mrs. Denvers refused to leave before Orson's plane had taken off, and she prayed on her rosary for him to have a safe flight. "The virgin Mary, she knows what it's like to lose a child, she won't take Orson from me." She spoke too loud, and I saw the gate agent eyeing her.

"People fly planes every day," I said.

"She's a mother, and only a mother truly knows. Mr. Denvers has his career, but all I have is Orson. I'd die if I lost him too."

The plane streaked down the runway, and then lumbered into the air like an overweight hen. Mrs. Denvers held her breath, and then softly exhaled once the plane rose out of sight. "Don't think me foolish," she said, now that she was able to focus on me again.

"You're not foolish, you're a mother."

"I am," she said simply. "Even though he didn't come from me, he is my son, and I'll love him always. A mother's love is different from all other kinds of love. It's even different from a father's love. A mother is right there, changing her baby's diapers, holding his hand as he toddles his first step. Orson used to run home from school and throw himself into my arms, then wiggle free and show me what he'd accomplished that day. He always loved school."

"He still does," I said. I took her hand, and guided her through the crowded airport. I was going to be a mother too, but I couldn't tell her. She'd lost fourteen pregnancies. How could I tell her that I, too, was more woman than her? No, I couldn't break Mrs. Denvers' heart like that. I needed her love. And it seemed to me that she needed mine.

That evening, while Mrs. Denvers rested in the parlor reading Jane Austen's *Persuasion,* I tied one of Bonita's aprons around myself and got to work on cleaning. Bonita had been gone for a week, but no one had made arrangements for another maid to be hired. I didn't mind picking up the slack; with Mr. Denvers and Orson both gone, I had very little driving to do.

I trespassed into Orson's room, and stripped the beds, cleaned the windows, vacuumed the thick white carpet. The clinical smell of my cleaning spray matched the clinical look of his room. I dusted off the books, scanning their titles as I went. I wouldn't ever cuddle up to *World Economies in the Twenty-First Century,* but *Women's Rights* looked intriguing. When he came home, maybe I'd ask him what he thought of that feminist text.

No, what was I thinking? Orson wouldn't be home for two months, not until his fall break. By then I would be four months pregnant, and my belly would show. Maybe Orson would be kind; he sometimes was. Maybe, if Mrs. Denvers lived through my pregnancy with me, some of her pain would heal.

And maybe not. More likely, she would push me away, and Orson would make some crude comment about procreation. I'd end up back on the streets, with no job, no medical care, and no place to sleep. And no one who loved me.

I shut the door on Orson's room, and entered the room across from it. It definitely needed a cleaning. Even in the darkness, I tasted the dust in the air. I fumbled for the light. My thoughts were on the future, but as soon as I saw the maroon crib in the middle of this room, my attention was suddenly, completely, focused.

Baby clothes hung in the open closet, both boy and girl outfits, spanning two decades of fashion. A Deer White mobile leaned against the far wall; I hadn't seen that familiar deer since my own childhood. Every pregnancy, she must have thought, this is the one who will finally join me. Every pregnancy, she had bought the accessories and toys that lined this room. And no baby had ever come to play with that Deer White mobile, or to sleep in this giant maroon crib. Maroon had been a popular color when I was ten, but even then I thought it looked like dried blood.

And I was wrong; the babies did sleep inside the blood-colored crib. Six ultrasound printouts showed six sleeping fetuses. The others must have died too young for ultrasounds. Their hands, their faces, their eyes, oh, they beckoned me, like little ghosts, they begged me to bring them back, to give them life, because it wasn't fair. They had died before they lived.

I dropped the printouts back into the crib, wrapped my arms around my stomach, around my own precious baby. Draped over a black rocking horse were maternity dresses, slacks, even a swimsuit. On the floor next to it lay a collection of baby rattles. Next to that were a stack of pink baby blankets, and then a leather bolster seat. It just went on and on, the accumulation of fourteen pregnancies, the preparation for fourteen babies that never came.

I stumbled back, out of the room, tripping over my own cleaning bucket in my haste. Even once I was in the hallway, I couldn't rid myself of the image of that blood-colored crib, with its ghostly fetuses cradled within.

I fished the cleaning supplies out of that room of loss, and I threw myself into cleaning the rest of the house, but no matter how hard I scrubbed, I couldn't wash away the tragedies that haunted this house.

Chapter Twenty-Two

I dreamed the same dream, night after night, and no matter how many covers I piled on, I was always cold in the dream.

I was cold. Tom and I walked hand-in-hand through ocean waves. The waves came as high as my waist, but they didn't slow us down. With my free arm, I held my baby girl, wrapped in her maroon fuzzy blanket so that only her big, blue eyes were visible. She cooed softly, and I cooed back. Tom looked at me in confusion, and I realized that he didn't know I carried his daughter, and I let go of his hand to hold Hope in front of us, beautiful Hope, my darling. She had his curly hair, his pug nose.

Look, Tom, she's beautiful, I said, but Tom shook his head, he refused to look, and when I held Hope directly in front of him, he backed away into the waves. He swam one steady stroke after another, away from me, away from the shore. I screamed his name, but he raised his hands, covered his ears. See no evil, hear no evil. He was going to die out there, but I couldn't follow him, because I had Hope in my arms – only I didn't have Hope. The maroon blanket trailed from my arms, wet at the end where it hit the waves. *Hope!* I screamed, and I scratched at the water in front of me.

I woke, tore my way out from under the sheets before I realized that they were sheets, not water, and that my daughter was safe inside of me, safe in the gentle waves of my womb. I had dreamed that dream again.

In my dream, I had called her Hope; it was a pretty name, and a fitting one as well. All my hopes of the future now rested on this tiny baby, no bigger than a fingertip but growing every day. Hope Laurice, if she were a girl. Thomas Jacob, if a boy. I felt the weight of the choice – whatever name I gave my baby, that would be a part of her identity, just as Anise was part of mine – but both Hope and Thomas were good names.

"See, Mommy's doing well by you," I whispered. "I promise, I will always think of you first, and me second."

I left my sunny yellow bed behind, and went as I always did to water my anise herbs, and check on Mr. Rat. The herbs looked fairly wilted, despite their indirect sun and my constant care. Mr. Rat slept in his corner, as usual. "Wake up, sleepy," I said, tapping the glass. He did not budge, and suddenly I noticed that he wasn't sleeping as usual, because his soft white chest wasn't rising and falling with every breath. Mr. Rat was not breathing, and, as I soon discovered, he was cold to the touch. Sometime during the night, Mr. Rat had slipped away.

I buried him in the garden, with Mrs. Denvers' permission. I packed the cool earth down over the tiny cardboard coffin, and tears fell from my eyes to muddy the grave. I had promised Jake that I would take care of his pet. I had failed. What if I failed as a mother, too? What if I lost my baby, just as Mrs. Denvers had lost hers? Everyone I loved, I lost.

His grave looked barren, the one brown patch in the teeming garden. I fetched my anise herbs, and planted them to mark his grave. That looked better. And I had included my namesake plant in Mrs. Denvers' garden. Even if she never knew what it meant, I knew. Among the ferns and roses and long-lost lilies, among the shadows of children that never were, that patch of anise claimed a corner of the garden for the child I once was.

The perfume of the garden lingered even after I went inside; I searched for Mrs. Denvers in the parlor, and the main hall, and the family room, and through it all I smelled the haunting trace of flowers. Only after I washed my hands, cleaned them of the grave-dirt, did the smell come away.

If Mrs. Denvers was doing all right today, I would ask for the day off, and visit the temp agency to find out how my medical benefits worked. I was going to take good care of my baby, starting with a visit to the doctor. If Mrs. Denvers wasn't doing all right, and it seemed to me she had looked pale when I asked her where to bury Mr. Rat, I'd do what I could to console her. Either way, I needed to find her.

The downstairs having turned up empty, I picked my way up the stairs, and peeked into Orson's room. She sometimes liked to sit in there, but she wasn't there today. If she was in the room across from his, the lost babies room, I wouldn't disturb her. And perhaps she'd retired to her bedroom; I couldn't disturb her there, either. Defeated, I headed back to the stairs.

And then a woman's angry scream rocked the hallway. I spun around, out of balance, almost falling down the long flight of stairs; even after I steadied myself, my heart pounded at what that long fall would have done to my baby.

The scream, and now a loud angry chatter, came from the elder Mrs. Denvers' room. I hurried down the hallway, my feet pounding the thick velvet carpet in rhythm with my wild heartbeat, and I thrust open the heavy door to the room at the hall's end.

"Does no one here know how to knock! Your knuckles are all too delicate to rap against my nasty oak door? No one has any respect anymore!" The elder Mrs. Denvers, her lips drawn back like those of a feral dog, hoisted the metal tray in her lap and threw it at me. A bowl clattered off of it, spilling strawberry oatmeal on the floor. The tray hit the door, missing me by mere inches. Mrs. Denvers hurried from across the room to take my hand. She was shaking. "I will not be manhandled downstairs so you can have someone to moan and simper at. So what if Orson's gone? He isn't even your son. You've got to control your emotions!" Coming from a seventy-year-old woman in a white-hot rage, it would've been amusing if not for how deliberately hurtful her words were to Mrs. Denvers. She couldn't even respond; she quivered like a willow in a storm, and she squeezed my hand tight enough to bruise.

"Control your own emotions," I countered.

The elder Mrs. Denvers turned on me, her teeth bared in that dog-snarl. "You're fired. Get out."

"You're not fired," Mrs. Denvers whispered.

"Yes, she is! You're not in charge here! You're just a fool girl who couldn't keep her panties on. You're the mistake we've had to put up with for twenty long years. But Jonathon has finally come to his senses. The only thing I don't understand is why he left, and you're still here. This is the Denvers' estate. This is our home, not yours." The elder Mrs. Denvers clamped a wiry hand down on the tiny jars of hand cream on her bedside table. She pelted one at us, and struck Mrs. Denvers in the stomach. The next one hit the mirror overhead; glass fragments rained down onto me and Mrs. Denvers. I pulled on her to leave, but she resisted long enough to say, "Jonathon still loves me."

"Don't come in my room again without knocking! Don't come in at all!"

I pulled the door shut behind us, safe in the hallway, just before another jar rocketed off the wall where we'd just been. Mrs. Denvers sank down onto the velvet carpet, and cradled her knees to her chest. I sat with her, holding her. "Her back is bad today," Mrs. Denvers whispered. "I shouldn't have asked her to come downstairs. She's in too much pain."

"I don't think so. I think she likes to cause pain so much, she can't possibly know what it really feels like." How could she have thrown her jars so hard, if her back ached? Either it didn't hurt as much as she let people think, or she didn't mind the pain if she could cause Mrs. Denvers more pain. Either way, she disgusted me. "Don't let her get to you, you're better than her."

"She doesn't understand," Mrs. Denvers said. "Jonathon loves me. But my miscarriage last fall hurt me, and it took several months to heal, and even then we didn't make love, because I can't bear to be pregnant again. That's why he turned to Bonita. He loves me, not her."

Bonita had even said as much. My lover does not love me, she had said, her words lilting prettily. "I understand," I said.

"No, you don't! My mother-in-law is right, I was a fool girl. I listened to her. Back when I was twenty, when I should have listened to my own priest, instead I listened to her. She'd had an abortion when she was young, and she went on to have Jonathon. I wanted —" She sobbed for breath. "I wanted to have my children in wedlock. I wanted to be thin and pretty in my wedding dress that summer. But I've burned those pictures. I hate that white dress, size eight and flat. It should've ballooned with child. It would've been beautiful that way."

"You've suffered so much. She must know that," I said.

Mrs. Denvers glanced at the door behind her. "She never liked me. My genes weren't good enough, my parents not rich enough. She gets mad just looking at me, and thinking of what better women her son could have married."

"He married you," I said. "He chose the woman he wanted."

"He'll come home if I ask him. If I forgive him for Bonita. He'll even get a vase. A vasette –"

"A vasectomy?"

"Yes, that's it. So I don't ever get pregnant again. I want him to come home," she said. With her head leaned against the corner, she looked like a punished child, hopeful for a reprieve. So very hopeful. "Do you think I should forgive him?"

"Do you really want to know what I think?"

She looked confused. "I wouldn't have asked otherwise."

From inside the elder Mrs. Denvers' room, a thunderous crash shook the floor. It sounded as if she had knocked over her nightstand, lamp and all. "I think you should bring Mr. Denvers home, and kick your mother-in-law out. She hurt your marriage before it even began. All she'll ever do is hurt you."

Mrs. Denvers looked shocked. "But it's her house. Her husband built it, just before he passed away."

"Then move out yourselves, you and Mr. Denvers. You asked for what I thought. I think you have a chance to make it, but not if you stay here. He's at the Hilton now, isn't he? Move in with him."

"My stuff wouldn't fit into a hotel room."

"Leave your baggage behind. Leave all your baggage, and go to him." I meant her emotional baggage, as well as the physical, and by the light in her eyes, she understood me.

Later that afternoon, I dropped Mrs. Denvers and her thin blue suitcase off in front of the Hilton Hotel on Regents Street. Her excitement and her anxiety combined to make her look younger than I had ever seen her. I could well imagine the twenty-year-old girl she'd once been. "If I don't call, that means everything went well."

"I hope not to hear from you, then," I said.

"And Anise. . ."

"Yes?"

"If I could have a daughter, I'd like her to be you." She disappeared into the hotel. I sat in the limo, stunned. She had called me by name. I knew Orson hadn't told her; he was true to his word. How long ago had she figured me out? Did it matter? I'd like to be her daughter. I just wasn't going to marry Orson to get there.

"Take back your marriage," I whispered. "Take control of your life." That's what I had to do, too.

From the hotel, I drove straight to the temp agency on Tamiami Trail. Mrs. Denvers and I were both seeing to the future today, her to the future of her marriage, me to the future of my child.

Ms. Hamilton, the same recruiting lady from last time, didn't look up from her computer when I entered the agency. Instead she typed faster, intent on finishing her document. Her lips were pursed, her hair in a tight black bun, and her clothes as dowdy as ever. "Just one more moment, please." She sounded as if she'd had an exhausting day too. It was only three o'clock, but it felt much later.

"Take your time," I said. She looked up when she heard my voice.

"Oh, it's you!" She pushed the keyboard aside, and came around to my side of the desk. "How is the chauffeuring job?"

"I haven't crashed the limo yet," I said with a smile.

"Please don't, you can't imagine the paperwork I have to do for an on-the-job accident. Seriously, now. Do you like your employer?"

"I like them," I said.

"Good, I knew you would. No more boy trouble?"

"No," I said, my heart twisting. I had more serious trouble than boy trouble. I had baby trouble. "I came to find out about my medical benefits. Do I need to do anything before

I go in for a check-up?"

She scooted back behind her desk, dug into a file cabinet, and returned triumphant with a stack of forms. "You need these. One goes to the hospital, one comes back to us, and one gets sent on to your employer."

"To my employer? Why?"

"Company policy," she said with a shrug. "Some degens abuse their medical benefits, visiting the hospital two or even three times a week. The poor dears are worried about degenerating, of course, but it's the employer who gets stuck with the bills."

I looked at the form she'd handed me. The blanks to be filled in included the hospital name and the doctor's specialty. I couldn't go see an obstetrician, or this form would fly right back to Mrs. Denvers' hands. If I closed my eyes, I could still see the blood-colored crib with its sleeping fetuses. Mrs. Denvers was just beginning to hope again, to reach out to Mr. Denvers, to live. If she found out that I was pregnant, she would withdraw right back into her pain, and it would be all my fault.

I carefully folded the form, and tucked it into the pocket of my slacks, knowing I would never use it. The phone rang, startling us both. "Just a moment," Ms. Hamilton said. She took the call. I'd taken care of my business, but I waited to say good-bye.

She cradled the phone against her shoulder, and called up information on her computer. I considered sitting down, but I was too tired; if I sat, I wouldn't want to get up again. A bulletin board posted near the door had job listings tacked to it, and I scanned them. Dog walker. Retail clerk. Night manager. What would I do once I gave up my job at the Denvers? Some of the posted jobs were for national companies. I could go anywhere, from Boston to Seattle, but the only place I wanted to go was Tom's apartment, and that was the one place I couldn't go.

Yoga instructor. Janitor. Cook. The last one caught my attention, not because I desired to be a cook, but because of the location. An onsite cook was needed for Bayshore Street. Nearly everyone but Daddy on our street used offsite cooks.

Ms. Hamilton settled her phone into its receiver, typed a

few more entries into the computer, and then sighed. "One of these days, I'm going to hire someone to work here in this office. Business has been booming lately, and I can't keep up with it."

I felt bad asking her to do more work, but I had to know. I handed her the listing. She shook her head when she saw it.

"I'm sorry, you're not eligible for that one. The employer specified that he didn't want a degenerative. It's ironic, because the man works at the Degeneration Institute. Seems to me he'd be more sympathetic to degens."

I clutched the listing to my chest. "He doesn't want to get attached to any degen, not even a servant. Not after Laurice." Ms. Hamilton gave me a curious stare, and I realized I had spoken aloud. The phone rang again, its shrill demand chasing away whatever questions she might have asked me. She answered the phone, and I stumbled out the door.

Daddy had placed a listing for a new cook, but Marce was our cook. Marce had made me and Laurice our birthday cakes, year after year. After Laurice's funeral, after everyone had said their empty condolences and Daddy had hidden himself away in his study, Marce had brought me hot soup, and she had stayed by my side as I ate. Daddy hadn't been there for me, but Marce had. For my entire life, Marce had been there when I needed her.

But she was old. Her joints ached, and her vision was failing, and last year she'd fallen ill with pneumonia. It had taken long weeks for her to recover. What if she were ill again? What if, in the three months since I ran away, Marce had died?

I climbed into the limo, but I wasn't steady enough to drive. My fear seemed palpable, an unwelcome passenger in this long limo. With its black leather, black windows, the limo reminded me of a hearse. I tried to imagine Orson sitting beside me; he'd tell me to get ahold of myself, don't assume the worse, don't give in to my fear. It was good advice, very Orsonlike, but it was impossible. Marce had always been there for me, but these last three months, I hadn't been there for her. What if she had needed me then? What if she needed me now?

I had to go to her. If Orson were here, he'd tell me no, don't be foolish, find a phone and call her, don't risk getting caught myself. Logical Orson. He didn't understand the first thing about love. Tom would understand. Tom knew what it was to sacrifice for a loved one.

Somehow I managed to hit six red lights in the five miles between the temp agency and Bayshore Street. I waited impatiently, and I maneuvered from lane to lane in my rush to get to Marce. A small Dodge Dean blared its horn as I swooped in front of it. The driver of the Dodge was right. I was driving recklessly, and even if I didn't care about myself, I needed to care about my baby. I slowed down, but I didn't relax my hold on the wheel.

Marce loved her job. She wouldn't have left it willingly, and she'd never given Daddy any reason to fire her. Oh, death lay in wait for us all, even Marce, even me. To a degen, it might seem like we live forever, but we were mortal, just like everyone. Only God was immortal. "God," I prayed. "Let me find Marce healthy, let me find her in the kitchen making apple syrup or lavender sauce. Let me find her, God, please."

Even as I prayed for the best, I imagined the worst. What if I found her, not in the kitchen, but in the small graveyard at the edge of our property? What if, past the Beloved Daughter headstone, past the Beloved Wife and the Second Wife, there lay a smaller headstone? Marce Cannings, it would say. Faithful Servant.

"My friend," I whispered, and I brought the limo to a stop just outside my Daddy's property.

When you live in a place, you become blind to its appearance. I hadn't lived in Tom's place more than a day before I stopped seeing the cracks in the ceiling and the sparse furnishings, and opened my eyes to the love that dwelt within those close walls.

The sunny yellow of my room at the Denvers had been deceptive; it seemed to be a refuge from my pain, but Mr. Denvers had still found me there, touched me, hurt me. Afterwards, my room had looked the same, but that was only appearances. Appearances are deceiving.

All my life, I had lived at Daddy's bayfront mansion, but I doubt if I had ever truly seen it before. I threaded my way through the willow tree barrier, and stopped to stare from just inside the shadow of the trees. Three stories high, made of ivory brick with pale green arches above the windows, it looked like a house anyone would love to live in. It looked pristine, as if no pain could cross that marble threshold. And yet the opposite was true. Everyone who lived in this house met with suffering.

Marce's cottage was just behind the main house, so that every day its cursed shadow spread across her small gabled roof. Of course she had come to grief. Living there, she hadn't had a chance.

The graveyard was off to my right, amidst a cache of oak trees at the edge of the property, but I studiously ignored it. Daddy's house looked empty, all the windows closed, all the curtains drawn. At three-thirty on a weekday, Daddy had to be at work. The curtains were drawn. No one would look out and see me, because no one was there to look. Except Marce, I reminded myself sharply. Marce was somewhere on this property, and not in the graveyard, not with her eyes forever closed.

I stepped out from the safety of the willow trees. The sunshine swept over me like a spotlight. I wanted to jump back into the shadows, but I forced myself forward over the sharp St. Augustine grass. Like a roach, I skittered across the lawn. Oh, I'd never had much sympathy for roaches, but I understood now how helpless they must feel, caught in the open, squashed underfoot. If Daddy were home, if he caught me, my new life would be squashed flat. A katy-bird trilled from behind, and I threw myself onto the grass, recognizing even before I landed that it was only a katy-bird and not my Daddy. No one exploded out the front door, no one came to hustle me inside. I reached the shadow of the house, and pressed myself against the cool brick, the comforting brick. I walked the rest of the way to the small cottage, but when the katy-bird called again, I cringed instinctively.

I knocked on Marce's solid wood door, and I waited. The call of the katy-bird had sounded mournful, dirgelike. Did the katybird know something I didn't? I knocked again, and no one answered, and my legs gave way; I tumbled down to sit with a thud on her doorstep. I could just make out the glimmer of the headstones in the graveyard, on the far side of the property. I didn't know if my legs had the strength to take me there. I didn't know if my eyes had the power to see what I would find there, or if I would go blind from the misery, the guilt. I had left Marce here, alone with no one but Daddy. I had abandoned her.

"Marce, forgive me, I never meant to hurt you," I cried.

The door swung open behind me then. "Child, is that you?"

It was Marce, oh, Marce was still here. I drank her in, all five-foot-one of her, from the white in her hair that was flour, not age, to the smile that forced back her wrinkles, to her dainty house-slippers, and she looked healthy, she looked wonderful; best of all, she looked alive.

Chapter Twenty-Three

The distinctive smell of orange scones drifted out of Marce's cottage. "You came home in time for tea," Marce said, and she drew me in for a tight embrace. "I've missed you so."

I found that I was trembling, and could not stop myself. "I thought you were dead. I thought I'd never see you again."

"Anise, darling, no, I'm fine. Although I worried the same about you. Come in, we'll talk, and you can let me know if you can taste the honey in the scones. It's a new recipe."

She led me into her homey cottage, with its overstuffed couches, red-and-white quilts, and hand-carved bears that lined the windowsills. Her kitchen took up one-fourth of the cottage, which was just the way she liked it. I settled into her couch, and curled my feet up under me like a cat tucking its paws beneath its chin.

I hadn't eaten Marce's food for over two months. The smell was driving me crazy, but Marce insisted that I remain seated and not help her in the kitchen. "If I trip over you, than we'd both be sconeless." It was something she'd said for years and years. *If I trip, then we'll all be milkless. Stand back, or I'll trip and we'll be birthdaycakeless, and your sister will be sad.*

"If you ever did trip, I'd be more concerned about you than the scones."

"Then that's another good reason to stay seated," Marce said. Seconds later she swooped the plate of scones down onto the small wooden coffee table. She perched on the other couch, such a small woman for such a large couch. "Now, where have you been?" she asked, but I had just bitten into a scone. I could taste the honey, and it combined marvelously with the orange and the cinnamon sugar. It tasted like home. Marce waited until I'd finished, and then she repeated herself.

"At first I stayed in the ghetto," I said. Marce, small already, seemed to shrink smaller with worry. "But the last few weeks, I've worked as a chauffeur, and I've lived in a mansion even bigger than Daddy's."

"Have you been safe?" she asked.

"Not always," I admitted. I dropped my gaze, taking in my own chest, still hating those traitorous lumps. "But I fell in love," I said.

Marce smiled so warmly, I found myself telling her all about Tom. It hurt to talk about, but Marce held my hand in her own tight grasp, and I poured it all out, even the hard parts like Jake's death and Tom's rejection.

"Oh, child," Marce said when I was done. "Sometimes love ends in heartbreak, but at least you loved. Many years ago, I loved and lost, too. Life does go on."

"I thought you never married," I said.

"I didn't. He was thirty years my senior, and we only had one bright summer together before he decided that he was too old for me, or I too young for him, or some nonsense. He took a job in England. I never fell in love again, nor married, nor had the children I always assumed I'd have."

"You have me," I ventured.

"And if I didn't, I'd have nothing," she said.

I loved Marce too, but even as I heard her words, I imagined Daddy saying them. *If I didn't have you, Anise, I'd have nothing.* He'd never say that. I wanted Marce's love, I needed her love, but I needed Daddy's too. "I'm lucky to have you," I said. Marce's smile dimmed, as if she heard my sadness.

"Your Daddy's been working crazy hours, ever since you left," she said. "From seven a.m. to eleven at night, every day, even weekends. Some nights he sleeps in one of the empty rooms at the hospital. He needs you, Anise. You gave him a reason to come home at night, even if it hurt him to see the one daughter without the other."

"I can't let him catch me," I said. I strained to make out the hands of the clock in the kitchen, but the angle was wrong and I couldn't see it. We'd been talking for quite some time already.

"Have another scone," Marce said. I couldn't resist. Some people combined paints on a canvas to make masterpieces. Marce combined eggs, flour, honey, and oranges, and made an edible masterpiece. I savored every bite.

Ever since I sank into the couch, I hadn't wanted to get up. Today had been so tiring, and I wasn't eager to return to the Denvers mansion where only the elder Mrs. Denvers waited. But I had to go soon, even though I didn't want to.

"You look pale, child," Marce said. "Are you in good health? Have you been eating right?"

"Better than ever," I said, thinking of the veggies and vitamins that I took for my baby's health.

Marce looked hurt. "I tried to cook healthy meals for you, but your Daddy always wanted something rich. If I didn't sneak the fruit and vegetable into the meals, he'd never eat it. That's why you always got banana pancakes and zucchini muffins, you know. It was a compromise."

"Marce, you're the best cook ever. Of course I haven't been eating as well without your food. Didn't you see me devour your scones?"

"You only had two," she said primly. I hadn't placated her. Cooking was more than her livelihood, it was her passion, and I had insulted her.

"What I meant was, I've been eating my vegetables even if they aren't hidden in breads and soup. I've been taking vitamins, too."

"The only vegetables you'll eat straight are carrots," Marce said suspiciously. "Even your first baby food, you spit out the pea mush, and the broccoli mush, no matter how I tinkered with the recipes, but you'd eat carrot mush until your little belly ballooned out."

I blushed, and looked down at my stomach. It was still flat, but soon it would balloon out, not with carrots but with child. Marce followed my gaze, and suddenly she gasped. "You said you made love with Tom. Anise, honey –"

"Yes," I said. "I'm carrying Tom's baby."

Marce joined me on my couch, held me, smoothed my hair. I expected her to ask about his genes, just what had he scored, and I'd have to tell her that Tom was no ninety-nine point eight five, no, far from it. I'd have to tell her that yes, my baby would be a degen. But instead Marce asked, "How far along?"

"Nine weeks," I said.

"Have you been to a doctor?"

"I don't have medical insurance."

Marce withdrew into the kitchen, and returned with a sugar canister. She struggled with the latch, at last giving it to me to open. It popped open, revealing the bills stuffed inside. All hundred-dollar bills. Hundreds of them. "This should cover the hospital bills," Marce said.

I tried to give it back, but she wouldn't take it. I set it on the table. "That's your money, Marce. You earned it. I can't take it."

"It came from your Daddy. It's as much yours as mine. He always paid me twice as much as I'd make elsewhere, because he knew I took good care of you girls, and he didn't want to lose me. Let me take care of you. Take the money."

"But you're not working for Daddy anymore. He's hiring a new cook. I was so worried."

"Don't worry about me, child. With you gone, and him working all the time, I had no one to cook for. I retired, but he'll let me have this cottage for as long as I live. I don't keep all my money in a sugar canister, nor the flour can either. No, I've got most of it in stocks. Old people have far fewer needs than young people. Take care of your little one." She pressed the canister on me again. I accepted a single hundred-dollar bill, but that didn't satisfy her. "It costs thousands of dollars to have a baby," she said.

"I better leave before Daddy comes home."

She set the money canister aside. "I just found you again, and now I lose you already? But at least I know you're safe. Write me, call me, please. I want to see your little baby just as soon as he or she makes an appearance."

Appearances are deceiving, I thought. The cottage suddenly seemed too enticing, the couch too comfortable, the scones too delicious. I had stayed longer than I should have, just because it appeared so safe. I was like a girl in a fairy tale, led astray by a candy house, not aware that danger lurked nearby. I jumped to my feet.

"Wait, please, I need to write down my phone number for

you, it's a separate line to the cottage," Marce cried. I waited, impatient, as she found a scrap of paper, and a pen, and carefully inked the numbers. I kissed her soft, flour-dusted cheek, hugged her one last time, and then hurried out the door.

And I bumped right into my Daddy on the doorstep, his hand already raised to knock.

Chapter Twenty-Four

Daddy looked tanned, handsome, healthy, so good that even a movie star would be jealous. For a moment we simply stared at each other, and then he remembered himself, and clutched me with both hands. It wasn't a hug, no, it was a clutch, like how you'd hold a disobedient dog that wanted to chase the seagulls.

"Let me go," I cried.

"No." He held me tighter. "You'd only run away again."

"I just came back to visit," I said. "If you want me, I'll visit every day. I've got a job now."

"You need to be in school. You'll quit your job."

"I can do both," I said.

"But can you do both well?" He nodded, as if it were all decided, as if I couldn't possibly disagree. And then he talked over my protests. "Marce, I need you in the house. There's a young woman coming to interview for your job, and I'd like you to show her around the kitchen."

"Isn't it wonderful to see Anise again?" Marce prompted. "Her new hair style makes her look very grown-up."

"It looked better before," Daddy said.

That was because I had looked more like Laurice when my hair was long and brown. "It sounds like you're busy, Daddy. I'll come back tomorrow to visit."

He didn't release me. "You can help with the interview. You spend more time at home than I do."

"Not anymore, Daddy. I moved out."

"I remember," he said sharply. I cringed at his tone; there was no love in it. "But now you're back, and you're coming inside."

"No," I cried. Had I ever said no to Daddy before? He looked as shocked as I felt, and his grasp on me loosened. I pulled free, and ran. The St. Augustine grass stabbed my bare feet.

Seconds later, Daddy tackled me. We fell to the ground with me beneath, trapped against the sharp grass. He was so heavy! I struggled, clawing my way forward, but Daddy only pressed down harder. Behind us Marce's screams finally registered as words. "Don't hurt the baby! She's pregnant! Let her up!"

Daddy's weight slackened at once. "You're pregnant?" he asked. He sounded like a little kid, baffled, awed.

"Yes," I said.

"Who is the father?"

I couldn't tell him, and I couldn't lie, and so I said nothing.

"You can trust me. I know that girls your age have sex, I'm not going to be mad about that. Just tell me what the father scored on the degen measure."

I struggled to free myself, but Daddy restrained me. I choked on the taste of grass and earth. Marce caught up to us, and tried to pull him off of me.

"What did he score?" Daddy asked.

"Leave her be, this isn't good for the baby. You don't want her to have a miscarriage."

"Don't say that word," I cried. It was bad luck to say miscarriage, and bad luck to even think about Mrs. Denvers' poor lost babies. Bad luck to remember the maroon crib cradling eternal the unborn babes. "My baby's healthy, my baby's just fine."

"Then it's not a degen?" Daddy asked.

"Mr. Hunt, I've worked for you for twenty years, but I'll leave this property forever if you don't let her up right now. You're not just sitting on her, you're sitting on the baby."

Daddy relented, pulled me to my feet, but kept his hand locked around my wrist. "You understand, don't you, why I can't let you run away again? Being pregnant changes everything. You need good food, good doctors, and you're not going to get that on East Street in the ghetto."

"I'm not there any longer. I left weeks ago."

"You're here now, Anise, and here is where you belong."

He dragged me forward, onto the back porch, into the house. The air conditioning hit me like a solid wall, as if I had to leave all warmth and comfort behind in order to enter the house.

"Please, let me go."

"I'm only doing what's best for you. And for the baby. Think about it from my perspective. I'll give you lots of time to think about it." He took me upstairs then, and forced me into his bedroom suite. Before I even realized what he meant to do, he'd shut the door behind me and locked it from the outside. I heard his heavy steps back down the stairs, and then he greeted the interviewee with his movie-star voice, as if nothing were the matter, as if he hadn't just locked his runaway pregnant daughter in his bedroom. I pounded on the door, but no one came, not even Marce.

When my fists grew tired from pounding, I let myself sink down on his plush rug, and leaned back against the door. Daddy wanted me to sit here and think about his perspective, but that was what he always wanted from me. Why couldn't he think about my perspective for once? Why was I always wrong, and he always right? I tried to learn from it, tried to tell myself that at least I'd know better than to treat my own child this way, but the pain was too fresh. I couldn't turn it into a life lesson. I didn't even know how to deal with it myself.

I couldn't sit still, either. Daddy's bedroom was enormous, bigger than the entirety of Tom's apartment, almost as big as Mrs. Denvers' vast garden. One alcove was lowered, with soft brown chairs before the bay window with its view of the deep blue bay. A bay window of the bay, I thought. Laurice would've liked that. If only Laurice were here, Daddy would let me go. He didn't want me, he wanted her, but he could never have her back. Laurice was gone forever, just like Jake, just like my mother.

Out in the bay, a pelican skimmed the surface of the water. I couldn't see if it had gotten the fish it had been after. The bay led out to two keys, Feeler's Key on the left, Weston's Key on the right. The bay channeled between the two, with no bridge to impede its clean sweep out to sea. That was where my mother had swam, the day she swam away from us. An impromptu search team had found her body, miles out to sea, with a smile stiffened upon her face.

I closed the curtains, blocking out that tragic view. That Daddy could bear to look upon it told me all I needed to know. He hadn't loved my mother, and he didn't love me. He had locked me in here like a piece of property, as if I had no more feelings than his walnut dresser. I was the daughter of the woman he hadn't loved, and I couldn't compare to Laurice, the daughter of the woman he had loved. It wasn't fair. He had married without love, that was his sin, and yet my mother and I were the ones who had suffered for it.

Across from the bed, Daddy's dresser was impressively dark against the ivory walls and carpet. Daddy had spent lots of money on it, as he did on everything, but that didn't make it any more than a possession, a thing. I crossed the room, tore out the drawers, pounded on them, but the dresser couldn't feel the pain. It was just a dresser. I was a woman, hurt and angry. I kicked his bed, and only succeeded in stubbing my toes. I wanted to destroy Daddy's things, to prove that they were only things and I was something more. But I was no match for a dresser made of hard walnut, or the expansive bed, or the door itself. If I wanted to destroy something, I'd have to settle for something glass, like the chandelier or the framed picture of Laurice that stood on his nightstand. Laurice seemed to look at me out of the picture, out of the past. She was smiling in the picture, but sadly, as if she loved me and longed to help.

I couldn't destroy anything with Laurice watching. I paced through the suite; he had a walk-in closet with all his clothes hung neatly, he had a tiled exercise area and a marble shower in the bathroom, he had an enormous cushioned bed, and yet he had no one with whom to share all this. He had to be lonely. Was that why he wanted a grandchild from me?

Oh, it was no good to think about this. I didn't understand Daddy, and he didn't understand me. I sat on his bed, and tried to read one of his medical journals, but they bored me, and the thought of what was to come made me anxious. I cracked open the window, but the ground was two stories down. My baby wouldn't live through a jump that far. I cranked the window shut again, and locked it tight.

At a quarter to eleven, long after the sun had set, there came a soft tapping at my door. "Child, are you all right?" Marce's exaggerated whisper was loud enough for me to hear where I lay on Daddy's bed. I leapt to my feet at once, hurried to the door. "Let me out," I begged.

"Listen to me, child. You haven't had any stomach pain, or spotting?"

"No," I said. "No, my baby's fine."

"Thank God for that. Thank God."

"Why didn't you come earlier? I've been alone, and afraid."

"Oh, child, I'm here now, even though I'm not supposed to talk to you. Your Daddy wants you to think about his perspective, as a father and now a grandfather. He's going to talk to you again tomorrow."

I pressed my cheek against the cool door. "He's going to keep me imprisoned until tomorrow? Why haven't you called the police?"

"Child, you're not imprisoned. I know it's unpleasant, but he's your father. He grounded you."

That's what this was? I was grounded? "For running away? Or for getting pregnant?" I spoke sarcastically, but Marce answered in earnest.

"For running away, and scaring us both to death. Your Daddy's right about one thing. Your baby needs medical care. You said yourself that you don't have any. He's arranged for a house visit from one of the doctors on his staff. I wouldn't feel right about letting you out, even if I had the key. Not until after the visit." I fell back, away from the door, stunned by Marce's words. What could I say to that? She had turned against me. She had taken Daddy's side. "Child, talk to me," Marce pleaded, but I crawled back onto Daddy's plush bed, pulled up the sheets, and tucked my head beneath the down pillow. If Marce said any more, I didn't hear her.

In the morning, I regretted what I had done, but the door remained locked; I couldn't seek out Marce, couldn't apologize. I was angry at Daddy, not Marce, but I had taken my anger out on her. I only hoped she would forgive me.

At noon precisely, the door swung open. I left the treadmill to hurry over, but it wasn't Marce, and it wasn't Daddy. I blinked, and blinked again. The young woman who stood in the hallway had Laurice's dark curly hair, and Laurice's perfect body. "Here's your food." She spoke through lips as rounded and pink as Laurice's, but she had a clipped New York accent. When I didn't move to take the tray, couldn't move, she frowned, thrust the tray inside, and relocked the door.

Even with her gone, I remained frozen where I was, ten feet from the door. The thick smell of tomato soup wafted over from the tray. I hadn't eaten since Marce's scones the day before. I had been hungry, but I wasn't now. I had seen a ghost, and it talked with a New York accent.

Chapter Twenty-Five

Late that evening, Daddy came at last. He opened the door just wide enough to fit through, then closed it behind him as fast as he entered, as if I were some speedy squirrel that might zip past him. I remained where I sat, cross-legged in the middle of the floor. He had locked the door behind him, and that meant he hadn't come to let me out.

"How are you doing?" he asked. His black suit and gray dress shirt were sleek, unrumpled, despite the long hours he must have put in at work today. He was fine. I wasn't.

"I want to be let out," I said.

"I can't do that. You've got an appointment tomorrow with Dr. Jamison." Daddy smiled winningly, but his arm twitched. He was holding something behind his back. "Jamison agreed that you should have doctor visits every week until your last two months, when you'll have visits twice a week. Your baby is very precious, Anise. We've got to take good care of her."

"Or him," I said.

"Of course," he said lightly. "We won't find out whether it's a boy or a girl until Jamison does the chorionic test. That won't be this week, but possibly next."

I blanched. Any genetic testing would reveal that my baby was a degen. What would Daddy do then? I slowly rose to my feet, and held out my hand. "Give me the key," I said. "I'm leaving."

Daddy brought his own hand out from behind his back, revealing a twined silk rope, its tassels dangling nearly to the floor. "You're not leaving me," he said, his voice so low it barely reached me. I stared at the rope, and at the trail of sweat across Daddy's brow. Daddy never sweated. Daddy always had everything together, under control, perfect.

"You don't have to do this," I cried, but he never even hesitated. He grabbed my arm, dragged me to the bed, threw me down. Just like Al, Scar-lip, Sicko. I screamed, and Daddy put a finger to my lips and said, "Shush, honey. This will be over soon."

He looped the rope around my left wrist, pulled it tight. I screamed again, but Daddy ignored me. He didn't even seem to hear me. Intent on the rope, like a scout going for a badge, he knotted the rope to the left headpost, stretched it across to the right post, knotted, and came back for my other wrist. I fought, twisted, hid my arm beneath me, but he dragged my arm out, he tied me to the bed. From his pocket, he drew out my engagement ring, and gently placed it on my finger. He sat on my legs then, trapping them, as if I'd kick my own Daddy. Maybe I would. Maybe he deserved it.

"It's done," he called. The lock clicked from outside, and the door swung open. Someone was coming to rape me. That was the only possible reason for me to be tied, arms spread, on the bed. Now he would tie my legs, one to each bedpost, and I would be helpless to stop it, helpless to say no.

"No!" I screamed. "Let me go right now!"

The girl at the door chuckled. It was the new cook, not a rapist, but still my blood ran cold. Daddy watched her with the same look on his face, the same familiar longing, which he always wore when he stared at Laurice's picture. She looked so much like Laurice. Her long brown hair was pulled behind her, but her curls fought against the hairclip and poked victoriously out at various angles. She even walked like Laurice, a smooth glide across the room, like a ballerina floating across a stage. Daddy watched until she disappeared into the closet, and then he gave his head a funny little shake, as if to wake himself from a dream. He looked down at me, seeming almost surprised to find me there. "You're shaking," he said. "Don't be scared. I wouldn't let anything bad happen to you. We're just going to switch out our rooms, yours and mine. You'll have more space here."

The girl emerged from the closet, a pile of clothes stacked high enough to hide her face. Even so, despite her heavy load, she glided, and Daddy stared. "She's not Laurice," I shouted. She stopped, shifting the clothes to the side so she could smirk at me. That smirk diminished the resemblance. My sister had been easy-going, with a smile for everyone. This girl was hateful.

"Of course she's not Laurice," Daddy said, but he blinked repeatedly at her, as if in doubt. "Rachel, Anise, have you met each other? You'll be seeing a lot of each other in the coming months."

"Pleased to meet you," Rachel said. Still she smirked. It was as if she'd taken the beautiful clay of my sister's face, and twisted it into something ugly. Even her eyes seemed hard and cold, as if they were made of marble. She didn't wait for me to reply to her pleasantry. She hoisted the clothes back into position, and carried them out the door.

"Daddy, if you love me, please untie me," I said. With Rachel gone, he was able to see me again. I knew how awful I must look, because I knew how awful I felt.

"Did I tie the rope too tight?" he asked, confused. He leaned over me to check the knots, and I screamed. It was Daddy, and yet it was also Mr. Denvers, trapping me with his body. Daddy shook me, and my breasts bounced. It was Daddy, and yet it was also the guys who had attacked me on the street. I felt a warm trickle between my legs, a warm touch against my most private parts, and I choked on the air screaming from my lungs. Daddy slapped me hard, and I remembered to breathe. The warmth between my legs quickly cooled, and I caught the sharp odor of urine. In my terror, I had wet myself. That had been the touch I'd felt.

"I didn't mean to scare you." Daddy remained stretched over me, his hands working the knots, but now he wasn't checking them or tightening them; now he was untying me. My left hand fell free, and I was able to wipe the tears from my face. Rachel stood in the doorway, gaping at us both. Daddy caught sight of her and paused. "Nothing's changed. I still need my things and she needs hers. I'll have to watch her now, so I'm afraid all the work falls on you."

Rachel nodded, and carelessly dropped a load of books to the floor. My books. Normally I would have cared; I would've wanted to know if their bindings were hurt or their covers knicked. Normally my books were like friends I'd made or adventures I'd had, but right now they were only blocks of dead paper, dead wood. The adventures I'd truly had had all been frightening ones. The friends I'd truly made – Tom, Orson, Mrs. Denvers – were all far away from me. Except, of course, for Marce, whom I had snubbed the night before.

"Carry on," Daddy said. He lay his arm around my shoulders, holding me, but he kept his attention focused on Rachel. When she went out the door, he watched for her return, without even seeming to know that he was doing it. He talked of many things, told me how nice this bedroom suite was and how he was going to keep me well entertained during my months of confinement. Told me how hard his job was lately, and that the promising research for a degen cure had turned out to be false hope. Told me that he had already subscribed to Baby Care Magazine and American Motherhood in my name. He never told me that he loved me, though. He never told me that he'd love my baby even if it were a degen, because of course he wouldn't.

When all Daddy's things had been replaced with mine, Daddy brushed my forehead with a kiss, and slipped out the door. I heard the heavy click of the lock, and the footsteps as they left me. I was alone. I changed into clean clothes, and tucked myself behind the heavy curtains, where I had a view of the nighttime bay. I had thought I'd feel safe behind the curtains, but I didn't. If Daddy or Rachel returned, they could still find me. I wasn't truly hidden.

Out on the keys, the lights of the houses made the sweep of water appear even darker. If only my mother would swim back to me, out of that damp darkness. If only I had someone to lead me through the months that lay ahead.

Wind sighed past the palm trees. The trees stood apart from each other, each one a lonely sentinel. They could take the night's light winds, but it was summer. Hurricane season. Alone, unable to escape to safer land, they had only themselves to depend on. Their only option was to dig in their roots and weather out the storms, because eventually all storms pass, even hurricanes.

I will weather out this storm, I thought. For my baby's sake, I will make it through.

Dr. Jamison arrived the next morning with a black doctor's bag, just like you see in old movies. He smiled, but the smile never reached his eyes. He looked weary, as if he'd seen too many young mothers, too many degen babies, and too much death. "So you're Anise," he said, and by the way he weighted my name I knew he'd heard all about me from Daddy, which meant he knew all of Daddy's side and none of mine.

"Don't believe everything you hear," I said.

"You're either Anise, or you're not Anise," Dr. Jamison said. "And if you're not Anise, I've made a very expensive house call to the wrong bedroom." He smiled again, and this time his eyes, beneath those big eyebrow bushes, were included in the smile. "I'm Dr. Jamison. Call me Jamie if you like. I may be your father's employee at the Institute, but when I'm here in this room, I'm your doctor, not his. You can trust me." He set his doctor's bag aside, and shook my hand. "Seven months from now, I'll be among the first to shake your little one's hand, too."

I studied him, from his balding forehead to his polished shoes. Both shone like silver in the strong overhead light. It was hard to distrust someone who shone. "Daddy will want you to tell him everything. He might fire you if you don't tell."

"Well, then I'd have excellent grounds for a lawsuit, wouldn't I? Unlawful firing, interference with medical ethics, attempted violation of a patient's privacy. No, don't you worry about any of that. My sister is a lawyer, and she'll watch out for me. Sisters always do." His eyes strayed to the picture of Laurice on Daddy's nightstand, and then back to me. I looked away. He undoubtedly knew all about Laurice, too, and he could see for himself how beautiful she had been, how deserving of Daddy's love.

"I'm nine weeks pregnant," I told him.

"Was the father a degen?"

"No," I said. My lie came out too emphatic, too loud. Dr. Jamison raised his eyebrows, but only said, "That must be a relief to you. It's especially hard for young mothers, who know just what it's like to be seventeen, to give birth to a child who's likely to die at seventeen, or thereabouts. You know how much living you still have in you, and how much is denied to a degen baby. If a mother decides to have an abortion, it's most likely because the baby was a degen, or otherwise genetically deficient."

"Degens aren't deficient," I said hotly. I wrapped my arms around my stomach, as if to shield my baby's ears from Dr. Jamison's cruelty. "My sister was a degen, and she was the smartest person I knew."

"I offended you," he said. "I'm sorry. I see a lot of sad situations, working at the Degen Institute. Your Daddy does too. It affects how we think. Never mind what I said. I'm not here to talk about all that, I'm here to give you your first maternal exam." From his bag, he pulled a paper gown, and a pair of plastic gloves. I went into the bathroom to slip on the gown, which opened in front, and when I returned Rachel was in the room, that slight smirk on her pink lips.

"Rachel here has agreed to supervise me. To make sure I don't take advantage of you. Which, of course, I wouldn't, but we've got to follow the rules, or even my sister couldn't protect me from that lawsuit." He talked smoothly enough, but his gaze crept down the length of my body, to the slit of the gown that I held closed. "Up on the bed," he said, too brightly.

I lay down on Daddy's bed. Dr. Jamison removed his silver wedding ring from his finger, and then slid his hands into the slick plastic gloves. My heart pounded faster. For my baby's sake, I was going to have to let this man touch me, but I didn't have to watch. I clenched my eyes shut.

"Relax," Dr. Jamison said. "Trust me." Could I trust him? My instincts had said no, which was why I had lied about my baby's father. "I'm going to peel back the top of your gown now, and examine your breasts. Have they been more sensitive than usual?"

"Yes," I whispered. Like in a nightmare, I couldn't get my voice to raise above a whisper. "They've grown bigger too, just this past week."

"That's quite normal," he said, only his voice didn't sound normal. His voice sounded excited. He peeled back the gown, and my right breast was exposed. He ran his fingers over my breast, above and under it, pressing hard. "Sometimes a woman's nipples invert during pregnancy, but yours look healthy." He moved on to my left breast. I kept my eyes clenched shut, and waited for this storm to pass.

When my chest was covered again, he lay his hand on my thigh. "I need to do an internal exam now, after which we'll do a pap smear. Spread your legs as wide as you can."

I bit the inside of my lip, and I spread my legs for him. His plastic-shrouded fingers forced their way inside of me. He pressed against me from the inside, and it hurt. It seemed that he stayed inside for a very long time, but at last he withdrew. The pap smear was nothing in comparison, only cold metal, not warm flesh. Where I bit my lip, I'd drawn blood, and I nursed on that coppery taste as a distraction from my discomfort. When all was done, he drew the gown down over me again. I opened my eyes, and saw Rachel leaned up against the wall directly behind Dr. Jamison, where he couldn't see. She sucked suggestively on her middle finger. I couldn't believe her nerve. She was taunting me.

"Next week we'll do a chorionic villus sampling," Dr. Jamison said. "The week after will be the ultrasound."

"A chorionic villain sample?"

"Chorionic villus," he corrected. "That'll get us a sample of your baby's genes. We'll learn what its degen score is, and whether it's a girl or boy. I suppose you want a little girl, like most young mothers do?"

"I want my baby, whatever it is," I said. Rachel pretended to gag on the finger in her mouth. "I don't need that test."

Dr. Jamison paused. "There's very little risk. Only one mother in a thousand miscarries after a CVS."

"Please don't say that word," I said, and even though I was Lutheran, not Catholic, I crossed myself. Dr. Jamison seemed taken aback. Rachel rolled her eyes.

"Your father insisted that I do the CVS as early as possible. He wanted me to do it this week, but it's still too soon."

"You're my doctor, not his. You said so yourself."

"So I did," Dr. Jamison said, seeming bemused. "Very well. If he fires me, at least I've got my sister handy." He raised his eyebrows, giving me a moment to change my mind, and then he took my blood pressure, which was low, and my pulse, which was high. He weighed me on Daddy's scale, then pricked my thumb for a drop of blood. "I'll also need a urine sample. You're not opposed to that, are you?"

"No, of course not," I said. I took the plastic sample cup with me into the bathroom, and I emerged fully dressed, my white cotton shirt buttoned all the way up to the collar.

"I'll see you next week," Dr. Jamison said. He'd see me every week from now on, whether I liked it or not. And I didn't like it. The schedule reminded me of how Daddy had made Laurice go to the doctors twice a week, even though there wasn't anything they could do to save her. Laurice could have used those hourly visits to play on the beach, or to kiss her Jimmy, or to write more poems, but instead she had wasted her precious time on doctor visits.

Dr. Jamison exited the room, leaving me alone with Rachel. She still lounged indolently against the wall. She might be just a servant, but she had the power to come and go from this room, and I didn't. She had more power than me. "The show is over," I said to her.

"I saw your face. You liked it." She clipped her words in her odd New York accent. She couldn't possibly believe I had enjoyed that exam. Could she? "Your precious Daddy would be amazed to know what a pervert his little Anise really is."

"I doubt Daddy cares one way or another," I said. I couldn't hide my trembling though. The exam had drained me of energy, and Rachel was stealing more away.

"You've got that right. He doesn't care about you. He only cares about that dead Laurice. Yesterday I counted how many pictures of her I could find. Forty-three. And only two pictures of you, both with her in the picture too. Yeah, I got this household figured out. You rich folks are freaky." Rachel bustled past me out the door. She hadn't known me more than a few days, and already she disliked me. I had done nothing to her. It didn't make any sense, unless she was just a mean person who did mean things and didn't need to make sense. Worst of all, I had to depend on her to bring me my food, clean clothes, everything.

As if to punish me, Rachel didn't bring lunch until late in the afternoon. The chicken was cold, but I ate it anyway. My baby needed the nourishment, and who knew when Rachel would bring me more.

Daddy didn't come that evening, and I grew bored reading my old books. They used to seem like adventures, but now it seemed that I was really avoiding adventures when I read, withdrawing into worlds that didn't exist to escape the world that did. I set aside the books, and pretended that Tom, Jake, Kelly, Kenny and little Honey, the whole family, were gathered before me. "What does Honey want?" I asked the empty air. Honey wanted to be held, I decided, and I spun a story filled with loving arms, soft kisses, and warm chests.

But if Tom were truly there, I wouldn't be able to talk at all, because the moment I opened my mouth the truth about our baby would spill from me, uncontainable, and Tom's heart would be broken. Dr. Jamison had been right; I knew what it was to be seventeen, and to have years of living ahead of me. I knew exactly what our baby would miss out on. I only hoped that Tom would never know.

Chapter Twenty-Six

One late afternoon that week, a workman on a ladder appeared outside my windows. He refused to look at me, refused to listen, and he nailed my windows shut. There would be no escape that way, even if I'd been willing to risk a fall. My door wasn't nailed shut, but it was locked, and I had no control over it. Daddy had all the power over my life, and I hadn't any power at all. It was just like that phrase the media liked to use when they talked about degens. Daddy was a have, and I was a have-not.

I needed to concentrate on getting out. Early the next morning, before anyone else was awake, I examined the door from top to bottom. It was walnut, to match the dresser and the bed, a gleaming dark wood, just as dark as my chances for escape. No light came through the keyhole, no way to see the lock inside. I took a wire hanger, straightened it out, fumbled it into the keyhole. Nothing gave within, but the hanger did meet against resistance here and there. It would take time, but maybe I could figure it out. Maybe I could get my baby and me out of this prison.

After a persistent hour, I hit against a thick wall inside the lock. I pushed against it, but my hanger gave way, and came nearly out of the keyhole. The door handle turned, and the door banged open against my forehead.

"Hey, what're you doing?" Rachel said, her New York accent stronger than ever.

"Nothing," I said, but the hanger in my hands was as visible as the silver tray in hers.

She shook her head, looking more amused than angry. "I'll

trade you," she said, taking my hanger, giving me the tray. Then she ducked back out, but instead of locking the door again, she came in with another tray. "You're getting a feast today. I wanted to apologize."

"Apologize?" I said, surprised. She certainly had reason to apologize, but I hadn't thought she would.

She pulled the silver cover off her tray, revealing stacks of waffles, fruit, and sausages. "I'm not perfect. Everyone's a sinner, me more than most people. I treated you bad during that doctor visit. Where I come from, people tease each other, only you didn't tease me back when I tried to tease you. I didn't know what to do, so I slammed you. I'm sorry."

"Forgiven," I said. I opened the cover on my tray to reveal a bowl of fruit, which I could enjoy all day long, and a plate of broccoli hash browns, just like Marce always made.

"Marce gave me the recipes," Rachel explained.

Oh, maybe that meant Marce had forgiven me, too. "Tell her I love the meal, and I love her."

"Okay," Rachel said. She joined me, and nibbled at the fruit while I flitted from waffles to hash browns to fruit and back again to the waffles. It was the best meal I'd had in days.

"I'm not really a cook, but I'm trying to learn. I don't know why your father hired me," Rachel said, looking embarrassed.

"I know why," I said without thinking.

Rachel leaned forward. "Because I look like Laurice?"

So she'd noticed the resemblance too. "Daddy loved Laurice so much. All the passion that goes into his work used to go into being a father. He inherited more money than he'd ever know what to do with, so he really doesn't need to work. He used to work in my grandfather's law office in the mornings, when we had our tutoring, and then hurry home to be with us. Everything changed when Laurice died."

"What was so special about her?"

"Everything," I said. "There's some old home movies stored in Daddy's office, if you really want to see for yourself. Laurice was so kind, so smart, everyone loved to be near her."

"I wish I was like that," Rachel said wistfully.

"I do too," I admitted, and smiled at her. Rachel and I had a lot in common, it appeared. "You said you had friends back in New York. Why did you leave?"

"I got family back there, too. My momma, three brothers, four sisters. I'm the oldest. We're not degens, not one of us," she said with pride. "But we live in the degen part of town. It's a nasty place. I'm sending all my money home to Momma, so she can get them out of there."

"That's noble of you," I said. My opinion of Rachel increased with every word she said.

"No, noble's something that you rich folks do. What I do is necessary." She met my eyes, a hard gaze. "I gotta admit, I'm jealous of you and your Daddy. I think that's also why I treated you bad. Can you forgive me for that too?"

"Of course," I said. "I'm jealous of you too. You get to come and go, while I'm locked in here. And you're so beautiful. I wish I had your face."

"That's crazy." She took an orange sliver, and said, "Anyone with eyes could see that you're prettier than me. I got no hips, and an ugly chin."

Her chin looked just like Laurice's. Her lack of hips only made her look slender. "You're beautiful, trust me," I said.

"Do you mind this? I know I'm acting more like a friend than a servant. I don't know how to be a servant. The only cook I ever had was my own Momma."

"Marce was always a cook and a friend, too. You can be both."

"Then I will. So long as you can be a rich girl and a friend at the same time, too." She paused for a moment. "I'm teasing again. You're supposed to say something like, 'I'm richer than you'll ever be,' or 'It's hard to be your friend when you make waffles this bad.'"

"When you make waffles this delicious, I'm your friend for life," I said.

"That's not really what I meant," Rachel said, but she smiled anyway. She looked more like Laurice than ever when she smiled, so much that it wrung my heart to be sitting here with her. It wasn't betraying Laurice, was it, to enjoy a conversation with this girl who looked just like her? Was it a betrayal if I confided in Rachel that I was lonely, and afraid, and in need of a big sister's guidance and love? She had said she was the oldest in her family, after all. She was a big sister, just like Laurice.

"I hate being locked in here," I said. "I don't know what to do."

"Don't be thinking I'm gonna let you out. We're friends, but we aren't family. My momma's depending on my paychecks, and I'd be fired this fast if I did anything." She snapped her fingers for emphasis.

"I wasn't asking you for anything. I was just saying –"

"Don't say it," she said. "It puts me in an awkward position."

"I'm sorry," I said.

"Forgiven." She mimicked the same tone and pitch I'd used when I forgave her. It was eerie, hearing my voice coming from her mouth. I must have gaped, because she laughed. "Do you like it? Up until a week ago, I read my brothers and sisters stories every night, and I did all the voices."

"With a voice like that, you could be an actress, or a comedian," I said.

"Or a telemarketer," she said. "You gotta be realistic about things like that. No good getting my hopes up, when we both know I wouldn't make it as an actress."

I didn't agree with her, but she refuted my protests. After she left, I looked for notebook paper for a journal. I didn't find any. I wanted to write a diary entry to Laurice, but my diary was back in my room at the Denvers.

I settled for a prayer, sent up to whoever might be listening. I asked for guidance, and a way out of this room. No answers came. Maybe there wasn't anyone listening. Maybe Rachel was right, and a person shouldn't get her hopes up. If Daddy had anything to say about it, I'd never get out of this room. I'd deliver my baby right here on this bed. And what then? Sooner or later he had to learn that the baby was a degen. I didn't know how he'd handle that blow. He had wanted me to marry Orson, just so he could have grandchildren with perfect genes; it mattered that much to him. It mattered more than I did. I had failed him, and he might never forgive me for that. He might never love me.

I couldn't bear to think about it, but all I had in this room was time and thoughts. The thought of Daddy not loving me, Daddy hating me, kept circling in on me, like a vulture circling over a dying man. I had seven months to think of a way out, but suddenly seven months didn't seem like much time at all.

The following day, at half past eleven, Daddy threw open the door to my room, squeezed through with a dozen pink and blue helium balloons, and caught me in a full bear hug. Over his shoulder, I saw the door, standing open, inviting me to escape. "I should've known," Daddy was saying. "I should've known I could count on you, you've always done what's right. I taught you well."

"What did I do?" I asked, breathless from the hug and from the praise.

"What did you do? Oh, Anise, you clever girl! But I know now." He released me, and bent to talk to my stomach. "Grandpa can't wait to meet you, Grandpa loves you already. Grandpa, that's me, isn't that incredible?" He caught me again in his hug, twirled me, until we were both too entwined in the balloons to move. Pink and blue balloons, to celebrate my baby.

"Did Dr. Jamison have news?" I asked.

"Yes, everything's fine, you and your baby are in perfect health. But that's not the big news. I'm so proud of you, Anise. I understand now that you didn't want to marry Orson, which makes what you did all the more wonderful." Daddy shook loose of the balloons, sending them up to rest against the ceiling. One popped, loud and sudden. "I know who your baby's father is, and I couldn't approve more," Daddy said.

I caught hold of his arm, suddenly dizzy, barely able to steady myself. I heard what he was saying, but couldn't make sense of it. I had worried so much about this, and somehow he knew, somehow he approved? "How can that be?" I asked.

"I love you," he said. "And I love your baby. Orson's baby. It's going to be a perfect child." He didn't seem to notice how weak I'd gone, only talked on, as excited as I'd ever seen him. "The limo gave you away, of course. It was parked in the street, just outside our property, and no one came to claim it. It was a simple thing, really, to track the license plate to the Denvers household. Mr. and Mrs. Denvers are away on a second honeymoon, but I talked to the grandmother, and she had plenty to say about the young woman who'd been working there these last few weeks. You can't deny that, now. She described you, right down to the clothes you were wearing the day you came home, and the uppity attitude she claimed you had. Of course you were uppity! You didn't belong in the servants quarters, you belonged in the guest room."

"Did you say Orson's baby?" I asked.

"I can see it all now. You ran away, first to the ghetto, but you didn't like it there, and so you figured out how to please me without going through with the marriage. You went to live with the Denvers, and you seduced Orson. Not a hard task, I'd imagine. I saw how he looked at you. He's a lustful boy, but then most boys are. And then you came home to me. It's perfect." His voice caught with emotion. "I get the grandchild I wanted. You don't get stuck with a marriage you didn't want. You can even go off to school, and leave the baby with me. Oh, Anise, you were very smart to find this solution. I can't tell you how proud I am of you." He hugged me tight, and twirled me around like a little girl. I let my head rest against his chest, and he held me there. "I love you, Anise, I have always loved you," he said.

His words were like nectar. Like sunshine on eyes newly opened. "I love you too, Daddy," I said. How I wished I had done what he said, that I had earned this love he now poured on me! He'd find out the truth, I knew he would, but oh, he loved me, he approved of me, and even if it was all based on a falsehood, it was exactly what I had dreamed of. He ran his hands through my hair, kissed the top of my head.

"We'll talk more this evening. I cancelled a meeting to come home and see you. It was too good of news to wait, though. Orson's baby! Who would have guessed it!"

Certainly not me, I thought.

"It feels like a new beginning. So many sad things have happened in my life, so many loved ones lost, but this baby will be a new start. It's all because of you, Anise. You've given me more than I can ever repay." He kissed my forehead again, and held onto me a little longer, not wanting to let me go. Finally, he said, "I'll see you tonight," and headed out the door. In his hurry, he forgot to lock it, forgot to even shut it.

I walked over to the threshold of the door, and peeked out into the hallway. No one was out there, but I drew back quickly anyway. Daddy loved me. Daddy wanted to see me tonight. It was all I'd ever dreamed of.

I closed the door after him, and then I went into the bathroom to curl my hair for tonight. I wanted to look my absolute best, for Daddy.

Chapter Twenty-Seven

Daddy came through the unlocked door at three o'clock, far earlier than his usual return time. He'd brought me a bouquet of yellow chrysanthemums. "Mums," he said. "For my little mum-to-be." Rachel trailed after him, a vase filled with water at the ready. He didn't even glance at her, even when she crossed between us to set the vase and flowers on the nightstand. Daddy only had eyes for me. "You've done your hair, and your make-up, haven't you? It's strange how different you look with light hair. It's as if I'm living with some Dutch princess, not my own Anise."

"I'm your Anise," I said. "I'll always be your Anise."

"Well, with you all done up, we certainly can't stay in tonight. Rachel, forget about dinner. I'm taking Anise out."

"But I already put the roast in the oven. I spent all day making it." Oh, Rachel didn't know about being a servant, she'd said so herself. She didn't know that talking back was just going to make Daddy mad.

"Finish cooking the roast," I said, trying to smooth the way. "We can have it tomorrow as leftovers." Daddy wasn't even bothering to wait, but rushed me toward the door.

"Okay, rich girl," Rachel said. Was she teasing me again? It didn't sound like teasing; it sounded too harsh. I didn't know how to respond, and Daddy didn't give me a chance. We were down the stairs and out the door before I could even say good-bye to Rachel.

The sunshine on my skin felt better than ever. Up north, people had to last long winters without the sunshine. They were used to it. I was used to year-round summer, and had missed the sun for the days I'd been trapped in Daddy's room.

Daddy opened the passenger door to his black Beijing convertible. Oh, he was being the gentleman today, and I was the lady, the focus of all his attention. He drove at a comfortable speed, not so fast as would mess up my hair, and he asked me several times if I wanted the top up, or the air conditioning on. I didn't. I wanted things just the way he had them.

We went first to Zasheen's, and Daddy escorted me past the fine silk dresses and designer bath towels to the baby section. No other department store had so many fine baby clothes, and handcrafted cribs, and such expensive price tags. Daddy didn't care about the prices. Daddy wanted my baby to have the best of everything.

I stopped to examine a tiny baby dress, all pink lace and lavender silk. The tiny sleeves, and tiny skirt, made me imagine the tiny person that would fill this dress.

"Let's buy two," Daddy said. "My grandchild will look like a princess in that dress."

"Any real baby would destroy this dress in minutes. It's not made for wearing, it's made for looking at."

"Well, then we'll have to take a picture of her in this dress, and I can look at it forever." What he said made me shiver. Twenty years from now, would a picture of my daughter or son hang next to Laurice's picture? Would Daddy stare at both pictures with that same desperate longing? No, I couldn't think about it. If I thought about the future at all, I had to think about everything. I was living in a bubble, and as soon as Daddy learned the truth about the baby, my bubble would pop. I refused to think about it. I let Daddy pick out a whole pile of maternity clothes for me, all in the best cottons and silks. The sales clerk, her hair piled decorously high, filled her arms with our choices, and made several trips to the checkout counter before we were ready to go. Daddy paid for it all, and arranged for it to be delivered to our home, so that we could go on to Dillinger's, and BabyLove, and Tanner's.

I grew tired, but Daddy didn't. He would've gone on to another dozen stores, and spent thousands more, if I hadn't grown faint at Tanner's and fallen back against a swimsuit mannequin. The mannequin's outstretched arms were all that kept me from sliding to the floor. Daddy had me in his arms in seconds.

Instantly he was contrite. I was pregnant and he'd been overdoing it, but he was going to make up for that. He bought me a health juice, and made me rest and drink it. Passing shoppers saw us and their expressions softened. Daddy was so handsome, and so focused on me, that anyone who saw us had to want the same for themselves. Maybe it was bad of me, but I wanted them to be jealous. I had my Daddy's love, and that was something no one could buy in any of these fancy stores.

"Should I take you home?" he asked.

"No, I don't want the day to end," I cried. "Just give me a moment, and I'll be ready for more."

The day had to end sometime, I knew it, just as Daddy's love for me would end as soon as he learned the truth. I had to stretch the time I had, make it last forever, and so I sipped slowly on my health drink, parsing out the tastes of carrot juice and apple cider. Daddy sat next to me. An older woman, as she passed us, was so intent on smiling at us that she didn't look where she was going, and ran right into a shoe display. Daddy didn't even notice. But when I so much as closed my eyes, Daddy asked if I was okay, if I needed anything, if I was feeling better yet.

"I'm just savoring the moment," I said. "I feel better now. My baby must've been thirsty."

Daddy bent before me, ran his hand over my stomach. I was just barely showing. Most people wouldn't have even known I was pregnant. "Baby, are you thirsty? Are you hungry? Is there anything I can get for you?" He smiled up at me and shrugged. "What can I do? Baby's a little taskmaster already. She insists that she wants an Italian dinner. And it just so happens that there's that new restaurant, Diablos, that I've been wanting to try."

I hesitated. Diablos had been the restaurant he'd promised to take me to, the day he forgot, the day I ran away. Obviously he didn't remember. I'd prefer to go to any restaurant but that one.

"Baby has spoken," Daddy said, but really, it was Daddy who had spoken.

The whole week was filled with wonderful days like that one. Our purchases arrived, and suddenly I had a whole wardrobe full of clothes that accommodated my new figure. My stomach didn't stick out yet, but it no longer curved inward, either. I filled Daddy's dresser with the new baby clothes, and I loved to hold the tiny articles and imagine the little baby that would someday wear them.

I stayed in Daddy's room, but the door was unlocked. Only once did I sneak out, and that was to Marce's cottage. She greeted me with kisses. Daddy had said I didn't want to see her, but I told her that hadn't been true, and I asked for her forgiveness for what I'd done my first night here, when I refused to talk after she said she wouldn't free me.

"Nothing to forgive, child. I've known you too long to let anything get in the way of my love. I've been worried about you, and worried that you wouldn't forgive me."

"Marce, I forgave you the very next morning, and have wanted to see you ever since."

"I've wanted to see you, too." Marce glanced behind her, toward the kitchen. By the smells drifting from the cottage, she was making butterscotch nut cookies. They were my favorite. "Join me for tea," Marce asked, but I couldn't. I wanted to get back to the room before Rachel noticed I was missing.

"I can't stay," I said.

Marce caught my arm to stop me from leaving. "Child, don't go yet. You told me that Tom, a degen, fathered this pregnancy. Your Daddy tells me that it's Orson. Which is it?"

"It's Tom," I confessed.

"Anise, child, what game are you playing? Your Daddy will learn the truth. Think about it. As happy as he is now, that's how angry he'll be when he finds out. He's falling in love with this baby. Tell him now. It'll be harder later." She released my arm, leaving flour marks where her hands had been. I brushed them away, using that as an excuse to avoid her eyes.

"Maybe I'll tell him. Maybe after a few more days."

"Tell him today," Marce said.

I backed away from her. "He's taking me to the opera tonight. He's bought me a thousand dollar dress, and a diamond necklace to match. It's a mother necklace, with a teardrop sapphire hanging off to represent my baby. Don't you see, Marce, I can't tell him. He loves me now. I can't ever tell him."

Marce pressed her floured hand to her own lips, and blew a kiss to me. "I love you, child. May God see you through this, because it's beyond me."

I fled back to my room, but Rachel followed ten minutes later with a plate full of Marce's cookies. Rachel didn't want to join me. She didn't care for butterscotch, and she had a load of chores waiting. "We can't all be like you, rich girl," she said.

"Who would even want to be," I said. Talking to Marce had made all my worries boil to the surface. Even dressing up for the opera, and putting on my new necklace, failed to reassure me. I was playing with fire, and I hadn't needed Marce to tell me that I was going to get burned. But when Daddy appeared at the door, his black tux gleaming, his face lit up in a smile just for me, my worries fell away. Whatever was to come didn't matter, I told myself. I deserved Daddy's love, and I was going to enjoy it, just as long as it lasted.

Chapter Twenty-Eight

Daddy went beyond just coming home early, and decided to take a day off to spend with me. It was a Friday. When the day came, we sat out on the back porch, where the breeze off the water played with my hair and salted my lips. Daddy talked about my baby's future, and I dreamed along with him. I imagined my baby a newborn, a toddler, a schoolgirl. Or a schoolboy. Daddy had begun talking about the baby exclusively in female terms – we'll put her in the guest room; she'll grow up to be a doctor – but I might be carrying a boy just as easily as a girl. I wouldn't know for months yet. If I had it my way, I'd have twins, and then I'd have both my Hope Laurice and my Thomas Jacob to love.

Daddy jumped up to survey the back yard. "I was thinking of putting in a swimming pool, in case she has ambitions for the Olympics."

"Daddy, listen to yourself," I said.

"I am listening. I hear a man who loves his daughter, and loves the grandchild that's on its way."

I heard that too, which made it hard to chastise him. "I'm just saying, let's wait until the baby arrives before we decide we need a pool. For all we know, the baby won't even like to swim."

"All babies like to swim," Daddy said. "I'll build a wading pool first, and then a full-sized one when she's old enough. If she really takes to it, I'd build her an Olympic-sized pool. Nothing's too grand for my grandchild."

Just as Marce had said, he was falling in love with my baby already, even before she was born. Marce was right. I had to tell him, had to do it right now before I lost my nerve. Right now. "Daddy," I began, but I couldn't get the rest out.

"What is it, Anise? You look faint." Daddy knelt at my side, took my wrist and felt for my pulse. It was weak. I did feel faint. I looked away from Daddy's eager, loving face, and it helped me breathe easier. I couldn't tell him in person. I resolved to write him a letter tonight, and slip away before morning, but even as I resolved, I doubted that I could actually walk away from Daddy's love. Daddy raised my wrist and kissed it, just like a lover. "Did you want to tell me something?" he asked.

"No," I said, denying the truth, denying Tom. I would write Daddy a letter, that's what I'd do. Sooner or later, Daddy had to learn the truth. I would write the letter tonight, or maybe tomorrow, or next week at the latest.

"Are you unhappy? Is there something I can do for you?"

I had no idea what lie to tell him. I couldn't meet his eyes. I was completely happy, reveling in his love, but I was also miserable, knowing I'd lose him. How do you explain emotions like that, without giving away the truth?

Rachel stepped out onto the porch, and looked surprised to find Daddy kneeling beside me like a suitor. I was glad for the interruption. "Somebody's here to see Anise," she said. Her New York accent made her words sound clipped, disapproving.

"Unless it's Dr. Jamison, send him away," Daddy said. "Anise is mine today. I stayed home from work, just for her."

"Who is it?" I asked.

"Hello, Anise." Oh dear God, it was Orson. "I assume you don't mind a visit from your fiancé." He brushed past Rachel, and casually settled himself onto the open porch chaise. His dark brown slacks and blue polo shirt didn't match, and they were rumpled, as if he had slept in them.

Daddy ignored all of that. His face lit up as if Christ himself had joined us. He leapt to his feet, and made a show of shaking Orson's hand. "Orson, back from Harvard! I'm so glad to see you –"

"No," I cried. "We weren't expecting you. You can't be here now."

"Anise, what's gotten into you? Control yourself," Daddy

said.

"Why such strong emotions?" Orson asked. He looked unaffected by what I'd said, as if how I felt didn't matter one way or another. And he didn't leave. He peered past Daddy, taking me in from head to feet. Too late, I remembered the baby rattles Daddy had brought home with him. They lay on the ground near my feet. Orson saw them, and for a moment he sat very still. Then he left his chaise, left Daddy, to pluck all four rattles off the ground. Two were silver, two gold. Orson shook them as if in disbelief, and discordant notes tinkled forth.

"Congratulations, son, you're going to be a father." Daddy clapped Orson on the shoulder, and Orson dropped the rattles. One broke open against the pavement. A little ball rolled forth, and jingled all the way across the porch.

"Should I get him a drink?" Rachel asked, but no one answered.

"Our baby's due in six months," I told Orson. Oh, how I hoped he'd play along! I took his hand, and brought it beneath my shirt, to the curve of my stomach. "I must have gotten pregnant the first time we made love."

"That's impossible," Orson said.

Daddy beamed. "It's true. Your child is on its way."

Orson drew his hand away from my stomach, and took my hand. He knelt beside me, looking as much a lover as Daddy had just moments before. He looked more like a lover, because he stared wide-eyed into my eyes, as if his whole life hinged on how I would answer his question. "Tell me, Anise. Tell me the truth. Is it my father's baby?" I tried to pull away from him, tried to run away, but he held fast to my hand. "If it is, I'll disown him. We'll take him to court. I thought you said he only touched you. He raped you, didn't he?"

"No," I cried, but Orson didn't believe me, I could see it in his eyes. He squeezed my hand tighter. "No, it's not Mr. Denvers' baby," I cried.

"What's this? Whose baby is it?" Daddy asked. He crouched over Orson, over me.

"Is it Tom's?" Orson asked. My whole world crashed down around me. Of course he knew about Tom. I'd told him myself.

Daddy pushed him aside, and pulled me from the chaise. "Who is this Tom?" Daddy said. "Is he a degen?" I didn't answer. He shook me, and I bit my tongue.

Orson wrestled with Daddy, but failed to free me from his grip; Daddy had the strength of a maniac, and the will of a tiger. "Is it Orson's baby or not?" Daddy demanded, and Orson answered, oh, Orson gave it all away.

"It can't be my baby," he said. "I've never slept with Anise. I've never even kissed her."

Daddy dropped me then, let me fall onto the chaise. I hit my back, and twisted in pain. Orson scooped me up into his arms, shushing me. "It's Tom's baby," I cried. "You've got to get me out of here. It's Tom's baby, and Daddy will never love a degen, not after –"

"Of course I'll love the baby," Daddy said. His voice was strangely calm. He knelt beside Orson, tried to take me, but Orson didn't relinquish his hold on me. "Tom," Daddy said, testing out the name. "That's the guy I saw you with at the Degen Institute, right? The good-looking fellow?" Orson's grip loosened, ever so slightly. Daddy kissed my forehead, but it was a cold kiss. I pulled away, closer to Orson, and Daddy frowned. "We better get you inside, and call Dr. Jamison. I dropped you. I'm sorry. A fall like that could cause a miscarriage."

Oh, there was that word again! "I won't have a miscarriage," I cried. "I love my baby too much."

Orson scooped me up in his strong arms. "Which way?" he asked. Oh, even though I fought to resist, he carried me into the house.

"Not here," I cried. "Take me home with you, don't leave me here."

"I know about miscarriages. My mother had them nearly every year, all my life. If you're in danger of miscarrying, you can't go for a car ride. It's too jarring." Up the stairs we went, at Daddy's direction. Orson carried me as if I were as light as air.

"Please," I begged.

"Orson's right," Daddy said. "Your baby's safe here, and only here. It is too precious to risk." For the first time in days, he had called my baby it rather than her.

Daddy opened his bedroom door. Orson lay me on the bed, but I wouldn't stay down. If Orson left me alone with Daddy, I didn't know what would happen. Daddy was far too calm. "You better go," Daddy said to Orson, and I cried out in protest. "Once you're gone, she'll stop being hysterical. I'm going to call the doctor right now." Orson hesitated, and Daddy took his arm. He was stronger than Orson. "I'll see you out," Daddy said, and it no longer sounded like a choice.

"Anise, please rest, for the baby's sake," Orson said.

"Come back," I cried, but the door shut behind them. I was alone. My back cramped, and I cried out again, this time in pain. I couldn't chase them. I gripped the edge of the mattress, and waited for the pain to pass. I would not have a miscarriage. I loved my baby too much.

Scant minutes after Daddy and Orson left, footsteps returned, but no one came in. I heard a solid click as Daddy locked the door from the outside. He wasn't going to call a doctor. He wanted me to miscarry, and if I died along with my baby, why, all the better.

Chapter Twenty-Nine

Daddy's love had lasted exactly nine days, five hours, and fifteen minutes. It had gone so quickly.

My back pain lasted thirty-four hours, a terrifyingly long time. At every cramp, I thought, this is going to be the one, this is the cramp that'll steal my baby away. I slept briefly, and I dreamed that my sheets were coated with blood, but when I woke, it was only sweat.

Daddy did not come to see me. Rachel came, and fed me water, and told me stories of her brothers and sisters back home. Little Erdine, five years old, loved an old polyester dress that served as her blankie. Gregory, at age seven, climbed off the balcony and fell to the apartment below. Baby Rose, born with a heart murmur, had recently learned the alphabet, but still wasn't walking. The stories stuck with me like fever dreams, taking on more significance than I knew they had; if I clung to these stories, then someday my baby would be a five-year-old with a dress for a blankie, or a seven-year-old covered with bruises from a dreadful fall. "Tell me more," I begged Rachel, and she sponged me with cool water, and told me of a Momma with a shiny pink prom dress still hanging in her closet, never worn. Told me of a brother with a bullet wound through his hand that looked just like one of Christ's wounds, and that he was always threatening to get his other hand shot to match. She told me of a dog and a cat, always fighting, and a sister who never smiled. When she talked of her family, her voice grew warm and loving, and I soon stopped listening to her words and heard only that tone, that love.

Love got us through, my baby and me. When at last the pain passed, I knew that we had been through the fire and come out stronger. No miscarriage would come between us; my baby and I were invulnerable, like Superman. We were reborn, before my baby had even been born to begin with. I tried to explain it to Rachel, but she only hushed me and took my temperature. I had run a slight fever, nothing high enough to hurt the baby, and it was gone now.

"Will Daddy come visit me today?" I asked Rachel.

"I'll let him know you're feeling better," she said. It was an evasion.

When she left, she locked the door behind her. That solid click felt like a bullet wound, taken directly on my heart. Daddy had left the door unlocked while I was in favor, but once again I was nothing to him.

No Daddy came to see me, no Orson, no Marce. Not even Dr. Jamison. Only Rachel, day after day. Only Rachel saw how my belly grew, and my spirit waned.

She changed, too. She showed up one morning wearing Laurice's green floral sundress. It wouldn't have fit Rachel when she first arrived, she'd been so skinny, but she'd gained weight since then. I couldn't take my eyes off her. She'd parted her hair in the middle, just as Laurice had. Laurice's diamond earrings dangled from her ears. Laurice's jelly thongs displayed Rachel's green painted toenails. Laurice used to paint her toenails, just like that. In fact, this entire get-up was exactly what Laurice had worn to her fourteenth birthday party.

"I don't understand," I said.

Rachel set the tray, with its bowl of grits and green banana, on the bed. She'd included a can of soda, when she knew I couldn't drink soda during my pregnancy, and she hadn't given me any water or milk. I'd have to drink from the bathroom faucet today.

"Why are you wearing Laurice's clothes?"

She vanished into the bathroom, to empty out the garbage can. "Why not?" she called from out of sight. "Why are you wearing Anise's clothes?"

"I'm Anise. You're not Laurice," I said.

She crossed back through the room, pausing at the door

to say, "Daddy asked me to wear these clothes. I just do what he asks. He's the boss."

She was gone, and I was left to eat my tasteless breakfast and worry about Daddy. I hadn't seen him since the day Orson came and blew my cover. I had no idea how Daddy was doing, but I imagined the worst. Oh, sometimes I was so angry at Orson for not keeping his mouth shut, and sometimes I was desperate for him to return and save me. But a month had drifted past since that day, and Orson had to be back at Harvard. If he thought about me at all, it was probably to think about how fat I must be getting, and how lucky he was to get away with not marrying me. Rachel had taken Orson's engagement ring back from me, days ago, because Daddy had canceled the promise contract. That chilled me. I had longed for Daddy to call it off, but not this way. It was as if he'd given up on me, didn't care, but then why was I still a prisoner in this room?

Over the next few weeks, Rachel's accent softened every day, until the day came when her voice seemed not to be hers but Laurice's. I couldn't talk to her when she came in, could only stare, because she looked so much like my sister, and sounded like her, and even smiled like her, that I found myself wanting to believe that it was her. It wasn't, of course. It was only Rachel, even if she did insist that I call her Laurice from now on. "Daddy's orders," was all she'd say about that. She was calling him Daddy now. Oh, I longed to go to him. I listened each day to the sounds of him leaving and coming home; he left early, but he returned at five o'clock each day. That was quite early for Daddy. Rachel would tell me the next morning about the lovely gift Daddy had brought her, or the museum they had visited, or the long talks they had enjoyed. He came home early to see her. He pretended that Laurice had come back to him. Oh, if only I could go to him, I'd tell him what a dangerous game he played. Maybe that's why he kept me locked in here. Maybe he didn't want to hear what I would say.

Rachel refused to grant me notepaper, saying that Daddy didn't want me to slip a note out to anyone. I was many months pregnant before I thought of writing in my books. Oh, I'd been writing all along on the back inside cover of

Dickens *The Christmas Carol* – I made notches to keep track of the days that passed – but writing on the inside cover and writing on the pages themselves were two very different things. To my old self, it would've been sacrilege. I'd read *The Christmas Carol* repeatedly in the years since Laurice died, and each time it had done what I'd wanted; it turned my mind away from my troubles, and gave me a respite from worry.

I no longer wanted to withdraw from the world. After months of being trapped in this room, I was desperate to rejoin the world. I turned to the last page, pressed my pen to the paper, then paused. I had no idea what date it was. *Day One,* I wrote in between the lines of Dickens' text. On this page, just above the picture of Tiny Tim throwing his crutches aside, the text read that of all men, Scrooge knew how to keep Christmas alive. As I made my journal entries, I'd follow Scrooge backward through his progression; he'd turn from a generous man to a heartless miser. Just like Daddy, I thought, and it pained me like a betrayal. Daddy wasn't a miser; he was indulging Rachel generously enough. And he wasn't heartless, no, he was too heartful, just like me, so heartful that the loss of Laurice had struck so hard he might never recover.

Day One

Daddy will lose Laurice all over again if he fires Rachel, as I think he should. What if that loss drives him over the edge? Oh, Daddy, I love you, but I think you need to face your grief, rather than taking joy in this Laurice substitute. She might look like Laurice, but she's a very different person inside.

Anise

At last I was able to work my thoughts out on paper, rather than let them twist interminably in my mind. I had little else to occupy my time. It wasn't long before Scrooge had said good-bye to the Ghost of Christmas Yet To Come and was on to the Ghost of Christmas Present. I suited my journal entry to fit.

Day Nine

If the Ghost of Anise Present visited, what would she show me? I'd love to see how the Denvers are doing, or Tom's family. Yes, the Ghost would surely show me Tom's family, and I'd remain happily invisible as I watched them gather in the living room for story-time.

My own present is much more dreary. I'm over five months pregnant. I look as if someone cruel has tied a bowling ball to me, but in truth someone wonderful is growing inside. My breasts are uglier than ever. My feet have swelled, which makes it hard to motivate myself to exercise on Daddy's treadmill. If Dr. Jamison ever visited, I could learn what sex my baby is, but he does not come. I try not to think about what will happen in a few months from now, if Dr. Jamison doesn't come then. Will I give birth here, in this room, all alone? No, I mustn't think about it. If I concentrate on the present, the future will take care of itself. It has to.

Anise

That was the last journal entry I wrote in *The Christmas Carol.* The next day, I emerged from the shower to find Rachel furiously packing my books into a trash bag. I clutched my towel to myself, too stunned to look for clothes, too pregnant to try to physically stop her.

"What are you doing?" I asked, my voice as calm as I could make it.

"I found your scribblings," she said. "I know what you think of me. Daddy should fire me? I'm not good for him? Who do you think you are?" Her anger had brought back her New York accent. She shoved a gilt-edged, leather bound copy of *Romeo and Juliet* into the trash without even looking at it.

She hoisted the trash bag over her shoulder like Santa Claus, only this Santa was taking away gifts instead of giving them. Struck by the thought that she might not come back, that she might leave me here to starve, I hurried after her, but she slammed the door and locked it, right in my face.

From outside the door, she said, "You're under my care, you know. You should have thought about that before you wrote those things. You should've thought." Then she was gone.

Not only had she taken my books, but my pen was gone, too. I couldn't write, and I couldn't read. I hated her. Who was she to come into my family, steal my Daddy, and deprive me of my things? Where was Marce? It had been months since I had seen her. She was my friend, not Rachel.

For the first time in weeks, I drew open the curtains on the bay window. The channel between Feeler's Key and Weston's Key sparkled in the morning sunshine. I forced myself to look away. My mother must have looked at that channel from this very room, looked at it again and again until she gave in to the temptation and swam to her death.

I turned my gaze away from the bay. The window fogged where my breath hit it. I was breathing hard. Below me, I could barely make out the entrance to Marce's cottage. I had plenty of time. I waited for Marce to come out, and when at last she did, I signaled wildly, and banged on the glass, and screamed her name. She locked her door, and trudged through the grass to the front yard, out of sight, all without seeing me. At least she was healthy, and still living in the cottage.

I tried to open the window, but it was still nailed shut from the outside. The window itself was hurricane-proof, too strong for my mere arms to break. I pounded on it with a drawer from Daddy's heavy walnut dresser, pounded and pounded without making any impact. Two hours later, Marce walked across the yard again, and again she did not look up. "Marce," I shouted. "Marce, I need you." The cottage welcomed her back; she vanished inside, no doubt to the smells of cookies or scones or peppermint tea. Oh, I'd even drink her Brussels sprout cider, just to be with her again. But the window, and the world, kept us apart.

I grew hungry again that afternoon, but Rachel did not come. That night, I filled my stomach with tap water, and for a short time had the illusion of fullness. The next day, I drank more water, and I soothed my baby with assurances that all was well. All was not well. I had angered my keeper, and she wanted me to suffer. Now I waited by the door, not the window, and I listened for the sounds of footsteps. When I heard them, I yelled and banged, but the footsteps only sped up, hurried away.

To pass the time, and keep my mind off my hunger, I played Tom's wanting game. "What does Anise want?" I asked myself. I wanted to be free. I wanted meatloaf and potatoes. I wanted someone to hold me, someone to love me. I wanted Laurice, just like Daddy did, but that was something I knew I'd never have. "Can't have it" was the answer to all the things I wanted. Can't have freedom. Can't have food. Can't have love.

"What does Hope Laurice, or Thomas Jacob, want?" I asked the life within me. Food was the answer, please Mommy, just a nibble, just a bite? How could I say no to that? But all I had was water, endless water.

At Tom's, our stories had been simple; as soon as a person declared what they wanted, the character in the story got it, and everyone lived happily ever after. But real life wasn't like that, and neither were most stories. If Scrooge had gotten his wish – I want to be left alone – then no ghosts would've plagued him, and he would've continued on, the most miserly of misers. If Lizzie from *Pride and Prejudice* had gotten what she wanted, then the detested Mr. Darcy would have been banished from her life, and that life would've been drear indeed.

I turned the thought over and over, as I sat by the door. Laurice had crafted such beautiful poems and stories. How I wished I could talk with her, and find out if she'd known the secret I had only now discovered. To make a story, deny the poor characters what they wanted. It was so simple. Of course Laurice had known it. If she had lived, she might have gone on to write all kinds of great stories. She might have written novels. It wasn't just my family and me that suffered from her loss; it was the entire world.

The next morning, my third morning without food, I woke with an idea - or rather more a fascination, an obsession, than a mere idea. What if there was a secret way out of this room? A hidden passageway, an escape chute, the sort of thing you see in movies but never in real life. It seemed unlikely that my father had such a passageway and had never mentioned it, but what if he'd used it to sneak a mistress in? Never in the last twelve years had he even mentioned another woman, but it wasn't impossible. Or what if he'd used it himself, when he was supposedly gone working, so that no one had known he'd come back - a horrible thought, that he had avoided me like that, but what if? Or what if he liked to sneak down to the bay all alone late at night? The what-ifs led me along, countering my every objection, until I could see the secret passageway and believe in its reality just as clearly as I could see the locked door.

And what if I starved to death, when all along this hidden passageway was right here?

That got me out of bed despite my hunger and exhaustion. I felt along the walls of the main room. I looked for seams in the carpet that could be pulled up to reveal trapdoors or escape chutes. I bent down awkwardly, careful of my pregnant belly, to peer under the bed, and there lay the twined silk rope, its tassels now hopelessly tangled, that Daddy had used to tie me to the bed when he had switched out our rooms. It reminded me of a snake, and I dropped the bedspread quickly, hiding its coils from view.

The bathroom with its modern fixtures and exercise area seemed an unlikely spot for a hidden passageway, but I searched anyway, finding nothing but soap and towels.

Only the closet remained. I was getting tired and losing hope - oh, if I had learned nothing else in my life, I'd learned the importance of hope, how it gives energy and life, and how futile everything seems once hope is lost - but I pressed on, more now to prove to myself that there was no passageway than out of the lingering belief that I'd find one.

I poked around in the corners of the closet and found only a box of ties that Daddy had left behind. Familiar ties, including a blue and white-hearted tie that I had given him for some birthday or Christmas. I had spent hours picking it out, and it really was a wretched thing, too garish for someone of Daddy's tastes, and yet he had worn it on several occasions.

I held the tie, wondering how to reconcile the Daddy who would wear such an ugly thing just because it was a gift from his daughter, and not from Laurice, but from the other daughter, the lesser daughter, with the Daddy who had abandoned me here because I was pregnant with a baby with degen genes. I couldn't do it; it didn't make sense. Daddy had loved me once, that's what the tie said. It was obvious when you stopped to think, which maybe I hadn't been prone to doing. And yet Daddy had locked me in here and never came to see me. Because he didn't love me? Or because he had Rachel now, pretending to be Laurice, and if he came and saw me, then he wouldn't be able to deny her death? That seemed more like it. I held the tie. He couldn't deny me forever. His fantasy world, his dream that Laurice had come back, would pop once I confronted him, once I escaped, and then he would hold me and love me and send her away. Because that was what was right. Because I was his daughter and Rachel was not. Because Laurice was gone but I was here. Daddy and I had both been hurt, deeply horribly hurt, by her death, but we could recover. I even knew something my father did not; I knew not to focus on the eventual degen death of this baby I carried, but to focus on the life she would have, the love. I had learned from Tom and his family; I had learned from Mrs. Denvers.

I set the tie down with the greatest of care, as if it were a treasure, as if it were a newborn baby. However I got out of here, and I would get out, even though no secret passageway had revealed itself here in the closet, I would take the tie with me, so that I would remember.

After giving the rest of the closet a cursory search, I admitted to myself that there was no hidden passageway out of here. The silk rope and even the box of ties were pointers to a different escape, the same as the escape my mother had chosen when she swam away into the bay.

I had assumed that Daddy hadn't loved my mother, just as he hadn't loved me, and that was why she had killed herself. But the tie was physical, irrefutable proof: Daddy had loved me. What if proof existed that he had loved her, too?

I was too tired to search for such proof, although if it existed anywhere, here in Daddy's room would be the place to find it. A picture of her from their courting days, lovingly saved. . .a lock of her hair. . .even a cross. She had been religious, while Daddy was a scientist; if there was a cross left in the house, it would be because of her, not him. And in fact Daddy had gone with us to church on Sundays for many, many years after my mother had died. He had done it out of respect for her values, even though they were not his own, even though she was long gone.

I looked out towards the bay, which gleamed innocently. If I could accept, or even just consider, that Daddy had loved my mother, then I did not know why she had killed herself. It was a mystery, one that I had lived with all my life without even suspecting.

The dizziness I felt might be from the lack of food, or from the thoughts I was having today, thoughts that challenged all that I thought I'd known about both my parents. I had learned the truth of Mrs. Denvers' sad secrets; surely I could learn the truth about my mother, too. Not all the answers could have drowned with her.

Marce had been our cook since we were little. I pledged to myself to ask Marce as soon as I got out. Surely she could tell me something.

Drawing strength from my pledge, I pounded on the door and yelled for Rachel. I kept it up for hours. Eventually, footsteps stopped outside my door. The smell of soup wafted in. Chicken noodle soup. A very distinctive smell. "You in there?" Rachel called. As if I might have stepped out for a movie, or a trip to the beach.

"I'm starving," I said.

"I've got soup for you. Breadsticks, too, and a tall glass of milk. It looks delicious," she said.

"Do you know what I've been through?"

"Of course I do. When I was a kid, we went without food all the time. It's good for you. Keeps you focused on what matters." The tray clinked; she had set it down. She wasn't bringing it in. She meant to torture me first. "Do you understand now? Daddy put you under my care. He never mentions you anymore. It's like denial or something, it's weird. It's like you're dead to him, and if you die for real, he won't even notice."

When I didn't answer, she opened the door. I looked at her, blinking slowly, and what struck me was how young she looked. She was my captor, yes, but she was also another child, a young woman like me, brought into a situation that she did not create.

I did not want my life and the life of my baby in the hands of someone so young. The temptation of Daddy's money, even Daddy's love, must be so strong for her. And what was this - me feeling sympathy for her, thinking of what it must be like for her, when she was abusing the situation, abusing her control over me? I shook my head, trying to focus on what was at stake.

"I'm not going to die in here," I said.

"Are you sure about that? Are you very sure?" Rachel slid the tray in. I grabbed at the door. Escape mattered more than food, no matter how dizzying the smell. Rachel shut the door hard, on my fingers. Oh, how it hurt! An agonizing minute passed, and then she loosened the door, and I slid my fingers back out. "Eat up," she said.

"Go to hell," I said, before I could stop myself.

She laughed again, a real belly-chuckler. "That's more like it, rich girl. Show your spirit."

I took my first sip of soup, my hands trembling so much that half my spoonful spilled onto my chest, but what I got in my mouth was delicious. The breadstick was easier to hold, and I dipped it into the soup. It was paradise food, like what St. Peter hands you when you step past the pearled gates; welcome to paradise, here's your soup.

The bowl was nearly empty when my stomach turned. I dropped the spoon, and ran for the bathroom, but I didn't make it in time; all the soup spilled back up, out of me, onto the floor. I had eaten too fast. I had eaten more than my shrunken stomach could handle, and I had deprived my baby of the nourishment she needed. I had done this. The sodden mess on the carpet wasn't just rejected soup, it was a condemnation of me as a mother.

I returned to my bowl, and slurped what remained, but it came back up at once. My stomach twisted, and I knew better than to try the milk; even warm water might not stay down.

Rachel sympathized when she returned for the tray, but she left the mess for me to clean up, and she denied my request for settling foods. That evening, she brought me a taco salad that dripped with hot salsa. My mouth watered just looking at it. It tasted divine. Welcome to paradise, here's your taco salad. But it didn't stay down. Nor did the next morning's pancakes, or the noontime sandwiches. Rachel grew frustrated, and threatened not to bring me food at all. I asked for Dr. Jamison; I was denied.

Days drifted past. I tried to eat, but very little besides water would stay down. I grew weaker. The treadmill stood untouched, a testament to my enervation. I lost weight, at a time when I should've been gaining weight. Rachel looked me over each time she came with her impalatable food. Whatever she saw must have been to her liking; she often left my room humming softly to herself. "It's only morning sickness," she told me one evening. "All pregnant women get sick. My Momma did, every time, all pregnancy long."

But I hadn't had any morning sickness, not until now. I needed a doctor, but Rachel had no plans to bring me one. She had claimed that Daddy didn't care if I died, but really it was Rachel who didn't care.

I tried again at the window to get Marce's attention. I saw her twice more, but she never looked up, never saw my waning face. I had to get out of this room. It wasn't just me that would die without food, but my baby too.

I couldn't lock pick. Rachel had already taken the metal clothes hangers away. She had taken the weights from the exercise area too. That didn't matter; I was too weak now to hit her with a dumbbell. The only possible weapon I had was the twined silk rope that I had retrieved from under the bed. It had been used in violence before, when Daddy tied me to the bed. Yes. The rope had a history of violence; the rope had the cruelty in it that I lacked.

I tied the rope to the headboard, and then I lay in bed, and did my best to look dead.

Chapter Thirty

Rachel slid the tray in, as usual; I listened, my breath held. Rachel was humming something, a happy little tune. "Lunchy-lunch," she said. Oh, it was hard to stay limp, when every muscle in my body wanted to tense for what was to come. I listened for her to approach me, but what I heard was the door's soft close. She had left.

Long minutes passed. I needed to use the bathroom, but I stayed in bed. If I got up, that's just when she would return. At last, the lock clicked open, and Rachel stepped back into the room. Her humming caught off abruptly; she'd noticed the tray, and noticed me here in bed.

"You okay?" she asked. She crept closer to me. My eyes were closed, but I heard each soft footfall on the carpet. She stopped by the foot of the bed, and then she gasped.

"Lord is my shepherd, I shall not want," she whispered. The baby kicked within me. I did not move. I held my breath, just as if I were underwater. "He anoints my head with oil, and strikes down my enemies." She tiptoed closer, to the side of my bed, her heavy breaths coming a foot from my face, and then for a moment her breathing stopped altogether.

"I'm sorry, Anise." She spoke in a whisper. "I saw the opportunity, and I took it. Fancy dresses for me. So much money to send back home, more than I could've made in years. Just for pretending to be a dead girl." She laughed sadly. "You didn't see what I saw. You didn't see him cry. Daddy loves your baby, degen or not, and it kills him to love a degen again."

She reached for my wrist, feeling for a pulse. I grabbed her hand. Quickly I looped the silk rope around her hand, knotted it. I had the advantage of surprise, but she recovered fast. She attacked the knot with her free hand, and I looped that hand too. I tied it tight. Rachel was half on the bed, half off; she screamed as if being slaughtered. I bound the rope tighter around the headboard, until she was entirely on the bed, facedown, screaming. The rope's tassels draped festively near her hands, as if she were holding pom-poms.

It was over that fast. I collapsed to the ground, breathing heavily, hardly able to believe that it was her trapped in the bed, not me. Her legs flailed, but her arms were tightly bound. Oh, her legs! She wore Laurice's white slacks. She wore Laurice's red drawstring t-shirt, too. I wanted to rip them right off her. If I'd had the strength, I would have done it.

"Daddy!" Rachel screamed.

"He's not your Daddy." I tucked Daddy's tie, the tie that proved he had loved me, into my pocket.

"You can't leave me like this!"

"Watch me," I said.

She was watching me – I could feel the heat on my back, right where she'd stick a knife if she had one handy.

The doorway stood wide open, the hallway bright beyond it and the morning's tray of food just inside. My conscience twinged. She had been bringing me my food for months now. I owed her that much.

Rachel had craned her head to the right, watching me, but when I brought the tray over to her, she hid her head into the pillow. "Go away," she mumbled, barely audible.

"I'm not going to leave you hungry. I'm not that cruel," I said.

"Daddy!" she screamed. She could scream all she wanted. It was mid-day. Daddy was at work.

I couldn't just leave the tray for her; with her hands tied as they were, I'd have to feed her. She still had her face hidden in the pillow. My patience was wearing thin. I caught her beautiful curly hair, so much like Laurice's, and dragged her head to the side. "This is for your own good." I took a spoonful of watered-down tomato soup – not a very hearty meal, but it was what she'd deemed fit for me – and forced it into her mouth.

She gagged on it, then spat what she could back out. She didn't seem to care that I held her by the hair; she twisted violently, nearly tearing the hair from her head in an effort to get away from me. Her whole body twisted to the other side of the bed, but she was bound to the headboard; she couldn't get far. Her response left me speechless. It was as if I were trying to hurt her, not feed her.

I scooped up another spoonful. This time my hand shook, and some dripped down onto the bed, staining it red. Rachel resisted, but I pulled her head back. Her face was violently red, her eyes wild. "I won't eat it," she screamed. "I won't eat it, it's poisoned, you can't make me. You knew, didn't you? You were dying for the day when you could poison me back."

The spoon fell from my hand. I let go of Rachel's head, and she fell forward into the pillow. The tray was knocked from its perch on the nightstand, and the bowl of soup splattered red against my legs, down to a puddle on the floor, like blood, like a miscarriage. I stumbled backwards. Rachel craned her head, and smiled victoriously. "Poisoned you," she said softly. "Poisoned you, to get rid of you, because I could."

The hallway no longer seemed bright; it was dim, and spinning, as I stumbled out of my prison. I pulled on the door, heavier than a thousand rocks, and slowly it shut behind me. I moved to lock the door, but I didn't have the key. It was inside, in the white pants Rachel wore, the white pants that were Laurice's. I couldn't go back for them. Rachel had poisoned me. But it had been all her, only her; she had lied to me about Daddy. Daddy didn't want me dead. As soon as he knew the truth about her, he'd turn her out, and he'd love me again. That's why she wanted me dead, because I could take away what she'd gained. And I would, with joy. I'd send her back to the ghetto she came from. I'd send her to jail.

From inside the room, Rachel screamed her hate at me. That got me going. I made my way down the stairs, as fast as I could go; now that it was all over, now I was awash with fear and trembling. I had escaped, but a part of me would never leave that room. She had poisoned me. I'd known she was willing to let me die – she had starved me, then refused me a doctor's care – so why was it so hard to believe she had actively tried to kill me?

"Because I don't understand," I said aloud. "Because I would never poison anyone, not even if they deserved it. Not even her."

I was weak, my head dizzy, my heart pounding. Maybe once I ate, maybe then I'd have the strength to understand. I headed for the one place I knew good food awaited me, yes, food and friendship too.

At Marce's cottage, I didn't even knock, I went right in. "Marce, I'm free," I cried.

"Child, is that you?" Marce was in her living room, but not alone. Orson and Marce both rose from where they sat on Marce's couch. In Orson's hand was an atlas, with notes scribbled all over it.

"Orson?" I gasped.

"Anise, you look terrible," he said. I raised a hand self-consciously to my face. He looked more handsome than ever, despite his mismatched khakis and bright Florida shirt. His white-blond hair was combed back in a wave. He looked like a male model, and I looked terrible.

"Don't mind him," Marce said. She dragged me to a seat on her oversized chair. "You look alive, that's what matters most." She sat down again, alongside Orson. For the first time I could remember, she had failed to offer me food.

"I haven't eaten in days," I mentioned. Orson let go of the atlas, which fluttered to the floor. Marce leapt back to her feet, a look of horror upon her face, and vanished into the kitchen.

"Why? Where have you been?" Orson leaned across the coffee table to take my hand. "I've looked everywhere."

"I've been right here," I said.

In the kitchen, Marce dropped a bowl of Jello salad. "Right here?" she said in a strangled voice.

"Trapped in Daddy's bedroom, for months now. Only Rachel decided she didn't like keeping me alive. She poisoned me."

Another crash came from the kitchen; this one sounded like broken dishes.

"What about the baby?" Orson asked.

"None of the poisoned food stayed down," I said. "My body knew better, even if I didn't."

Orson let his head droop, coming close to the curve of my pregnant belly. "I went to the Carolinas, I went to New Orleans, I even went to Omaha. And you were right here all along, and in danger too."

"Your Daddy told me you'd run away again," Marce said. "He said Dr. Jamison took you to the hospital and you escaped him. He cried when he told me. He spent thousands of dollars on a search for you, and you were here all along?"

"Daddy isn't himself. He pretends that Rachel is Laurice come back to him. He knows my baby has a degen father, and he can't accept that. He needs help," I said.

Dish fragments crunched under Marce's feet, and she tracked pink Jello across the linoleum. Orson drew back, and I accepted the plate heaped with mango bread, carrot cookies, and cold shredded beef. I swallowed a bite of everything, and paused for a moment, but my stomach had no objections. "Don't eat too fast," Marce cautioned.

"Why aren't you in school?" I asked Orson, between bites of the delicious mango bread.

"Because of you. What was the last thing you said to me, that terrible day when he knocked you down and nearly gave you a miscarriage? As far as I knew, you had miscarried. You told me to come back, and that's what I was trying to do. Only your father got rid of me with his lie. I tracked down seven runaways, four of them pregnant, but none of them were you."

"It wasn't all wasted effort," Marce said. "Three of the girls let Orson buy them a bus ticket home. He got them off the streets, and may have saved their lives."

Orson blushed, embarrassed by her praise.

"Then you saved their babies' lives, too," I added.

"But I didn't save you. You managed that all on your own. I should have known you had it in you."

Now it was my turn to be embarrassed. I finished the last of the cookies, and held the empty plate firmly. "I'll bring more," Marce offered, but I declined. My stomach was still sensitive, and there would be time for more food later. Besides, I had promised myself I'd ask Marce about my mother just as soon as she was available, and yet I hesitated. I did not fear asking, but I did fear her answer.

"While I was locked in that room, I had a lot of time to think," I began slowly. Marce settled into the chair next to me, leaning forward, clearly interested in what I had to say. Oh, how I loved her. I reached across and hugged her, surprising her and myself with the strength of my grip.

Even after I released her, I found it hard to go on.

"What did you think about, child?" she prompted. It seemed she could tell how important this was to me without my even having to say so.

I rested a hand on my belly, thinking of the life within. "You've worked here since I was born. You must remember my mother better than I do. She gave me life, and then she took her own life away. From the room, I could see the bay where she did it, and I can close my eyes and see her swimming away, swimming into death. But I can't see why she did it. I used to think she killed herself because Daddy didn't love her, but now I don't think it was that simple."

Marce took my hand and squeezed. Orson sat close enough that his arm touched mine. It felt good to be touched after so many days of isolation.

"Why did she do it?" I asked Marce, pleading with her to tell me, and when she shook her head gently, I looked to Orson, but of course he didn't know either.

"She had a sadness to her. That's all I know. It was there even before she married your father, so it wasn't because of him."

I composed myself, and nodded.

"She was beautiful, I remember that. And she liked the number seven," Marce added.

The number seven. Perhaps she had been superstitious.

"She loved me," I said.

"Very much," Marce agreed.

We sat in silence for a few minutes. I accepted another cookie, and the sound of my chewing was embarrassingly loud. I hadn't meant to make them uncomfortable by asking about my mother.

"Orson, do you have a car? I'll feel safer once I'm out of here, if you don't mind."

"I've got the limo. I'll take you anywhere." He laughed softly. "After all, I've already been everywhere, looking for you."

"I'm coming too," Marce said.

I got up to leave, but Orson held me back for a moment. "There's something you should know," he said.

I looked up into his eyes. He was going to tell me he loved me. Any man who'd search for me all across the country had to be in love. He was standing so closely. "Yes?" I said.

"I talked to Tom. I thought maybe you had gone back to him. He's a very nice fellow," Orson said.

"Oh," I said. Yes, Tom was extremely nice, and loving, and responsible. I was in love with Tom, not Orson. He was my baby's father, too. Of course I loved Tom. "Oh! You didn't tell him that I was pregnant?"

"No, I wouldn't do that to you. Don't you know me at all?"

I was beginning to feel dizzy. "I know you. You believe in doing what's right, and you don't like secrets."

"Not bad," he said. "You're right, I think he deserves to know. He was very concerned about you. But it's up to you to tell him, not me."

"We should talk about this in the limo," I said.

Orson opened the cottage door for me, and kept pace at my side. We followed Marce through the back yard. My chambray dress wasn't warm enough for the cool air. It was December already. A robin twitted from a palm tree above me, as if to remind me that up north, where the robin came from, everyone was much worse off. At least my bare feet fell on grass, not snow.

"Are you cold?" Orson asked.

"No," I said, but my shivers betrayed me. He put his arm around me, pulled me close to him. He was very warm. We rounded the building; I wasn't watching where I was going, and neither was Orson, and we both walked straight into Marce.

She had gone completely still, her hand raised to her mouth. Daddy stood in the front yard, home from work, holding Rachel tightly. She was crying. Daddy saw us, but he didn't come after me.

"I thought you locked Rachel in the room," Orson whispered.

"I did," I whispered back.

"Child, hold my hand, and we'll walk right past him," Marce declared. She didn't see a need to whisper, apparently. We joined hands, with me in the middle. I couldn't take my eyes off Daddy. He held Rachel so tenderly, as if he never wanted to let her go.

Parked in the driveway, ten paces back from Daddy and Rachel, the Denvers' black limo waited for us. The sight of it gave me strength; I had driven that limo, I had earned my living, if only for a few short weeks. Daddy hadn't been a part of that life, and I had managed to be happy without him.

"Let's go," I said. "Now, before I lose my nerve."

Marce and Orson obediently marched me forward. Coming close to Daddy was like being caught by gravity. We were a few steps past him, almost to the limo, when I couldn't take it anymore. The last time I'd seen Daddy, he had looked at me the way he now looked at Rachel. I broke free of Marce and Orson's grip, and I ran to Daddy.

"I'm your daughter," I cried. Rachel was an imposter, and as soon as he understood, he would love me again. I reached for him, but Rachel was in my way. "Me, not her. She's just the cook. She tried to kill me."

He swung Rachel behind him, out of my reach. He was protecting her.

"Daddy, she's the one who tied me up," Rachel said.

"He's not your Daddy!" I cried.

Daddy slapped me, hard; it stung, but his rejection stung me worse. Orson tried to drag me away, but Daddy punched him, right in the eye. Orson fell back against Marce, and Marce fell to the ground.

"I'm your daughter," I shouted; maybe if I said it loud enough, maybe then he'd hear me. "I'm Anise. I'm the only daughter you've got left."

"Don't let her get away," Rachel moaned.

He grabbed my arms, started dragging me back toward the house. Oh, not the house, I couldn't bear to go back in there. We had all been happy in the house once, me and Daddy and Laurice. The real Laurice, not this imposter. Rachel was nervously fingering the necklace she wore, a chain of connected diamonds. She was rich now. She had all the money anyone could want, and she had my Daddy's love, too. It wasn't fair. I yanked my arm, hard enough to hear my shoulder give softly, and I slid free of Daddy's clutch.

Running hard, I glanced back to see Daddy, striding purposely after me. Orson was dragging himself to his feet, his eye now a swollen red. Daddy had hit him hard. If Daddy hit me like that, if he hit me in the stomach, my baby could die.

I wasn't looking where I was headed, and my shins bruised up against an unexpected headstone. I had run right into the graveyard. Past the graveyard was the small forest, and then the tall metal fence that marked the neighbor's property. There was no escape this way. I backed up, and Daddy caught me from behind.

"Look down," he said smoothly. "I don't know who you are, but it's obvious you're suffering. I run a hospital. I can get you the help you need. Look down."

I looked down, at the small square headstone, so much smaller than the other headstones gathered here. Tiny block letters read: Anise. Daughter. Born 2030, Died 2046. Laurice's headstone was missing. I was standing on Laurice's grave, and my name was on the headstone.

Rachel had followed us, and even she looked surprised. Hadn't she known how well she had succeeded?

"It's wrong," I cried.

"How can it be wrong? It's carved in stone. Listen to me. I had a daughter named Anise, but she drowned four years ago. My daughter Laurice ran away once, but she came back to me." Daddy shot Rachel a loving look.

"Was Anise pregnant?" I asked.

Daddy glanced down at my waist. "It's hard to remember," he said. "But she might have been, now that you mention it. Then her baby died too?" It was a question, not a statement, but still it terrified me. "Maybe it needs a headstone too."

"No," I said. "No, my baby doesn't belong in a graveyard. My baby's healthy."

"No, it's not. It's a degen," Daddy said. His grip on me loosened, as he grappled with his memory. "Anise was pregnant, and it was a degen baby."

"Yes, yes, that's right," I cried.

His eyes met mine, and I could tell he knew me. But his voice grew cold. "I signed a contract for her to marry, but she disobeyed. She ran away."

"Yes, I ran away, but then I came back. Laurice died. She can't come back."

"I don't want Laurice to be dead," he said softly, like a little boy. He released me, bent down, and ran his hand over the misnamed headstone. "If one of them has to die, I want it to be Anise," he said. He looked at Rachel, and then he looked at me. "I choose her, not you."

I pushed away from him, covered my ears. "Anise is dead," he said, as calm as the bay's water. "As dead as her mother. Do you know what her mother's last words to me were? 'I am too happy here, and that's a sin against God.' She was happy because she was pregnant again. Both Anise and her mother, both pregnant when they died, and both their babies died with them. All dead. Everyone dead but not Laurice. All dead." Conviction had returned to his voice as he talked, and he looked down at me as if I were nothing more than a stranger. I ran from him, my ears still covered, ran blindly until I plunged knee-deep into water. I was in the bay. Behind me, Orson caught up to Daddy, and slugged him hard in the chest. Rachel screamed. Was she Rachel? If Daddy called her Laurice, and she looked like Laurice, didn't that make her Laurice?

"Anise," Orson called, running after me now. But Anise was dead. He was screaming a dead girl's name. I didn't want him to catch me, to hold my dead flesh in his warm hands. I ran forward, through the cold bay water, until it rose up to my neck, and then I swam. I knew just which way to head. Out through the bay, between Feeler's Key and Weston's Key, that was the direction my mother had swum. My strokes cut through the water easily, as if I were destined to swim this way, to die just like my mother.

"Anise, don't," Orson shouted far behind me. I dove under, my dress pulling at my legs, the water cushioning my ears so that I heard nothing. The current rocked me back and forth, unable to make up its mind which way to go; it was calming, like a baby's crib. Like a baby's –

I burst to the surface, coughed out water, sucked in air. The two keys remained before me, but now their sharp points looked like knives, ready to cut me if I swam between them. I couldn't go forward; there was no future out there, not in this cold gray ocean. Nor could I go back. No future there, either, not when my name graced that cold gray headstone. I had no future. I brought my hands up out of the water, and they were deathly pale. Cold, too. I paddled to keep myself up – I was out far past where I could touch – and I held my hands up to the sun, daring it to warm them. The sun declined. Dead hands don't warm, not even in the sunshine.

Orson splashed his way after me, expending far more effort than was needed to stay afloat. I swam backward, keeping a pace between us. He tried to move faster, but only managed to dunk himself under water. The water was dark, and it was as if he'd vanished. Moments later, he came sputtering back to the surface.

"Can't you swim?" I called to him.

A small wave knocked Orson off balance, and he spat out a stream of saltwater. "I haven't drowned yet. I must be learning."

"Go back," I cried. "You heard Daddy. I'm dead."

"No, Anise. It's your Daddy who is dead."

I didn't want to talk about this; I didn't even want to think. Daddy. His name tasted bitter in my mouth, like saltwater, like tears. I turned my back on Orson, and swam toward the keys. They were so long and thin, like a piano player's fingers, beckoning me.

Orson splashed after me, a victim to every wave. "He died long ago, when your mother died, maybe, or when Laurice did. Inside himself, he died," Orson shouted. "Not everyone survives that sort of pain. But you can."

"I don't want him dead," I whispered. Orson couldn't have heard me, not over the waves, but he answered anyway.

"You don't need his love. You have other people to love."

Oh, easy for him to say! He had always had his father's love and his mother's. Even his nasty old grandmother loved him. "You don't know what it's like." I spun to face him, so that he could hear. "You don't know how it hurts to love someone who rejects you."

He grew still, which actually helped him bob with the waves, rather than fighting them. He was a cold gray, like the ocean, like my gravestone. "I don't know anything about love? I'm just a heartless jerk, and I'm out here, half-drowning, because I thought a swim would be fun today."

"No, of course not," I said.

"You don't need him. You have me and Marce. She's on the shore, waiting for you. Don't you want to go to Marce?"

I did want Marce. I looked up, and was surprised to see how far away the shore was; it would be a long swim if I went back. I couldn't make out if Daddy was there or not. He didn't care if I drowned. To him, I already had.

"There's nothing you can do about your father. It's not your fault," Orson said. I treaded easily, but he was still splashing to keep above water. He had endangered himself by swimming out to me. I tried to listen to what he was saying.

"Nothing at all? Are you sure?"

"You did everything you could, and it wasn't enough."

But that wasn't true. There was one thing he had wanted which I hadn't done. "If I had married you, if I hadn't run away, none of this would have happened. It's my fault. When he thought I carried your baby, he was so happy."

A wave swept over Orson; he went under, long enough to worry me. When he came back up, he gasped for air. His face was long, grim, and he spoke with a hint of resignation. "If you hadn't run away, you wouldn't have met Tom. He's the love of your life, right? Come back to shore, for Tom's sake."

But when I closed my eyes, I could barely remember what Tom's face looked like. So much had happened since my time in the ghetto. Tom was wonderful, I remembered that, but the person I saw when I closed my eyes was the same person I saw when I opened them. Orson. He looked half-drowned, his blond-white hair plastered against his head, his face upturned in appeal.

"Why don't you know how to swim?" I asked.

He glanced at the dark water all around us, and smiled weakly. "Afraid of sharks," he admitted.

"Sharks?"

"Yeah, sharks."

"That surprises me," I said.

"I don't see why. Nobody likes sharks. Besides, there's a lot you don't know about me."

"Is there?" I teased, but he looked awfully serious. "Tell me."

"No. Sometimes it's best when secrets stay secret. You'll come in to shore, for Tom's sake?"

I peered back at the keys, and the channel between them. Maybe there were sharks out here. Maybe my mother had swum right past them, and they hadn't blinked an eye; they'd have recognized her as a fellow ocean dweller, never to set foot on land again.

My poor mother. She had killed herself because she was too happy. What a demanding God she had believed in.

"I'll come in to shore," I said. Unlike my mother, I would accept the happiness that my life brought me. But for a moment, I lingered. I felt close to my mother here. The waves rocked me just like she had when I was young. She used to hold me in her lap, and read to me, book after book, even after I fell asleep, so that I heard her comforting voice in my dreams. She was dead, but alive in my heart.

"I'll be beside you," Orson said. "If he's on shore, we'll walk right past him."

Daddy was alive, but in order for me to go on, he had to die in my heart.

Such a strange world we lived in.

Once we got close to shore, I saw Marce's small shape darting back and forth like a firefly on the beach. She was alone. As soon as I crawled out of the water, Marce bundled me across the yard, into the limo.

Orson lingered behind. Through the back window, I watched Orson hoist the small headstone out of the graveyard, and wade back into the bay with it. It sank down, into sand and seaweed. Over time, the current would wash my name off and leave the stone blank. Given enough time, the stone itself would crumble into sand. The ocean was a powerful force, stronger even than Daddy.

Orson rejoined us in the limo, and he locked us safely inside. As we drove away, I saw the parlor curtain rustle, and I whispered good-bye.

Chapter Thirty-One

Orson drove straight to the hospital – not the Degen Institute, but the Florida First Hospital. Its white tiled floors, white walls, and white curtains were just as oppressive as they had been years ago, when I accompanied Laurice on her weekly visits. Daddy had done a great service to all the degens in the area when he established the Degen Institute. I would always admire him for that, even if I never saw him again.

When I told the doctor about the poison, she went as white as the walls, and she hurried me in for testing.

"Wait," I cried. "My friends brought me here. Can they join me?"

"There might be bad news," she said.

If there was, I wanted Orson and Marce beside me. "Please."

"I'll send for them," the doctor said impatiently, but she went ahead and tested for the heartbeat at once. My baby's heart raced fast and high, like a tiny hummingbird.

"Very healthy," the doctor said.

After Orson and Marce joined us, the doctor coated my belly with jelly, then ran what looked like a computer mouse over my large stomach. On the monitor, my baby's image appeared. It was the most beautiful, tiny, life-changing little person ever. I glanced at Marce and Orson, to make sure they were watching. Marce was, but Orson watched me, with an unreadable expression upon his face.

"I can't tell what sex it is, when it's curled up like that," the doctor said.

"I'll know soon enough," I said. "A few short months, and my baby will be here."

The doctor prescribed vitamins, and Orson went to fill it, but he returned with two full bags. I peeked in one of them, and saw a baby thermometer, a first aid kit, a pacifier, baby wipes, and triple pack of Sesame Street bibs.

"Thank you," I said.

"Oh, you'll need so many baby things. This is only a start," Marce said. She took the bags, smiled approvingly at Orson, and then chattered on about baby cribs and baby toys, baby clothes and baby foods. Orson remained strangely silent. Once we were in the limo, I leaned against Marce's shoulder, and let myself drift on the currents of her talk. Baby diapers. Breast milk. Strained carrots, made from scratch.

I woke when the limo came to a stop. What I saw out the window made me gasp; I had expected the Denvers' mansion, but instead Orson had driven us into the ghetto, to the door of Tom's apartment building. A rat slunk along the side of the building, and disappeared into the garbage bin. Orson got out of the limo, and opened my door, but I stayed where I sat.

"Go to him," Orson said softly.

"But I can't. He doesn't know that I'm pregnant."

"He loves you. He won't care." Orson took my hand, pulled me from the car. "When I came here to look for you, he invited me in. He paced back and forth – if he wanted to move at all, he had to pace, in that tiny apartment. He said that he hoped you were far away and safe."

Oh, I knew that already, but it hurt all over again. "Don't tell me this," I said.

"But in the next breath, he said that he wished you'd show up on his doorstep, that he wanted you close where he could protect you. He'll welcome you back, Anise, I know that for a fact. It's what you want, and you can have it."

"What does Anise want," I murmured.

"He's one of the good guys. He works harder than I ever could. I'd go nuts, working at a factory like that, year after year. And he takes care of those three children, all on his own."

"Four children," I said, but I was wrong. Jake had been the fourth.

"He'll welcome your child, too. You won't even have to tell

him. Just let him see you, and he'll pull you close and cover you with kisses. It's what I'd do, if it were mine."

Marce rounded the limo to take my other hand. "Come, child. Don't be scared."

They led me forward, and I didn't resist. They both seemed so sure that this was what I wanted. The metal stairs to the third floor creaked more than ever, like a chorus of crickets. I never thought I'd see these stairs again, nor the hallway, nor the familiar door. Apartment 301. His home.

Marce hugged me fiercely, and pecked my cheek with a kiss. "I'm desperate to meet him, but I think this should be a private moment. Give me a call tomorrow, and arrange for an introduction, will you? I'll make him my grapefruit steak."

"You aren't going back to Daddy's?" I asked, worried.

"No, child. Orson's parents just bought a country home, with its own citrus glades that stretch on for miles. They're looking for a cook, and Orson offered to introduce me."

"She'll get the job. Mother wants someone older this time, and not a Brazilian. Prudent of her, don't you think? And I'm hoping for some delicious care packages while I'm at Harvard."

I fiddled with the handle of my bags to avoid looking up; inside the bag, a baby rattle rattled. Marce took the bags from me, and set them aside. "Don't look sad. I'll send you care packages too."

Orson glanced at the door, smiled sadly, and turned to go. I lay a hand on his shoulder to stop him. "Do you leave for Harvard soon?"

"Pretty soon," he said, but he avoided my eyes.

"Not until the next semester starts," Marce corrected. "That's two months from now. He dropped his classes to look for you."

Orson interrupted. "I'll make it up in summer school. It's no big deal. My father now says that he'll pay for all my schooling regardless of whether I marry or not. He says I could be a monk, and he'd still be proud of me." Orson smiled fondly, and I tried to be happy for him, tried to suppress the surge of jealousy, but oh, it was hard.

"Then you're off the hook. No marrying until you want to marry."

"I suppose," he said. "But if it was a hook, the bait was awfully sweet."

Marce looked from him to me, and said, "Oh!" Orson blushed. I couldn't think what to say, or what to think. I wanted to ask if he had meant what I thought he meant, but I couldn't find the words.

In the sudden silence, the door creaked open, and we all jumped. Kenny and Kelly ran out and threw themselves around my legs, one on each. "Anise back!" Kelly cried. Her dark hair was tied back with pink ribbons, and she wore pink jean overalls. This was the Kelly I remembered.

"Call me," Marce said. She glanced worriedly from Tom's apartment to Orson, and then to me. "We need to talk."

"Is there a present in the bag?" Kelly asked. She peeked into my baby bags, and set the rattle rattling again. It reminded me of a snake's rattle. "Present for me?"

"How come your stomach got so big?" Kenny asked.

"Good-bye, Anise." Orson kissed my cheek, a tender kiss. "I know you'll be happy here."

"Did you eat a basketball?" Kelly asked. She reached her small hand up, and tentatively touched my stomach.

"Aren't you glad she came back?" Orson asked them.

"Yes," Kenny said.

"Yes, yes," Kelly echoed.

"There you have it," Orson said. He left me there, weighted down by two small children and my own pregnant belly, unable to follow him even if I wanted. Marce blew me a kiss from the stairway, just before the metal door clanged shut behind them. I didn't know what I wanted. I didn't know at all.

"Kelly? Kenny?" Tom called out from the apartment. Seconds later, he rushed to the door, clad only in a towel. Water dripped from him onto the white carpet, soaking in like rain. He gaped at me. I brought my hands up to shield my rounded belly, but there was no hiding it.

"She swallowed a basketball," Kelly said.

"Hi, Tom," I said. "Can I come in?"

His nod seemed forced. He moved aside. My belly brushed him as I passed, and he exhaled sharply. His lively hair looked out of place on his grim, grim face. Had Orson really thought

Tom would greet me with kisses?

"This was a mistake. I'll go away," I said.

"Don't, no, of course not. I just need a moment," he said.

The children squeezed past us to get to the living room, leaving us alone in the entryway. Tom tightened his grip on his towel. A few droplets of water remained on his chest, and I dared to brush them away, one by one. He smelled like soap. I wanted him to kiss me. I wanted to feel his hands on my body, holding me close, loving me.

"Tom?"

He brushed my hair back from my cheeks, tucking it behind my ears expertly. "Yes?"

"I was your first lover, wasn't I? That's why you didn't want me, not because of me, but because you were afraid –" I cut off, but Tom knew what I was going to say.

"Afraid of getting a girl pregnant. Afraid of passing my genes on to an innocent baby." He touched my belly, bent closer, and kissed it. "Yes, you were my first and only lover."

"I'm glad for what we had," I said.

He closed the gap between us, and kissed my shoulder. My belly kept him at a distance, so that he had to lean in off-balanced. He kissed his way up my neck. I ran my hands through his hair, which looked and felt so much like Jake's. He kissed my cheek, but something was missing. His kisses felt more like a brother's than a lover's. Oh, Tom was putting forth a good effort, but that's what it was, an effort, and not what he actually wanted.

"You should get dressed," I said. I pecked him on the cheek, a sisterly kiss. It felt right. "I'll wait in the living room with the children."

Honey had grown so much since I saw her last. She was walking, and babbling, and more beautiful than ever. I didn't think she would remember me – how could she? She had been an infant – but she let me take her in my arms all the same.

Tom took a long time getting dressed. At last he returned, and Kelly swooped into his arms. After a quick twirl, he set her down gently. He was such a good father to them. That had been one of the things that had attracted me to Tom; he was all the things my Daddy wasn't – but then, maybe Daddy wasn't entirely to blame for that. If Laurice had lived, or my mother, either one, maybe we would have been a normal family too.

Tom sat in front of me and Honey. He had pulled on a black t-shirt and jeans; whether he meant it or not, he wore mourning clothes. From his pocket, he drew a small gold ring. Kelly grabbed for it, but he eluded her small hands. "I know this doesn't look like much. You deserve diamonds, not dime store gold. But it was my mother's." He rose to his knees. "It's yours, if you'll have me. Marry me, Anise. I'll take care of you and the baby."

I was stunned. I set Honey on the ground, and she toddled off toward Kenny. Tom held the ring in the palm of his upturned hand, like an offering in church. Like a sacrificial coin. He didn't want to marry me. This was a sacrifice. "Oh, Tom, no," I said.

He clenched his fingers around the ring. "Please, Anise? Let me marry you. Let me do what I can for the child, and for you."

He was doing the responsible thing, just as he always did. "No, I can't let you do this."

"Do what? I'm proposing. I want to marry you."

"What if it's not your baby? Would you want to marry me then?"

He hesitated. "Of course it's my baby. We made love. We didn't use protection."

"But what if it's not? What if it's Orson's baby? What if, when I left here, I went straight to his mansion, and he got me pregnant?"

"Then why did you come here?"

"To say good-bye." I stroked his outstretched hand, and folded his fingers down one by one around the ring. Touching him felt like touching a brother, not a lover. He looked so much like Jake, grown to an adult. I had loved Jake like a brother. I loved Tom too.

"Tell me the truth," Tom said. "It's not my baby?"

I didn't even hesitate. "No. It's Orson's. I'm sorry you misunderstood."

Slowly, slowly, Tom slid the ring back into his pocket; slowly, he relaxed. The warmth returned to his face. By that

I knew I was doing the right thing. "If it's Orson's baby, it won't be a degen. It'll live forever."

"Yes," I said, even though nobody lives forever.

"If you were my wife, in a few short years, you'd be my widow. I'd hate to do that to you."

I struggled to rise. My belly made it difficult. Tom leapt up to help. "Don't go," he said. "You're tired, aren't you? Spend the evening with us. One last evening. For my sake."

I stayed, not for his sake, but for mine. I stayed to hear Tom tell his stories one last time, to feel the comfort and the love that imbued this tiny apartment.

Kelly wanted a school friend, and Tom told a story where she was the most popular girl in kindergarten, and spent long hours chatting on her pink princess phone. Kenny wanted Jake back. That story was harder to hear. Tom had Jake come to Kenny as an angel, wings and all, and he said that he was always hovering over us, just out of sight, loving us. Kelly's hand found its way into mine, and squeezed tight. She missed Jake too.

"And you, Anise?" Tom asked. "What does Anise want?"

I knew the answer now. "All I ever wanted was love, and I have it." I thought of Marce, and Laurice, and my mother, and even Daddy - I still had the tie that proved he had loved me once - and I thought of Orson and Mrs. Denvers. "I had it all along."

"Of course you did," Tom said.

"All I want now is for my baby to be born safely. I want to kiss a tiny hand and a wrinkled forehead and know that I brought this person into the world, and that I will love him or her with all my heart, forever. Not just until she dies, or I die, but forever and ever."

Tom told his story. In it my baby shone like the heavens, and we danced together far above the clouds.

Chapter Thirty-Two

The next morning, I crept out of Tom's apartment before anyone was awake. In the garden at the Denvers' new country estate, I found Orson. He was on his hands and knees, attacking the ground with a trowel. He hadn't heard the butler pronounce, in heavy English tones, that Master Orson was right over there, and that he ought to come in before he was callused and sunburned both.

Orson wasn't likely to get sunburned, not in cool December. My dress had been cleaned and dried since yesterday, but it still wasn't warm enough. I crossed my arms in front of my chest. The butler would be pleased if I lured Orson in for a cup of hot tea, but then we wouldn't be alone. Marce was in the kitchen, and while I longed to talk to her, I needed to talk to Orson first.

"Hello, Orson," I said, from a few feet behind him. He smiled at the sound of my voice, smiled sadly, even before he glanced up and saw me. He left his trowel in the ground, and came to me.

"What are you doing here? Is there happy news?" He reached for my left hand, and I uncrossed my arms from my chest.

He was looking for Tom's ring, but he could see for himself that there was no ring there. "Did you know Tom was going to propose?"

"We talked," he said simply. "I asked him if he had any regrets, and he said he had only one. That he hadn't asked you to marry him after you and he made love. He said that even though he wasn't good enough for you, he should've let you be the one to decide that."

Did that mean Tom would have proposed even if I hadn't been pregnant? Did that matter? "I turned him down."

"I'm sorry to hear that," Orson said. A flutter of birds rose from the citrus glades behind him. They flew towards the sea. I watched until they vanished from the sky. "I'd say you're getting experienced at turning proposals down." A trace of his old irony scarred his voice.

"You don't have to be mean about it," I said.

"I'm not," he said. Maybe it wasn't irony that I heard. Maybe it was pain. "I thought he was the man for you. I thought you loved him."

"I do love him. Like I'd love a brother," I said. "He was my first love, but he's not right for me."

"But he loved you."

"I don't want that kind of love," I said. "I want –"

I saw then what Orson was planting – anise herbs, rows and rows of them – and I couldn't finish my sentence. On the far side of the garden, Mrs. Denvers had transplanted her roses from their old mansion. They took up a tiny corner compared to Orson's plantings.

"Marce says she can use them to make licorice," Orson said in a choked, strange voice.

"How much licorice is she going to make?" I asked. I counted the rows; there were twenty-five of them, each with anise herbs at one foot intervals. It looked just like a garden Orson would make, everything orderly and perfect. "You didn't use a ruler, did you, to get them that even?"

"Yes," he admitted. He pointed to the far side of the garden, at a red wheelbarrow stacked with more anise. A dirtied yardstick leaned against it. "I wanted it to be perfect."

"Why?"

"It's good to be orderly. They'll grow better –"

"No, I mean, why my herbs? Why anise?"

"If you have to ask, then you don't want to know," he said.

"I know what I want," I said. "What do you want?"

He hesitated, then searched my face. Whatever he saw there seemed to give him hope. "I'll show you," he said.

In the center of the garden, a small mound was crowned with a single herb. Orson crouched beside it, and dug down into the newly packed soil. What he pulled out sparkled in the December sun. He handed it to me. It was my engagement ring.

"I don't understand. You buried the ring?" It was worth thousands. It was crazy of him.

"I buried my love," he said. "It was easy. It's something I've done for years. Do you remember me telling you that my mother named me Orson because it sounded like your son? She told my father that to hurt him, but it hurt me instead of him. I couldn't trust the love she gave to me. I knew that she didn't really love me."

"But she does love you," I said. I reached for the ring, and he let me take it.

"You're right. She loves me. I finally told her what I'd overheard, and she told me that she had lied. She named me Orson after my great-grandfather on her mother's side. She showed me his picture. He had been a war veteran."

"It's a good name," I said. "When I first heard it, I thought it was old-fashioned. But now –" I swallowed, forced myself to continue. He had been honest with me. "Now I think it's a lovely name, and if my baby's a boy, I might just name him Orson Jacob instead of Thomas Jacob."

"But it's Tom's baby," Orson said.

"It doesn't have to be."

"What do you mean?"

"It's time for us to speak freely, don't you think?" I finished cleaning the dirt off of my ring. It sparkled so beautifully. "You first."

"See? You did it again," Orson said. "You catch me off guard. You get to the heart of the matter. And you bring out a better person in me, the one that I'm trying to be but don't always know how."

"Are you saying you love me?" I asked.

"Yes," he said. "Quite simply, quite truly, I love you."

I had thought that was what he was saying, and yet I wasn't prepared to handle how it hit me. Orson, my Orson, loved me. "You've been such a good friend to me."

"Friend," he said, and suddenly he kicked the mound of dirt where my ring had been buried. It sprayed out across the closest herbs.

"Yes, friend," I said. "Love should start with friendship, don't you think? First you're friends, and then you begin to notice that the other person's wit is actually a mask for his sensitivity, and that he's studious because he wants to learn and serve, just as I do. Whenever I need you, you're there for me. You never left me, except when you thought I was leaving you." I took in the field of herbs around me, and said, "Even when you thought I'd marry Tom, you still remembered me. You kept me in your heart."

"It's not exactly a choice," he said. "You are my heart."

He knelt before me then. I hastily gave him the ring, and he held it out in his strong hands. They were callused from all the planting, just as the butler had said. They were beautiful. "Anise Nicole Hunt," he said. "Marry me. I will love you always, and I'll make you proud of me."

"I already am," I said.

"Marry me," he pressed.

"Yes," I said.

He slid the ring on my finger. It had been loose before, but now it fit perfectly.

Epilogue

Our little house has shutter board windows, and a peaked roof, so that the snow slides off easily. Eleven pine trees grace the yard, with a tire swing and a hammock between them.

Inside our little house, in the foyer, our wedding picture is hung. I was eight months pregnant, and I positively glow. Orson looks nervous, but he came through all right. He later told me that he had feared I'd change my mind.

Further into the house, in the library, a black-and-white shot of Hope sits atop the grand piano. Hope is our daughter. Our son, Travis, came the next year. You can find his picture on top of the fireplace mantle.

Orson's degree, framed in black ebony, hangs in his office. It's cold in there in the winter, but he says he doesn't mind. He has thoughts of me to warm him.

Upstairs, in the hallway between the bedrooms, there's a formal portrait of the entire family, including Marce and the Denvers. Marce has been dating their English butler. She says they both enjoy an afternoon tea.

But in the master bedroom, tucked away in my bottom nightstand drawer, I still keep a picture of Daddy alongside the awful tie I had once given him and he had once worn. In the picture, he looks so handsome, so young. He's quit his job at the Institute now, and stays inside his house year-round, with only that invidious Rachel to care for him. He doesn't return my phone calls.

I have no picture to remember my mother by, but I have the memory of her love, and the knowledge of what life must have been like for her, and that is enough.

I do have one more picture, but I'm almost embarrassed to show you. I keep it in my purse. It's the picture of Orson that Daddy gave me, when he made our promise contract. I studied it so closely back then, and yet I never saw the kindness in his eyes. I took the tilt of his chin for pride, when really it was strength. He is a good man.

And there is one more picture. I have an office, too. My degree is framed in ivory. I majored in English, just as Laurice would have done. I love words and stories as much as she did. Orson knew. He said I always talked about how much Laurice would have liked a phrase, when really I meant that I liked it. I don't know if that's true or not, but I did love my English classes. I write for a living, now. You can see my Rodking Award up there on the mantle, draped with the red silk scarf. Red for victory, and for passion. Passion is important in a writer.

And there it is. Laurice's picture on the wall. Clad in a yellow sundress, diamond studs in her ears, she remains eternally sixteen. I grow older, and she does not, but she will always be my older sister.

Laurice, if you can read this in heaven, keep watching over me and my family. You live on in little Hope. I can see you in her eyes, hear you in her laughter. I haven't had her tested by the degen measure, and I don't think I ever will. So long as we don't know her score, we don't know what the future holds, and we can hope.

Pray for her, Laurice. Pray for all of us. We are so happy now.

www.ingramcontent.com/pod-product-compliance
Lightning Source LLC
Chambersburg PA
CBHW020612310726
48979CB00008B/1455/J

* 9 7 8 1 5 8 7 1 5 6 9 9 1 *